Losing Control
Guardian Security Book Eight

by

Desiree Holt

Losing Control

Contact Information: info@thewildrosepress.com

Cover Art by *Diana Carlile*

The Wild Rose Press, Inc.
PO Box 708
Adams Basin, NY 14410-0708

Visit us at www.thewildrosepress.com

Publishing History
First Edition, 2023
Print ISBN 978-1-5092-5272-5
Digital ISBN 978-1-5092-5273-2
Published in the United States of America

She needed answers…but the questions could send her life out of control.

"Can I help you?"

The deep voice sent shock waves through her. She whirled, her knees shaking. Oh, hell. It was him. The man in the truck. Wearing a uniform, for God's sake.

"I have to say," he went on, "you look a lot better when you aren't soaked through by the rain."

The first thing she thought was *cowboy.* He had the easy, relaxed yet alert stance she'd seen on men around horses and cattle. And his feet were shod in square-toed western boots. She was sure his hat was a Stetson.

But the way his eyes assessed her, the analytical gaze…*military.* Some kind of covert ops.

A dangerous combination in a man.

Dangerous to women. And to people who were misled by his friendly smile.

He was somewhere in his mid-thirties. At least six-four, broad shouldered, and lean hipped, the khaki of the sheriff's uniform looking as if it were custom tailored for him. His face was all angles and planes, with deep-set, whiskey-colored eyes framed by dark brows and lashes. Even in her high state of anxiety, she couldn't miss the sexuality that radiated from him.

The ultimate Alpha male.

And trouble.

I'll bet he has to beat women off with a nightstick. Well, he won't have to worry about me. Oh, wait. After last night, he probably thinks I'm a nutcase anyway.

She wet her lips. "I gave my card to the woman at the window. I'm Dana Moretti."

"I know who you are."

Prologue

There was a little girl who had a little curl,
Right in the middle of her forehead;
And when she was good, she was very, very good;
And when she was bad, she was horrid.

Carrie tried to hold absolutely still. The tape on her hands hurt and the hood on her head made breathing difficult, but she had to keep calm. She could hear Kylie crying, and she wanted to help her. She just didn't know how yet.

"There was a little girl…."

They were in a barn. She knew because she smelled the straw and animals. And wood shavings. She didn't think she'd ever smell wood shavings again without getting sick. And there was something else. Something she was sure didn't belong in a barn. The unseen man had brought them here after he clapped something evil-smelling over their faces. The vile smelling stuff had put them to sleep so Carrie wasn't certain how far away from home they were. When she woke up, the hood she now wore was already on her head, there was tape on her mouth, and her hands were tied behind her.

"There was a little girl…"

Over and over in that unnaturally high-pitched voice, the man recited the familiar nursery rhyme.

1

Carrie tried to wriggle around to see if she could get closer to Kylie, but she was trapped.

"No, no, no," the man cackled, alerted by the noise she was making. "You don't want to be a horrid little girl. You know what happens to little girls who are horrid."

They never should have talked to the clown. Only they were having so much fun at the fair. And there were lots of clowns talking to other kids. How were they supposed to know he was bad? They shouldn't have walked away with him. Mama and Daddy always told them "don't go with strangers."

But clowns weren't really strangers, were they?

"We're only going to walk a little way," he'd told them in a high voice.

But as soon as they were out of sight of the picnic area, the big clown grabbed Carrie under one arm and Kylie under the other. Before they could catch their breath to scream, he'd pressed something awful-smelling to their faces.

When she woke up, she was in this barn seated on a chair, hands tied behind her so tightly her wrists hurt. She couldn't see Kylie, but she heard her and even though she was scared, knowing her sister was with her had made her feel a little better. The feeling hadn't lasted long. Soon after she woke, the clown pulled off her underpants and hurt her. She tried not to cry and scare Kylie.

But then he'd whispered, "Your sister's next and I'm going to let you hear her."

In seconds, Kylie started shrieking in fear and pain. Hearing her sister's cries, Carrie began to cry, too, soundlessly, behind the tape over her mouth.

The hood on her head seemed tighter now, and it was getting difficult to breathe. Still, she had to keep calm. She had to put everything out of her mind except Kylie. She was the big sister. She had to try and get free so she could help Kylie. She *had* to. She just didn't know how yet.

Kylie shrieked in pain, and the sound echoed in Carrie's head.

Suddenly, Kylie's voice was cut off in mid-scream, and Carrie knew the clown was killing her. Knew it in her heart. Big fat tears rolled down her cheeks. She was more frightened than she'd ever been in her life.

His hands were on her body again, and he shifted her this way and that while he touched her in strange, frightening ways.

"Your sister didn't last too long, did she? That means I'll have to have fun with you again, little girl."

Carrie tried to flop herself off the chair, but it was hard to do with her hands tied behind her back and the clown man's hands holding her in place. Kylie, Kylie, Kylie, she chanted silently and bit her lip until she tasted blood. All the while she tried not to scream, not to frighten Kylie any more than she already was. Just in case—please Mama and Daddy and God—Kylie was still alive.

Then she heard it. A strange noise, an engine of some kind outside the barn. The clown man muttered some very bad words, but she ignored him as she strained to hear the noise.

Her whole body was on fire with pain, and her head felt as if it would explode as hands squeezed her throat. She fought to breathe, to cry out to whoever was outside. She listened hard, hoping someone would come and help them. Maybe it was Mama and Daddy. Please be Mama and Daddy.

Suddenly the hands were gone, so abruptly that she slumped sideways, and people were talking.

"We shouldn't be here, you dipshit. Whose place is this, anyway?"

"I dunno. It's just an old barn. Been here forever."

"I saw a light. Someone's there. Let's get the hell out of here."

"You're crazy. It's dark. Come on. I scammed this pot, and I'm going to smoke it."

A door creaked open and Carrie tensed.

"Hey, Skeet, turn on your flashlight so we can see in here."

The new voices were inside the barn now, coming closer. Closer.

"We can just... Holy shit!"

"What? What's the matter? Oh, Jesus. God!"

"Don't touch them. Go get someone. There's a house down by the turn."

Carrie forced herself to whimper. Help me, she screamed in her head.

"Hey, Skeet, I think this one's alive. Go call the sheriff. Don't just stand there. Hurry up! Now, dumbass. Move it!"

Hands pulled the hood from Carrie's head, and she blinked in the sudden light. Someone, not the clown man, placed her on the floor, and she began to shiver like she did when it was too cold outside.

"Kylie," she tried to say, to turn toward her sister.

"No, no," the person who'd freed her said.

"Help...Kylie." She forced the words out through swollen lips.

But nothing happened. The man didn't move. She tried to do it herself. Tried to go to her sister, but she couldn't make her body move. It seemed like forever before anyone else came to help.

She heard the car doors slamming. Heavy feet running toward her. Men's voices. More strangers.

"Holy mother of God," someone said in an angry voice.

Hands touched her. Turned her.

"Careful," someone said. "Her thighs are covered with blood."

"I'll move her as gently as I can," the first man said.

There were more voices and more hands, and she shrieked in terror. "No!" She tried to pull herself away from all the men touching her. Were they going to hurt her, too? One man had already hurt her and Kylie.

"Oh, little sweetheart. Oh, you poor baby."

A tall man crouched beside her, gently working the tape off her wrists. He tried to lift her from the floor, but Carrie struggled to get away.

"Kylie!" She screamed, kicking at the man, biting at him until he backed away.

"It's all right, honey," he was saying. "I won't hurt you. I promise."

"Help Kylie." Her eyes slid fearfully to her sister, but the image was so horrible she squeezed her eyes shut.

"It's all right, sweetheart," the man said. "I just want to help you. I won't hurt you. I promise."

She pulled away from him again. She hurt so bad. Everything inside felt like a big sore, but it didn't stop her from running to Kylie. Her sister's broken body lay on the floor of the barn, and she knelt beside her and tried to pull her into her arms. The nice man bent down to lift her away, but she kicked at him again, so he let her be.

That's how the sheriff and the deputies found her, cradling the small body of her sister in her arms.

The sheriff squatted down beside her, careful not to touch her. "It's okay, Carrie. We'll take care of Kylie now. Everything's all right, little one."

But everything wasn't all right and Carrie knew nothing would ever be all right again.

Chapter One

The cab driver honked for the second time, signaling his impatience. Grabbing her suitcase and her laptop, Dana Moretti set the alarm panel in her front hall and hurried out the front door. She considered herself lucky to get a cab to come out at this hour of the night and she didn't want him to take off. Having no idea how long she'd be gone, leaving her car sitting in long-term parking indefinitely didn't seem the best choice.

She barely remembered calling the airline, then haphazardly pulling clothes out of the closet and chest of drawers. She wasn't usually this impulsive, but tonight she was trying to outrun a memory. Make that more than one. And the twenty-five years that separated them shrank into nothingness.

Leaning back in the cab, she closed her eyes, trying to instill some calm into her chaotic mind. Tonight's episode and its painful conclusion were still too fresh. Grant Rushing got top marks for effort—fine wine, scented candles, soft music. Everything for the perfect romantic seduction. Too bad it was all wasted on damaged goods.

Like a rewound DVD, the memory of it played through her brain.

"Relax, Dana." His voice was soft, gentle. "This isn't a test. There's no pass or fail. It's okay, honey.

7

Just let yourself feel. You have such a beautiful body. Let me love it."

She swallowed and willed her tense muscles to unwind. God, would it ever be any different?

"It's not your fault," she told him, feeling sadness and defeat.

As if someone had thrown a switch, Grant rolled away from her, suddenly remote. "But not quite good enough, right? I should have known. It'll take a lot more than this to defeat the elephant in the room." The bitterness in his voice was unmistakable. "Tell me. Is it just with me or are you this way with all men?"

Dana squeezed her eyes shut, forcing back the tears that burned behind her eyelids. "It isn't you, I swear it isn't. You're really—"

"If you tell me I'm a nice guy I might be tempted for the first time in my life to hit a woman. Spare me, okay?"

"Grant—"

"Forget it." He climbed out of bed and headed for the bathroom. In the doorway, he paused and turned to her, his body backlit by the bathroom light. "There's too many of us in the bed, Dana. Get rid of the fucking ghost, or we have nothing more to talk about."

Grant certainly wasn't the first she'd failed with. Unfortunately. She'd been called everything from frigid to a cock tease to a waste of time. But the moment a man's hands touched her at the core of her sex, she was once again seven-year-old Carrie Nolan, blindfolded and tormented. Back in that barn again, so conscious of the scent of wood, of blood, of Kylie's screams and cries.

Her outer scars had long since healed, but the ones

on the inside were still raw and bleeding. She could change her name, but everything else had stayed the same. She was still a freak, terrified of men. All men.

Emotionally and physically.

The parade of therapists and volumes of reading material hadn't brought her any closer to what other women had. A loving fulfilling relationship. Oh, God, how she wanted it.

"When the time is right it will happen and you'll know it." In her head she heard again the voice of her current therapist, Dr. Summers. "The barricades will fall, Dana."

But she had her doubts.

Tears burned behind her eyelids, and her stomach pitched and roiled. Cold shivers skated over her body. For a moment, she was sure she'd throw up. The hatred for the man who'd made her into an emotional cripple welled up like poison. Clenching her fists in her lap, she forced back the nausea.

"Ma'am?" The rough voice broke into her mental fog, jerking her to awareness. "Ma'am, we're here."

Dana blinked her eyes and peered through the side window of the cab, realizing they were in front of one of the terminals at the airport. The roar of planes overhead mingled with the zing of tires on the interstate and the buzzing in her head. For a moment, she was tempted to tell the driver to turn around and take her back home, where she could hide forever behind locked doors. The only problem was, all that remembered terror would be hiding right along with her.

At the e-ticket machine, she swiped her credit card and punched in her information. It wasn't until she was buckled into her seat, waiting for the plane to take off, that her mind kicked into gear again.

What the hell am I doing?

This was a trip she never thought she'd take, to a place she'd unsuccessfully tried to banish from her mind. But she'd finally figured out that facing her demons was the only possible way to get rid of them.

Twenty-five years had passed since she'd had her last glimpse of High Ridge, in the rolling Texas Hill Country, through the rear window of the family car. Had the small ranching community changed much? Would people still remember what happened? Had they buried the horror and gone on about their business?

Now she was about to bring it all up again. How would they react?

****

"I'm sorry, I don't think we have those editions available."

Well, at least I have my answer about their attitude.

Handing over her business card, Dana had asked as nicely as possible for what she needed. As soon as she told the woman what dates she was interested in, she could feel the hostility rise up like a stone wall from the woman behind the counter at *The High Ridge Messenger*. Marion Jordan wasn't about to budge an inch. The pencil in her fingers tapped against the counter with an irritating cadence.

Tap, tap, tap. Pause. *Tap, tap, tap.*

Dana was beyond tired. Landing in San Antonio just after eight o'clock that morning, she'd rented a car and immediately drove the three hours to High Ridge, fueled with industrial strength coffee and anxiety. She hadn't even looked for a motel yet. And this woman was getting on her last nerve.

She tucked her hair behind her ears—a chronic nervous gesture—and tried to put on her best smile.

"Are you sure?" she asked, her voice cajoling. "Every newspaper I've ever worked with saves their editions all the way back to the very first one. Somewhere. Can you check for me? Please?"

Marion Jordan stared at her, lips thinned in disapproval.

Tap, tap, tap.

"Perhaps if you tell me what specific information you're looking for I can direct you to another source."

All right. If that's the way she wants to play it.

"The pedophile killer is the subject of my next book, and I need the newspapers for research. All of them during those dates I gave you."

Marion's eyes were frosty, her posture rigid. "I think writing a book like that would be a very big mistake. The people in this town suffered a great deal during that time. I wouldn't want to be the one helping you rake it all up again."

Dana mentally counted to ten. "Perhaps there's someone else here who could be of better assistance."

"I can promise you no one will want to discuss this with you," Marion assured her. "You can count on that. It took this town a long time to get over it. They won't want it all dragged out again."

The two women stared at each other.

"Is there a problem here?" A gravelly voice broke into the chill.

Dana hadn't heard the outside door behind her open, but suddenly a man stood next to her. Dressed in jeans and a work shirt with the sleeves rolled up, he looked to be about the same age as Marion Jordan. Mid-forties, Dana guessed. His hair, worn just a little long, was heavily laced with gray, with traces of its original sandy color here and there. His broad forehead was currently wrinkled in a frown.

Looking at him, her body tensed. Could he be the one? Was that possible? He was about the right age and height. Would she end up looking at every man in the county as a possible suspect?

Cut it out. Pull yourself together.

"I'm sorry, Mr. Garrett. I told this woman the editions of the paper she wants aren't available." Each word was an icicle dropping from Marion Jordan's lips.

Tap tap tap.

"I'll take care of it, Marion. Thanks." He held out his hand to Dana. "John Garrett. I'm the editor here." His smile didn't quite reach his eyes. "For my sins."

"Dana Moretti." She withdrew her hand as quickly as she could. Although she managed in pubic with rigid discipline, contact of any kind with men froze everything inside her.

"The writer." His sharp eyes studied her.

"Yes." She fished out another business card.

"Marion usually isn't so obstinate about requests." He ran his fingers through his hair in an absent gesture. "Can you tell me a little more about what you want?"

"I'm here to do research for my next book. When I made a request to look at some old editions of the newspaper, I discovered there's apparently some problem with me seeing them."

Garrett's eyes narrowed. "Here? What could possibly interest you in a small town like High Ridge?"

"She wants to see the newspapers from twenty-five

years ago," Marion told him, her face tight. "You know which ones. I said they weren't available."

Garrett studied the card for a long minute. "You want to dig up the pedophile killer case."

"That's right. If you've read any of my books, you know my interest is in old cases that were never solved."

He stuck the card in his shirt pocket. "Well, Miss Moretti, I don't think you'll be doing this town any favors if you go ahead with what you're planning. People here would just as soon not have to deal with it all over again. For many of them, it's still as real as if it happened yesterday."

Dana swallowed her frustration and tried to blink the grit from her eyes. A glance at her watch told her she'd been going for more than twenty hours, catnapping only briefly on the plane. The adrenaline that drove her this far was beginning to slide.

She moistened her lips, trying to tamp down her impatience. "I'm surprised that no one wants to find out who the pedophile really was. He could still be someone in this community, hiding behind his public face."

"We all agreed it was just some itinerant working in the area who's since moved on." Garrett's voice was hard. "Not anyone who actually lived here."

"You were here then?"

He nodded. "Lived here all my life."

"Then maybe—"

He lifted the flap in the counter and gestured for her to follow him through the main area. "Maybe we'd be better discussing this in my office."

Dana looked around the area at the small staff of

reporters and graphic artists, suddenly aware that everyone was listening with open curiosity. "All right."

She'd been stonewalled before and could play the game as well as anyone. But the knot in her stomach reminded her that this time the game was personal and far too important to let anything get in the way.

"Coffee?" Garrett asked, indicating a pot on a small table next to his desk.

"Yes, thank you. Black, please." Right now a good jolt of caffeine was exactly what she needed to jack herself up again.

"It's been a long time since all that nasty stuff happened," he told her, handing her a Styrofoam cup and lowering himself into his desk chair. "I don't know if you've done any research on Salado County or High Ridge itself, but they're nice friendly places. What happened scared the bejeesus out of everyone, and they were grateful when it was over."

It's not over and done with for everyone. "So they just want to keep pretending it never happened?"

Garrett leaned forward, set his cup down carefully and steepled his fingers. When he looked at Dana his eyes were like hard pebbles.

"The last...incident...was different than the others," he said slowly, "and then it just...stopped. Nothing's happened since then. As far as this town is concerned, whoever it was didn't come from around here. Maybe someone doing casual labor in the county for a couple of years. Someone who didn't call attention to himself. You know people like that don't appear much on the radar. Now he's gone."

Meaning he could have been one of the many illegals. But Dana didn't think so. And she couldn't say anything yet without giving herself away.

When she spoke she tried to keep the impatience from her voice. "What if they're wrong? What if that person is still living here, a member of the community, laughing at everyone because of what he got away with?"

Garrett shook his head. A little too vehemently? "Not possible. It was a stranger. No one in this county would do anything like that."

"But sometimes—"

"Everyone wants to bury the past and move on," he cut her off. "A lot of families whose children were molested and killed still haven't gotten past it after all this time. Talking to them would be nothing less than cruel."

"I can assure you, I'm extremely circumspect when dealing with survivors."

"I'm sure you are. Still..." He sighed and pushed back his chair. "All right. I've done my best. I guess there won't be any talking you out of it. Your reputation precedes you. And legally I can't keep you from looking at back issues."

"So you have them." She tried to keep the satisfaction out of her voice."

"Yes, but they're on microfiche and those rolls are packed away." He swallowed some of his coffee, made a face, and set the cup down again. "I'll need until tomorrow morning to get them out. Where are you staying?"

"Actually, I haven't checked into any place yet. Maybe you have a suggestion."

She didn't know if the expression on his face was a smile or a grimace. "You've got your choice between

Azalea Bed and Breakfast or the High Ridge Motel."

"Which one would you recommend?"

He grunted. "Neither, to tell the truth, but at the motel you won't have Betty Ann Morrison sticking her nose in your business."

Dana rose from her seat. "Thank you. And thanks for agreeing to help."

He shook his head. "Don't mistake what I'm doing for a blessing on this project. I'm just hoping you'll do your research, find nothing, and go away quietly. Ten o'clock tomorrow work for you?"

"That's fine."

Every pair of eyes followed her as she made her way to the front door. On the sidewalk, she stopped a moment and looked around. Her skin crawled, as if the predator was actually there, watching her. All these years, she'd been convinced he was still here, hiding behind a familiar face, concealing the evil that swirled within him.

Her mind still on her conversations at the newspapers, Dana barely glanced at the large black pickup parked across the street from *The High Ridge Messenger*. And the man watching her through the passenger window.

****

Just who the hell is she?

Sheriff Cole Landry sipped on the giant cup of hot coffee from Freddie's Gas and Go, watching the woman walk out of the newspaper office and climb into her car. Everything about her screamed "big city." She was maybe five four, with streaky blonde hair pulled back in a ponytail so tight it had to give her a headache and a slender body in jeans and a blazer. Her eyes were hidden behind huge sunglasses. Everything expensive. Even he could see that.

He was sure she wasn't from around here. As sheriff of Salado County, population twenty-five thousand, there were few people he didn't at least have a nodding acquaintance with. And with just five thousand people in High Ridge, strangers easily stood out. This one more so than usual.

She was definitely a different breed of animal. Tension radiated from every line of her body. He'd known plenty of women like her—tightly wound, obsessive about control even in bed, emotions locked down. Down and dirty sex, then get the hell away.

But something about her made the back of his neck itch. And worse than that, made his cock sit up and pay attention. What the hell was someone like her doing in his nice quiet slice of the world? The place he'd spent summers on his uncle's ranch. The place he'd retired to when he left the Marines—burned out from Iraq and Afghanistan—and bought a small spread of his own. And how lucky was it that Salado County was looking for a new sheriff at just that moment? And then the consultation offer from Guardian Security came out of the blue after he'd worked a situation with them. Life was good.

But he had a feeling this woman was going to kick him straight out of his comfort zone.

He took another swallow of coffee. Usually, he waited to reach the office before pouring his first cup, but he'd had to stop and see Freddie about some minor vandalism at the store and the coffee had looked and smelled better than anything Grace, his dispatcher, brewed. The stop put the stranger square in his sites.

17

Finishing the last of the dark liquid, he crushed the cup, turned on the engine, and headed for his office. He was barely inside before someone yelled to him, "John Garrett's on the line for you."

Good. Maybe he'd get some answers.

****

Needing something in her stomach besides airline peanuts, Dana took the time to grab a sandwich at a nearby diner. She had only vague memories of the town she'd grown up in, culled from the mind of a seven-year-old. But research told her High Ridge was just like all the other small Hill Country towns. Limestone buildings, ranches whose rolling acres held herds of cattle and horses, the local high school and weekend rodeo serving as centers of activity. As she drove down Main Street she thought she'd stumbled into a Charles Russell painting.

How many times had she Googled both the town and the county, searching for...she sure didn't know what. If it had to do with the children's murders, she didn't find it. Somehow, the sheriff at the time had been able to shut down the flow of news, and newspapers outside the county carried only a smattering of details of the crimes.

What had she expected coming back here? A sudden message from outer space telling her who destroyed her life and killed her sister? That certainly wasn't happening. Instead, what she got the minute she passed the boundary sign for Salado County was the familiar cold fist of terror that never released its grip. Not once in all these years. It was the single force that drove her.

The High Ridge Motel was every bit as dreary as

Dana expected, but no worse than dozens of others she'd stayed at. This one was distinguished by the fake antlers on the wall in the lobby, the terra cotta tile floor, and a potted cactus that had to be a hundred years old. The bedspread in her room was fake animal hide and the furniture a very cheap oak.

At least it would do for one night. She had a feeling she wouldn't be leaving this town any time soon. Tomorrow she'd do what she often did—find a short-term rental.

Parking in front of her room, she hauled her suitcase and laptop inside her room and flopped onto the bed, still fully dressed and exhausted. The lack of sleep the night before and the flight and the tension of the morning finally caught up with her, and in seconds, she fell into an uneasy sleep. A sleep haunted by dreams of an old barn and the high cackle of a man's voice.

Chapter Two

Dana pushed open the door of *The High Ridge Messenger* and hoped Marian Jordan didn't shoot her on sight. When she woke that morning, she was no more rested than when she fell asleep the day before. Her dreams were especially disturbing, and she had to look carefully around the room to be sure Kylie's little body wasn't lying somewhere for her to find. Sleeping in her clothes hadn't helped, and a shower had barely washed away the rumpled feeling.

When the grumbling of her stomach reminded her she hadn't eaten since lunch the day before, she made herself stop at the Gas and Go for coffee and a sausage biscuit. Now the food sat like lead in her stomach. She forced her mouth into a smile for John Garrett when he came out to greet her.

"I can't tell you how much I appreciate you doing this." Dana stood in his office, hoping he would give her what she wanted and leave her alone to work with it. Like every other man his age in the county, he was somewhere on her suspect list and being around him made her nervous and edgy.

"You won't thank me when you start reading this muck," Garrett told her. "But if you've got your mind set on it, I might as well get you what you need. I suppose you won't give me any peace until I do."

"I like to think of myself as persuasive," she told

him. "And I'll be fine. It won't be any worse than other research I've done, I can promise you."

He motioned for her to follow him. "Come on. I'll take you to the storage room where everything is kept. Lucky for you, those issues are on microfilm and not lying stacked in some box somewhere. Who knows what shape they'd be in by now? I'll set you up at a machine and leave you to it." He shook his head. "I wish you joy of it. I have to warn you, though. This town won't give you much cooperation if you try talking to anyone."

"I've already figured that out," she told him in a dry voice.

The room he led her to was obviously not used on a regular basis. A long table pushed against one wall held two microfiche machines, a printer, and dusty cartons labeled by years with rolls of microfiche in them.

"Help yourself to the coffee out there if you want," he told her. "Although after you start reading this stuff, you may need something a lot stronger." He walked away, muttering to himself.

Dana wiped her palms on the fabric of her slacks, her hands suddenly damp with perspiration. Setting a note pad, a pen, and her pocket PC next to her, she took a deep breath and loaded the first roll of film onto the machine. With the first turn of the handle, she crossed into territory from which there was no turning back.

She moved through the film one frame at a time, each story branding itself into her brain. By the time she'd been at it for two hours, her eyes burned, her shoulders ached, and she had to force herself to fight back the nausea.

She finished sooner than she expected. The paper

published weekly and they never ran more than two stories about each incident, as if by downplaying it, they could pretend it didn't happen. The stories were light on the details of the bodies, but even the flimsy descriptions were enough to rip her heart open.

Dana had read stories and reports of horrific crimes as she gathered research for other books. Been revolted by the inhumanity of what people could do to each other. But this. This created a special hell all its own. Even the barest of details of the mutilated young bodies, the scant particulars of the rapes were enough to give anyone nightmares.

Tears burned in Dana's eyes and her heart pinched, hard. What kind of monster could do something so hideous to innocent, unsuspecting children? To her and Kylie?

Oh, God. Kylie. Dana was supposed to have protected her, to make sure nothing ever happened to her. She'd certainly done a lousy job. Pieces of that night slammed into her like a fist, knocking the breath from her body. Kylie's screams echoed in her head, over and over, a reminder of her failure to save her baby sister.

Her stomach heaved, and she shoved her chair back from the table. Racing for the restroom, she barely had time to lock the door to the stall before the miniscule contents of her stomach roared out of her. She retched until there was nothing left, until dry heaves shook her and left her gasping for air.

When she heard the outer door to the restroom open, she flushed the toilet and leaned against the wall.

"Miss Moretti?"

She recognized Marion Jordan's icy voice.

"I'm here." She hoped her voice sounded stronger to Marion than it did to her.

"Are you all right? Mr. Garrett said he saw you hurry past his office and thought you might be ill."

And wouldn't you just love that.

"I'm fine. Thank you." She opened the door of the stall. "I think I ate something that disagreed with me."

The woman's face was rigid with disdain, as if throwing up was no less than Dana deserved.

"Well, if you're sure you're all right..."

"I'm fine. Thank you." Dana splashed cold water on her face, rinsed out her mouth, and blotted her skin with a paper towel. "Tell Mr. Garrett I appreciate everyone's concern."

"All right then." Marion turned to leave, then stopped. "Shall I tell him you're finished?"

"Yes. I'm getting ready to put everything back." Dana knew she had to get out of here for a while. Other cases she'd written about had been approached dispassionately. The details, no matter how gory, had not disturbed her on a visceral level. But this was different. This was personal. This had happened to her.

Back in the dusty room, she stored away the cartridges she'd been using, shoved her belongings into her briefcase, and picked up the stack of articles she'd sent to the printer. She'd pay for them on the way out.

As she passed John Garrett's office, she noticed the door was closed and heard the low hum of male voices. She wondered idly who he was meeting with that required a closed door and if it had something to do with her.

Paranoid much?

She swallowed a sigh as she went to pay for

printing.

****

"She wants to do what?" Cole tilted his Stetson back on his head and stared at John Garrett.

"You heard me."

Cole leaned back in his chair across from Garrett in the editor's office and stared at him. "Tell me again."

"She plans to dig into the old pedophile killer cases." Garrett dropped into his chair behind the desk. "I left her going through files in the storage room, so let's keep this conversation between ourselves."

Cole frowned. "You know how long it took the town to get over everything that happened. There are people who still haven't recovered."

Even as a kid, he hadn't been immune to the details of the horrific crimes. It had been impossible to avoid hearing about them.

Garrett picked up a book on the side of his desk and handed it to the sheriff. "Here. Her latest. A best seller, just like all her others. Her picture's on the back." He flipped it over.

The moment John handed him the book Cole realized why she seemed so familiar. Even he had seen her picture on the books in stores.

"Damn good-looking woman, despite everything," Garrett went on. "Maybe you can romance her out of this pickle."

Cole stared at the picture. The editor was right. Dana Moretti, even in a photograph, had a latent sexuality that made him want to find out just how deep it went. Except for the eyes. He'd never seen such cold eyes in a woman.

He handed the book back. "I think that falls outside

the demands of my job, John. But I'll have a talk with her about this. Maybe convince her what a bad idea this is."

Garrett shook his head. "No, let's just see if the gruesome details chase her away first. Maybe she'll decide she can't hack it after all."

Cole pushed his chair back. "If not, I'll think of something. I'm sure not anxious to have the county down on my head about her."

****

Barely able to tolerate the thought of food after her morning's reading material, Dana instead looked for the real estate office that had registered on her consciousness the day before. One night at the High Ridge Motel was one night too many. When research kept her in the same place for several months, she'd learned to search out the availability of short-term rentals.

Jane Milburn, the disgustingly perky real estate agent, was only too excited to sign a lease with famous best-selling true crime author Dana Moretti.

"The owner won't take less than six months, though," she apologized, pushing the contract across the tiny desk in the tinier office. "Will that be all right? You didn't say how long you plan to stay."

"I really don't know yet, but the six months is no problem even if I leave early." Dana signed both copies of the lease.

"The house is completely furnished with linens, dishes, and cooking utensils," Jane said in her best sales voice. "You'll need to stop by the municipal building to change the utilities to your name and have a phone line activated."

"Thanks. I won't need the phone. I can use my cell. But I'll take care of the others." She was anxious to get moving and see where she'd be living for a while.

"Are you here to work on another book?" Jane's eyes sparkled with avid curiosity.

"Yes, I am." Dana folded her copy of the lease and stuck it in her purse with the keys. In a voice as level as she could make it, she added, "I'm looking into the child abductions and murders that happened here some years ago."

The agent's face closed up as if a shutter had lowered. All the friendly sparkle disappeared. "I'm sorry to hear that. It was a terrible time for High Ridge, and I know people won't like having it dug up all over again."

"I understand the man was never caught." She watched Jane's reaction carefully.

"That's because it was some drifter or day laborer." Jane's tone was clipped and icy. "A person who hung around for a while and then moved on."

Dana raised an eyebrow. "*Hung around* for two years? Seems like someone would have noticed him during that time."

"Well, they didn't and now he's gone." She studied Dana with cold eyes. All the perkiness had disappeared. "Maybe you won't need that house after all. I'd be happy to tear up the contract."

"I think I'll take my chances." Dana's tone matched hers.

"Listen, Miss Moretti. I was just a little girl when everything happened, but I know what a terrible, terrible time it was for High Ridge. Everyone's tried to put it behind them." Jane slammed the desk drawer shut with a bang. "Don't expect anyone to talk to you about it."

Dana pasted on her best professional smile. "I usually have pretty good luck getting people to open up to me. Maybe I will this time, too."

The real estate agent swept the contract into a folder, a signal the discussion was over.

"I think we're done here." Her voice couldn't have been colder if it was chipped from a freezer. She looked pointedly at her watch. "You should probably get moving if you want to take care of the utilities today."

"Thank you for everything." Dana rose from her chair. "I'm sure I'll be seeing you around."

"Don't count on it." By now, the professional polish was completely gone.

As she was unlocking her car, she noticed a black pickup cruising past her and a thread of memory dangled in her brain. Hadn't she seen it someplace earlier? Like this morning? A shiver of unease skittered over her spine as she cranked up the engine on her little rented compact.

****

"This is stupid," Cole muttered to himself.

What in hell was he doing following this woman? He'd left his county vehicle in the lot along with his uniform shirt and taken his truck when he left the office. Strictly by chance, he'd seen her coming out of Jane Milburn's office and head for the Gas and Go. Now, he stayed far enough behind her, allowing two or three vehicles to ride in between, hoping he wouldn't tease her antennae.

Where the hell was she going? She was heading for the west side of town, but what could she be looking for? There wasn't all that much out that way. He muttered a curse when he saw her turn into the fairgrounds entrance. This was where the last two victims had been taken. Cole tried to remember if that tidbit had made it into the newspapers. Then he remembered she'd been going through old files this morning. Had she come to the last one already, the one about the little Nolan girls?

He watched her park her car near the concession stand, get out, and walk to the picnic area. She stood, nearly as still as a statue, just staring around her as if trying to visualize what had happened. How did she do what she did? Get inside the minds of dead people and killers to find answers that eluded everyone else.

He waited, wondering what she would do next. He was shocked at what he saw. She stumbled to a tree and vomited, then dropped onto one of the picnic benches and buried her head in her hands. From the way her shoulders shook, he knew she was crying and they weren't any ladylike tears. So she wasn't such a cold fish after all. Or was there something personal in all this? In the Marines, he'd learned to read people fast. Sometimes his very life depended on it. And his well-developed gut instinct told him. Something here just wasn't adding up.

He'd do a little more digging on Miss Dana Moretti.

Eventually the tears must have dried up, because she dug a tissue out of her pocket, wiped her eyes and blew her nose, and walked slowly back to her car. She looked up, and for a moment, Cole thought she'd seen him. Then she climbed into the little car, cranked the engine, and tore out of the parking lot like every demon in the world was after her.

****

The headache gestating since Dana got on the plane the day before was threatening to emerge full blown. After the episode at the fairgrounds, she wanted only to curl up in a fetal position and shut out the world. But she hadn't checked out her rental yet and she needed at least the minimum of groceries and supplies. Freddie's Gas and Go seemed the quickest answer.

As she moved through the small convenience store, she had the sense that every pair of eyes was glued to her. Mulling over the presence of the "muckraker," as she'd sometimes been called, and what it was going to mean to them and the county.

From what little she'd seen so far, it didn't appear that High Ridge had experienced a population explosion since she left, so she supposed it was just that a strange face piqued everyone's interest. She didn't know if John Garrett had mentioned to anyone what she was doing here, but she was sure Marion Jordan had.

Did they react the same way Marion had? Did any of them read her books and recognize her? Did the killer? Was he here somewhere?

Dredging up her best professional smile for the clerk, she paid for her purchases and carried them to her car. By the time she found the address on the directions Jane Milburn had given her and brought everything inside, Dana's head felt as if she'd stuck it in a vise. Digging two aspirins from her purse, she swallowed them with a glass of water at the sink, closed her eyes, and willed the pain in her head to subside.

The house was comfortably furnished and had

obviously been recently cleaned, but it still had the stale, closed-in feeling that suddenly made her claustrophobic. Dana opened a couple of windows, welcoming the rush of air. She took time to put away her groceries, knowing she should put something in her empty stomach, but even the *thought* of food made her stomach heave again. What she needed first was something to ease the mental strain gripping her body. Something mindless to make her forget for a while why she was here.

When her nerves were strung this tight, physical exercise usually did it for her. Deciding to take a run through her new neighborhood, she changed into shorts and a T-shirt and laced up her jogging shoes. What better way to familiarize herself with the area?

She glanced around as she moved from the front porch to the wide sidewalk. A nice, neat neighborhood. Well kept. Quiet. Exactly the environment she needed.

Taking a deep breath, she headed off, setting her pace, lengthening her stride as her body fell into the familiar rhythm. As her muscles stretched, she felt the tension ease. The evening air had a fresh smell to it, and a soft breeze teased at the tendrils of curls escaping her ponytail.

In a moment it all changed, the breeze shifting to a freshening wind, heavy clouds moving in. She was ten blocks from the house when fat drops of rain began pelting her skin, and in seconds, she was soaked.

She sloshed through the rapidly accumulating puddles and was wishing she'd opted for wine and a hot bath when a large, black pickup pulled to the curb and the passenger side window slid down. Dana began running faster, her natural fear of strangers, especially men, kicking in.

"Hey!" The voice was deep, heavy, masculine. "Need a ride?"

She glanced sideways. It was the same truck she'd seen earlier, she was sure. She didn't stop long enough to get more than a brief glimpse of the driver. Male, wearing the traditional Stetson. Was it *him*? Had he already discovered her and identified the grown woman who was once the child? No, he'd be older than this man.

But just like that, the familiar panic threatened to swallow her up. The pounding of her heart and the sensation of air trapped in her lungs had little to do with her physical exertion. This was the same kind of paralyzing fear that wrapped its tentacles around her whenever she was confronted with an unknown, unexpected male presence.

Dana pushed harder, strides eating up the distance back the way she'd come.

Just let me get to the house. Please. Just let me get away from him.

"You're soaked," the voice called to her as the truck slowed. "You'll catch pneumonia. Be sensible. I promise I'm harmless. Come on. Let me give you a ride."

Yeah, right. God, make him get away from me.

The voice didn't sound familiar, but that didn't mean it wasn't *him*. He'd have changed, gotten older like she had. She increased her speed, hoping that would be a signal to back off. Her heart was trip-hammering so hard she expected it to leap through her chest at any moment. She'd stupidly left her cell phone in her purse so she couldn't even call the sheriff.

At the corner, the truck turned in front of her and she had a vague impression of a man at the wheel, but the rain made it impossible to see him clearly. There was a big dog, some kind of shepherd, sitting up in the back seat. When the truck stopped at the curb, literally in her path, the fear was so intense it choked her.

Get away! Get away!

"Listen, it's all right," the driver called. "I'm…"

But she didn't wait to hear who or what he was or to get a better look. Fueled by a surge of adrenaline, she cut to the right and ran around the end of his truck. She headed through the yards of her unknown neighbors, knowing the truck couldn't follow her there and hoping no one would think she was up to no good and shoot her.

He won't get out of the truck and follow me on foot, will he? Faster, Dana. Run Faster.

Fear made her stride lengthen and her arms pump harder.

A giant streak of lightning split the sky, and thunder rumbled as if it were right beside her as she reached her back porch. Fishing the key from her waterlogged shorts, she shoved her door open and fell into the utility room. Slamming the door shut, she sagged against the wall, every muscle in her body trembling. Her pulse was racing, and she thought her lungs would never get enough air again.

I got away, I got away, I got away.

Over and over, like a litany, the words reverberated in her mind as they tried to convince her that she was once again safe.

Safe. What a joke. No place is safe.

Finally, aware that she was standing in a widening

puddle, she pulled off her soaked clothing and tossed it into the laundry sink.

She hurried to her bedroom and yanked her robe from the bed where she'd tossed it earlier, pulling it on and yanking the belt tight. Still shaking, she moved through the house, slamming shut the windows she'd opened, checking deadbolts and window locks until she was satisfied she was as secure as she could make herself. Safe enough at any rate to take a hot shower and chase the chill away.

When she'd caught her breath, she searched in the utility room and found a mop, using it to clean up the rain that had come in through the open windows. As she moved mechanically through the chore, images from her past clashed with those created by the articles she'd read today. She had to get this done before she turned into a complete basket case.

Tonight, she'd force herself to read again everything she'd brought home from the newspaper. Tomorrow she'd hit the sheriff's office and request copies of the files of those old cases. She just hoped she could get through all the explicit details without getting sick again.

Leaving the mop to dry, she headed into her bathroom and turned on the shower full force. With the hot water beating down on her, the tightness around her chest finally loosened and her pulse rate slowed. Leaning against the tiled wall, she willed the water to wash away both the memories and the ever-present dread.

Later, dried and wrapped in her sleep shirt, she managed to get down a bowl of soup. Finally, she crawled into the strange bed and tried to empty her mind. She closed her eyes, but the image of the ominous black truck wouldn't go away. Others might say, in a small town like High Ridge, the man was just being neighborly. He was harmless. What could happen in a nice town like this?

Dana knew. Oh, yes. She knew all too well. So she'd run, just as she always had. Old habits definitely died hard.

And fear never went away.

Chapter Three

He'd had a busy day, taking care of his public business so he could take care of his private activities tonight. In town, he'd heard all about the famous Dana Moretti, best-selling true crime author, who had descended on his small town. Gossip had her digging up old ghosts, but that didn't worry him. Still, it wouldn't hurt for him to check her out. Get a handle on her.

Meanwhile, he had things to do that required his attention. Things that satisfied his needs. He looked at the small prepubescent girl in front of him, barely able to stop from smacking his lips.

"Well," he drawled, "aren't you just the sweetest little morsel. We're going to have us some fun."

Watching her cowering in fear only ramped up the lust blazing through him. When she cried and tried to pull away, he just laughed.

"That's it," he crooned. "You go ahead and cry. I love it when they cry." Then he began to sing. "There was a little girl, who had a little curl, right in the middle of her forehead…"

Chapter Four

Her hair was spread out on his pillow like a silken fall, the low lamplight catching the golden streaks. He could still feel the anxiety running like a stream beneath her arousal, but the heat in her eyes told him she wanted this. God, he hoped he didn't fuck it up.

He brushed his mouth over hers then traced the outline of it with his tongue, licking the softness of her lips. When she parted them just slightly, he eased his tongue inside and glided it over the slick inner surface. Her small tongue danced with his, tentatively at first, then exploding like a banked flame.

His cock was so hard he had to grit his teeth to keep from ramming into her. Easy, easy, easy. This is a frightened bird you've got here. Don't attack like some berserker.

He kissed her cheeks, the line of her jaw, licked the soft spot behind her ear before trailing his tongue down the slender column of her neck. Her skin was like the softest satin, so smooth against his tongue. She moaned beneath him, delicious little sounds that made his balls ache.

Her hands fluttered against his back, then clutched at his muscles as his mouth found one stiff nipple. He sucked it, hard, pulling it into his mouth. Scraping it with his teeth. Nibbling then licking it to soothe the ache. When he had the one fully swollen and pebbled, he turned his attention to the other.

Beneath him, she moved restlessly, her thighs bracketing his, her body trembling as he teased and aroused her. He wanted her more than ready when he finally entered her. This would be it. The thrust that broke down all the walls. The moment that chased whatever demons kept her emotionally locked up.

In slow increments, he worked his way down her body, licking the soft flesh of her tummy, tracing the whole of her navel, until he reached the soft nest of pubic curls. He tugged them lightly with his teeth before moving lower and taking one long, slow lick of her slit.

Wet!

Soaked!

His cocked flexed and his balls tightened in anticipation.

Her moans were increasing, louder now and more frequent, as he took her clit between his teeth and tormented it. Sliding one hand between her thighs, he inserted two fingers into her drenched pussy, stroking her fluttering walls in cadence with his mouth, working her nub.

He worked her slowly, forcing himself to be patient, waking up all those dormant nerves. Unlocking the invisible manacles. Oh, yeah, she was soaking his hand and her hips were hitching upward, pushing herself against his mouth and his hand.

"Oh, oh, oh."

Her little cries were breathy and so arousing he was afraid he'd come just listening to her. He pressed her thighs open wider and replaced his fingers in her cunt with his tongue. The moment he thrust inside her, she climaxed, her legs clamping against him, her body shaking. Hands grasping his hair, yanking.

Before the aftershocks began to fade he grabbed the condom from the nightstand, rolled it on, and lifting her to him with his hands beneath her ass, drove home.

Oh, God. Oh, Jesus. Oh, holy mother.

She was so damned tight and slick and wet and hot, like a silken fist gripping his cock. Squeezing it.

He closed his eyes and clenched his jaw, trying to steady himself. But then she wrapped her legs around him, pulling him in tighter, and jerked her hips against him. The last thread of his control snapped. He drove into her, hips thrusting again and again, his cock dragging the walls of her pussy with each in and out movement.

He couldn't hold off release any longer. Moving one hand between them, he found her clit and stroked. Rub, rub, rub. And as she climaxed around him, he exploded, his cock pumping hot fluid into the latex reservoir.

Lights exploded behind his eyes and he felt as if someone had launched him into space. They shuddered together, over and over, the only sound in the room the ragged reverberations of their breathing.

I'm dead, he thought, collapsing at last, trailing kisses over her face and neck. But kill me again. Please.

At last, he lifted himself and eased slowly from the tight clasp of her body, his hand gripping his cock to keep the condom in place.

Cole woke to find himself clutching his erection with his own hand, his skin covered with the heat of semen where he'd jerked off in his sleep.

Swell. Just fucking swell. He was having wet dreams like a teenager over some woman he hadn't even met yet. So she intrigued him. Big fucking deal. A lot of women intrigued him, but he didn't have fantasies about them.

Good going, asshole.

The image of her in the rain was still burned into his brain. Soaked, with her thin T-shirt plastered to her breasts and her shorts clinging to her ass like a second skin, she'd looked like something washed up from High Ridge Lake. Even in the best of circumstances, he was sure Dana Moretti wasn't a woman he'd be anxious to get into his bed.

Yet there was the fucking dream.

He was losing his mind. That was the only answer. Or else he badly needed to get laid. Most likely the latter. But certainly not by anyone in High Ridge. Everyone in town would know within twenty-four hours, and five minutes later they'd have him married. He loved this place, but it exasperated him.

Awakened by the dream at five thirty, he decided to take a ride up into the hills where he could watch the day come to life. Yes, between his job as sheriff and the occasional mission for Guardian, life was good.

The sun was barely a whisper of gold in the sky when Cole had Thunder saddled and was riding him out of the yard. With a thousand pounds of sleek stallion beneath him running flat out, he felt the early morning breeze on his skin and inhaled the heady scent of horseflesh mixed with the crisp aroma of prairie grass.

He still wanted to kick himself for the stunt last night. Why in hell had he decided to hunt up Dana Moretti? Because Jane Milburn was telling people in the diner that she'd rented a little house and now they'd never get rid of her? High Ridge was small enough that

Cole knew exactly what property was available where, so locating her hadn't been difficult.

Renting a house had to mean she was planning on hanging around for a while. Causing a stir in his nice little community. His gut told him a big pot of trouble was about to boil over, covering all of Salado County with its sludge.

When it had begun to rain yesterday, he thought offering her a ride would be an easy way to meet her, but she'd run from him like a scalded jackrabbit. She probably thought he was some stalker trying to pick her up, and he couldn't exactly blame her. From her point of view, that's probably exactly what it had looked like.

Way to go, idiot.

He'd have to figure out how to talk to her without pissing her off too much. Just enough to get rid of her. Convince her there was nothing here to find. The killer was long gone and people wanted their kids to rest in peace.

Maybe he'd call Uncle Tate. See if he could drag him in early from the ranch for breakfast and tap into the man's instincts. They'd always been very good, an important trait for a man who raised cutting horses.

He held Thunder still for another long moment, trying to piece together all the bits of information about this woman. She still remained a puzzle. He'd have to find a better way to meet and assess her. He needed to keep his county safe from prying busybodies and at the same time figure out why those brief glimpses had aroused him so intensely and given him a hard-on like he hadn't had in months.

Loosening the reins slightly and urging Thunder with his knees, Cole took off across the pastureland, hoping to outrun his demons.

****

"I guess that probably wasn't the best way to try and meet someone." Cole took a swallow of the fresh coffee the waitress had poured in his cup and studied his uncle across the booth table. The man might be pushing seventy, but he was in damn good shape. All those years of ranching had kept his body lean and hard, his muscles nearly like those of a man many years younger. He still had a thick head of dark brown hair, although it was now liberally streaked with gray. Cole knew men a lot younger who weren't in half as good shape.

"I'd say you're right," Tate Bishop drawled, lounging back in the booth. "Seems pretty smart if she didn't want to get in a truck with a complete stranger. Seems like one of you has a brain in their head."

"Yeah, yeah, yeah. I know it was stupid." He stared at his coffee. "I don't know. It's just that she's been doing strange things since she got in town."

"Like what?" The look in Tate's piercing blue eyes was sharp. "And what have you been doing? Following her? Is that why you were in her neighborhood last night?"

Half embarrassed, Cole told him what he'd done the day before. And about Dana's strange behavior and her visit to the fairgrounds.

"What was she was doing there?" he asked, as much of himself as his uncle. "And what's up with the vomiting, anyway? I sure didn't expect to see her heaving her guts."

Tate idly stirred sugar into his own coffee. "Maybe she's not as hardboiled as she pretends to be and the stories she read really got to her. What did John Garrett have to say?"

"Not much more than who she is, an author of true crime books. Here to dig up all that stuff from twenty-five years ago. It's so far in the past, I can't figure why she's after it now?"

"Doesn't matter." Tate sipped the liquid in his cup. "There's nothing for her to find. And no one will talk to her." He paused. "You don't think she's got a personal interest in it, do you?"

"Like what?" Then a cold thought froze him. "You think she might be related to the pedophile? That she's trying to see if we ever found any evidence against him? Shit."

"I think that's very unlikely. But it wouldn't hurt to keep a close eye on her. Just in case." Tate smiled. "And use that smooth personality of yours to convince her she needs to leave High Ridge alone."

"Smooth." Cole snorted. "But I will talk to her. Make her see she has to leave these folks alone."

"You know good and well whoever it was has been long gone from here," Tate pointed out. "Otherwise, I'd say, yeah, go for it. But after all this time?" He shrugged. "There isn't even a trail to follow. And people want to keep their dead buried."

"I know. I know. Thanks for meeting me."

"Anytime. You know that, Cole. Maybe you could find time in your busy schedule to come out and have dinner with us. Your aunt sure would love to see you."

Cole slid out of the booth and clapped his Stetson on his head. "I'll see how the weekend shapes up. And I sure could use some of Adele's cooking."

"Come out Sunday. Plan on it."

"I'll let you know."

****

Dana dragged herself into the kitchen worn out from wrestling with the nightmares that always left her sleep deprived. The stranger in the truck last night had ignited a terror she usually kept a tight lid on. Every time she closed her eyes, memories of Kylie seized her in a tight grip, and with them came the choking scent of wood shavings. Sleep was a hell she didn't need.

She found the coffee maker and pulled the new can of coffee from the fridge. Leaning on the counter, she willed the machine to brew faster, needing the caffeine jolt to her system. When the last drop filtered into the pot, she poured some into a large mug and carried it outside to the small patio.

The chairs were still covered with dew, but the chilly dampness woke up her weary body. She settled in a lounger, leaned back, and watched two birds hopping from branch to branch in one of the crepe myrtles that guarded the corners of the tiny yard. If only her life could be that simple. She sighed and turned away.

She wasn't looking forward to her visit to the sheriff's office today. Would he be willing to help? After all, she might be able to find answers at last to an age-old case. He ought to be happy about that. Of course, if he gave her a hard time and was a real ass about it, she could always wave court decisions at him.

Assuming he gave her access to the files, reading the one about Kylie—and herself—would be the toughest part. She just hoped she'd be able to get through it.

Focus. Make an outline and focus. Think of it as an abstract story that piques your interest. Do what you always do. Stick to the facts, don't let emotion cloud your thinking.

Yeah, right.

When her mug was empty, she went inside, refilled it, and headed for the bathroom. Half an hour later she was showered and dressed in slacks and a tailored blouse, what she considered her non-threatening outfit. Grabbing a muffin from the box she'd left on the counter, she headed out of the house.

At Freddie's she bought a cold drink to wash down her muffin, chugging half of the liquid in her car in the parking lot. She could already feel the tension grabbing at her again, the expectation of conflict at the sheriff's office. Not to mention the image of that black pickup dogging her, crawling around the edge of her consciousness like some poisonous bug.

Despite swallowing three aspirin the night before and two more this morning, the headache still clung to her like moss to a tree. She rolled the half-empty can of soda against her forehead then pressed it to the column of her neck.

I can do this. I have to do this. For Kylie. And for myself.

She swallowed the last of the soda and tossed the can in the car's litter bag. Okay, enough with the pity party. Time to take on the law.

When she turned into the parking area at the sheriff's office, her hands tightened on the steering wheel and she nearly stopped breathing. That damn black pickup was parked at the side of the building. Sweat slicked her palms and the jackhammer in her head kicked up another notch. Surely, *he* couldn't be here. Could he?

The lettering on the glass door said Cole Landry, Sheriff, Salado County. Her research had told her he'd only been in office a short time, but unless the records had been destroyed, he'd still have access to them. The doors opened into a small, enclosed lobby with a reception window at one side.

"I'd like to see Sheriff Landry," she told the woman behind the glass. "If he's available."

And if he's not, I'll just wait until he is.

"May I have your name and the nature of your business?"

God. The woman was as frosty as Marion Jordan.

From her body language, Dana figured word was already circulating. Well, what did she expect in a small town?

"Dana Moretti." She handed a business card through the window opening. "I'd like to ask him some questions about an old case if he has the time."

"Let me just check."

She waited tensely while the woman spoke softly into a telephone. In a moment, she looked up and said, "He'll be right with you."

Dana wasn't sure if she should be surprised or grateful that Sheriff Landry had agreed to see her so easily. She'd have bet a year's royalties John Garrett had called him, filled him in, and asked for his help in shutting her down. A lock snicked as a door opened behind her.

"Can I help you?"

The deep voice sent shock waves through her. She whirled, her knees shaking. Oh, hell. It was him. The man in the truck. Wearing a uniform, for God's sake.

"I have to say," he went on, "you look a lot better

when you aren't soaked through by the rain."

The first thing she thought was *cowboy*. He had the easy, relaxed yet alert stance she'd seen on men around horses and cattle. And his feet were shod in square-toed western boots. She was sure his hat was a Stetson.

But the way his eyes assessed her, the analytical gaze...*military*. Some kind of covert ops.

A dangerous combination in a man.

Dangerous to women. And to people who were misled by his friendly smile.

He was somewhere in his mid-thirties. At least six-four, broad shouldered, and lean hipped, the khaki of the sheriff's uniform looking as if it were custom tailored for him. His face was all angles and planes, with deep-set, whiskey-colored eyes framed by dark brows and lashes. Even in her high state of anxiety, she couldn't miss the sexuality that radiated from him.

The ultimate Alpha male.

And trouble.

I'll bet he has to beat women off with a nightstick. Well, he won't have to worry about me. Oh, wait. After last night, he probably thinks I'm a nutcase anyway.

She wet her lips. "I gave my card to the woman at the window. I'm Dana Moretti."

"I know who you are." His smile, like John Garrett's, was professional and didn't reach his eyes. "I've been expecting you. Come on."

He swung the door wide.

"If you'd identified yourself last night," she told him, trying to keep the acid out of her voice, "I might have been more willing to accept a ride. I don't make it a habit of jumping into trucks with strange men."

"You don't know me better now than you did a few

hours ago. I looked up your books, and I'll tell you. There's nothing here that fits in your category."

Oh, yes, there is. You just don't know it.

His body brushed hers as he let the door swing shut, and lightning shot through her. What the hell? She knew what unexpected lust was. She often wrote about it, but it wasn't a feeling familiar to her personally. Certainly not in a situation like this. Maybe this was a bad idea, after all.

"So, what kind of men *do* you jump into trucks with?"

She blinked. "Excuse me?"

His smile was a little softer as he ushered her into his office. "If not strange men, what kind?"

"None." She made her voice as clipped and professional as she could.

"This is a small town, Miss Moretti," he said once they were seated. "People are very neighborly and reach out to help each other. If you stick around for any length of time, you'll find out we don't have marauders prowling the streets."

"But you did once, didn't you?" she shot at him.

His face tightened and all traces of the smile disappeared. "You're talking about the pedophile cases, which happened a very long time ago. Folks aren't happy about the fact you want to dig it all up again. May I ask why all this interest in a case that's been dead for twenty-five years?"

Dana took a deep breath to center herself. "It's what I do. Researching old, unsolved cases. It's how I make my living."

His lips thinned. "Raking through other people's misery?"

47

And sometimes giving them answers.

"Isn't that what *you* do?" she shot back at him.

"I investigate crimes as an officer of the law." His voice had gone from being polite to hostile. "I'm not in it for the publicity."

"Publicity is a byproduct that helps me sell the books," she snapped. "I examine old, mostly unsolved crimes. Look for new angles. Try to form a psychological profile of the killer or killers. Put it all into a book. Let people know we let the monsters out of the closet and destroy them with enough work."

He tapped her business card lightly against one hand. "You know, I've actually read some of your books."

Dana lifted an eyebrow. Was that grudging admiration in his voice? "I'm surprised."

"That I can read or that your books would interest me? I hate to admit it, but you do a pretty good job with unpleasant subjects." He leaned forward, his eyes pinning her. "But I don't understand how you can go back years later, when people have finally come to terms with tragedy, and rip them open again. Doesn't that bother you?"

Dana sat straight in the chair, her posture matching the aggressive line of Cole's body. Now that she was in familiar territory, where the tension wasn't sexual. "If you've read my work, you should already know that people are usually happy to cooperate with me. They see it as a way to get closure. I would think the people involved here would be more bothered by the unanswered questions."

"Really." His face was carefully expressionless. The man was doing his best to press all the wrong buttons.

She forced herself to speak calmly. "Doesn't anyone want to know who did such terrible things to those children? Don't they care that a pedophile got away with terrorizing and killing children? Don't you all want answers?"

I certainly do. Hell, if I don't get them, I might as well crawl in bed, pull the covers over my head, and call it a life because I won't have one left to go back to.

He stared at her for a long moment. "That was twenty-five years ago. It's over and done. There's nothing left to investigate."

Dana tightened her hands into fists. "I'm getting the feeling there's some kind of conspiracy here to keep the lid on this. As if you all know who it was and no one wants to admit it."

That thought had plagued her ever since she'd made herself face the truth of that terrible night. Was it really possible? Could it have been someone they were all familiar with and an entire town had bonded together in a conspiracy of silence? Her stomach roiled at the thought, and she swallowed hard.

Cole's eyes blazed, the corded muscles in his neck evidence of his effort at control. "Don't toss that kind of crap at me, *Miss Moretti*. If we knew who it was, he'd have been skinned alive long before this. That's a shitty thing to say."

Not as shitty as having to live with the nightmare all these years.

"Then let me do what I'm here for. I've had success before in finding evidence that slipped through the cracks. Flushing people out who thought they were home free."

His eyes narrowed as he held her gaze. "You think this is going to be another one like Clyde Montauk? You nearly bought the farm on that one, I heard."

Clyde Montauk was a man who preyed on lonely women for years. After wooing them, he took them to a secluded place and raped them before cutting them up and leaving their body parts all over Palmetto County, Florida. No one had a clue who he was until she came along. She dug hard enough and brought enough new information to light that he'd come after her and walked right into a trap.

She shuddered as the memory swept over her. Not something she wanted to do every day. But she'd do whatever it took to get the answers in this particular case.

"Having second thoughts?" His voice was mocking.

Dana stiffened. "Not at all. I came here, hoping for some cooperation, but I can work without it. I have before."

He studied her for a long moment. "Exactly what is it you want of us? Of me?"

"To start with, I'd like to look through the reports on each of the crimes. Make copies of them if you'll let me. Talk to any of the deputies who were working then. See what they still remember."

"And I suppose visiting the families and questioning them." His voice was flat and a muscle twitched in his cheek as he studied her. Okay, so he didn't like her or what she wanted to do. Well, too bad. She wasn't here for a popularity contest.

When he leaned forward again, she felt the room shrinking and his presence growing and enveloping her.

She'd been through this before. Men who tried to intimidate her. Make her back off. Who unknowingly lit a fire under the fear always lurking near the surface.

But there was something else in the room that unsettled her, an unfamiliar feeling of awareness. Something that skittered over the surface of her skin and made her pulse unexpectedly ramp up. Something that stunned her, that she couldn't afford to acknowledge and didn't want to. She swallowed a hysterical laugh. After all this time, sexual awareness of a man had decided to jump up and smack her at the most inopportune time?

She wet her lips, reaching for her usual and familiar control, unwilling to let him know he rattled her. "Sheriff, no one has ever complained that I acted insensitively or disrespectfully on my other projects. I can assure you it will be the same here."

Their gazes locked for what seemed an interminable length of time. Dana was damn determined she wouldn't break first, and she didn't.

Cole leaned back in his chair, fighting a grin. "Feisty, aren't you?" He held up a hand when she opened her mouth. "No offense. That's a compliment, okay? I like feisty women."

"I think whether you like me or not isn't the question. What's important to me is whether you decide to help me."

His whiskey-colored eyes darkened. The hard look was back on his face, and every trace of humor disappeared. "I'm guessing it will save me a lot of trouble if I just give you what you want instead of hassling with a court order. Which I'm sure you'd get." He stood up, his body ramrod stiff. "But you'll have to work on the files here. They don't leave my office. No copies."

She swallowed a sigh of relief. At least she would get to see them. "I understand. And thank you."

"Don't thank me. I'm not doing this because I want to. The files are so old we had them stored over in the archives. After I talked to John Garrett yesterday, I figured you'd be knocking at my door. To save us both some time, I had them lugged over here this morning and set up a place for you to work. Let's go."

Chapter Five

He sat in his den, pouring another shot of his favorite, aged whiskey, hoping it would calm his nerves. His hand trembled slightly as he lifted the glass to his lips again.

The whiskey burned as it slid down his throat, but it was a good sensation of heat. Comforting. Settling his jittery nerves. Last night's little *adventure* had soothed him for a while, but seeing her this morning had jacked him up again. Brought all those tiny lovelies back.

She had returned, his elusive little flower. This morning, he'd seen her entering Cole Landry's office. So sweet, just like he remembered.

He'd googled Dana Moretti last night, and the face looking back at him made his blood run hot again. He'd never forgotten his little Carrie. She'd been special. The only one who hadn't cried out. The only one who'd struggled against him, turning him on with her odd sense of bravery. Now, she was back. After all these years. She wasn't getting away from him. Not this time.

He leaned back in his comfortable chair and closed his eyes, letting the images from those first two years drift through his brain. His body jerked with pleasure as he remembered them one by one. So young. So sweet. Flesh barely touched. Like flowers not yet ready to bud.

But he'd opened those petals. Oh, yes. And those little flowers had been so sweetly delicious.

Until it was time to shut them up. The ultimate pleasure had been snapping their necks.

If only those fucking teenagers hadn't stumbled onto his cozy little nest. He'd barely gotten away. Good thing he'd left his car where he could roll it to the road without headlights. God, he could still remember pulling into a grove of trees and sitting for hours, shaking and sweating at the close call. Of course, after that, everyone was on such high alert that he'd had to call a halt to his little hobby.

It was a damn good thing DNA testing hadn't been around all those years ago. He'd covered his tracks easily enough over the two years, but DNA would have screwed him royally.

Then Fate visited him, and very quietly, he found another game to play. Oh, yes. This one wasn't quite as delicious, but it was a lot less risky and still gave him pleasure. And again, no one suspected a thing.

She was meeting with the sheriff, his Carrie, probably hoping to twist his arm so she could see all the case reports. Good. Let her take all the time she needed to do her research. She wouldn't find out a thing, and he'd have time to finesse his plan. Figure out a way to accomplish it that wouldn't identify the girls he chose as anything more than random victims. Everyone would panic, thinking another predator had invaded their precious slice of heaven. For damn sure, it wouldn't lead back to him.

He was smart. Oh, yes. He'd outfoxed everyone more than once. He could do it again.

He tossed back the last of his drink and poured another. Unzipping his pants, he pulled out his erection and thought of Carrie/Dana as he stroked himself, a satisfied smile on his face.

Chapter Six

Dana closed the last file folder and leaned back in her chair, rubbing her eyes. Her shoulders ached, her eyes were gritty, and her stomach felt as if she'd poured acid into it. Well, maybe that wasn't so far from the truth. Cole Landry made sure someone brought her coffee on a regular basis, probably hoping it would poison her, as bad as it was.

If she'd had trouble sleeping before, she wondered if she'd ever close her eyes again after forcing herself to read every horrific detail of every crime, every autopsy. She didn't know how the sheriff's deputies who found the bodies had managed to deal with it. Here were all the details that never made it into the news reports.

But with all that, there was still no clue to identify the pedophile. Nothing. All she had, besides the reports and articles, were vague memories and the song.

The damn song. Surely, it had to have some significance, maybe something that would click in someone else's mind if she told them.

If she told them.

She really didn't know why she never mentioned it to anyone, not even the police or her parents. Maybe subconsciously, she was afraid the killer would know, find her, and finish the job.

And isn't that just so stupid.

"I give you credit." The deep voice behind her

startled her, and she jumped. "I figured you'd quit long before this."

When she turned in her chair, she found Cole Landry standing almost directly behind her. That same sensation of heat and sizzle—the one she'd given up hoping she'd ever feel—pounded through her. Her breasts tingled, and the pulse between her thighs rocked with an unfamiliar throbbing. Over the years, she'd schooled herself not to panic when men she didn't know well came too close. Except this wasn't panic.

Although it probably should be.

She tried to conceal how shaky she was as she gathered her things. "I thought it would be easier if I just plowed through it all in one day. Then I wouldn't have to bother you again."

"And you could start on the next phase of your work."

"Something like that." She still hadn't looked directly at him. Why wouldn't he go away? The tiny flicker of attraction between them was going to be trouble for her if she didn't squash it.

"Let me get these folders out of your way." He moved to stand next to her, almost touching her as he reached for the pile on the table.

Without thinking, Dana flinched.

The sheriff took a step back, a look of curiosity flashing briefly across his face. "Sorry."

She took a deep breath and let it out slowly. "No, *I'm* sorry. I'm just a little jumpy from reading these files."

It wasn't so much the touch of a man affecting her as it was *this* man's touch. The unfamiliar heat. The heaviness in her breasts. Dampness between her thighs.

God, she never got wet for anyone. That was part of her problem. Did it have to be this macho asshole who woke up her pheromones? She drew in a deep, steadying breath.

"I can understand." But his eyes, studying her face, were filled with questions.

She snapped her briefcase shut, hitched the strap of her purse over her shoulder, and hurried toward the door. She had to get out of here. Quickly.

"Thank you for letting me see the files," she called over her shoulder and literally ran down the hall to the front doors.

Gasping, she shoved them open and hurried to her car, slid inside, and slammed the door shut behind her. Leaning her head back against the seat, she closed her eyes and drew in long cleansing breaths. When she ran shaking hands over her face, she discovered a fine sheen of perspiration had formed on her skin.

Taking another deep breath, she managed to get the key in the ignition and glanced up through the windshield. Cole Landry stood at the entrance to the building, watching her. A breeze dusted over the parking lot and lifted the edges of his dark hair. Even at this distance, the aura of sensuality he projected was obvious and the irrational fear coiled around her again.

Fear of what, Dana? That you don't want him to touch you? Or that you do?

She managed to back out of the parking space without banging into anything, then pulled onto the street. She'd go home and lock herself in the house and manage to swallow some food. No jogging tonight. No exercises. No thinking of Cole Landry.

Especially no thinking about Cole Landry.

Hot tea with brandy, a steaming shower, and her warm, snuggly bathrobe—that's what the doctor ordered. Once her nerves were back to normal, she'd sort through her notes from today and the articles she'd copied and try to get an outline started.

Focus. Focus on the project.

Chapter Seven

"The boss says we have to cool your fringe benefits for a while."

The younger man known as Tony looked at him from across the table in the highway diner as he delivered his message. The remnants of their meal were scattered across the table, and Tony was on his third soft drink.

"How can you drink that crap with breakfast?" he asked. "Why can't you drink coffee like normal people?"

Tony grinned, as if the kid knew it irritated the crap out of him. "It's just cold caffeine, old man. Try it sometime."

"No, thanks." He finished the coffee in his cup and signaled for a refill. "And tell your boss we don't need to make any changes just yet."

Tony cocked an eyebrow, another mannerism that irritated him. "Are you kidding me? The word's out everywhere about this Moretti bitch, and it's only been a couple of days. She's too nosy for her own good. And ours."

He waited until the waitress had poured his coffee before he spoke again. "I think you need to let me worry about that."

"Now, that's where you're wrong, old man. We all need to worry. The boss is getting itchy. She's digging around in old shit that could get people looking around in places we don't want them looking. It could even lead to you, and ruin a good thing for all of us."

"Tell your boss to pay no attention," he said in a flat voice, pushing back the surge of anger. "She'll be gone before long."

"But—"

"I'm telling you, no one will want to help her. Trust me on that. They'll blow her off." He swallowed some coffee and made a face at its bitter taste. Probably the bottom of the pot. "Besides, I plan to see that she doesn't hang around too long."

"How are you going to do that without attracting attention?" Tony crunched an ice cube. "We've got a good thing going here, you know. Everyone's making good money. Including you. We don't want to screw that up."

"And we're not going to. We'll just continue with business as usual. No one's looking our way, and with what I've got planned, they'll be too busy to pay attention."

"You better not be doing something to get us all in trouble." His lips twisted in a nasty replica of a smile. "Anyway, like I'm sayin', how about laying off for a little while on the extras, or are you so far gone you can't take a breather?"

He frowned at the little shit. "My business is my business. Your boss gets paid plenty for this, and so do you. I don't think you want to take a cut in your income."

"I don't want to lose a nice source of money, either," Tony said. "The top man says he don't want no more little side trips for a while. That's that."

"You tell the top man to let me worry about my end of the deal. I'll take care of that nosy bitch, you can count on it. We're not changing anything."

"Okay, I'll tell him, but he ain't gonna like it." Tony picked up his check and slid out of the booth.

"Just be sure we meet up as usual this week or there *will* be trouble."

Tony stared at him. "You threatening me, old man?"

"Just giving you some information to pass along."

He watched Tony head for the door with his usual arrogant walk. The kid was getting an over-inflated idea of himself. Someone needed to take a chip or two out of him. Later.

First, his plan. He needed to put it into action soon. To take Carrie/Dana out of the picture before she began digging around any more. Her reputation was that of a bulldog. She'd be all over the past like green on grass unless he got rid of her. But he had to do it right. One single death would be suspicious. A string of them would have the county on edge, especially because it would be such an anomaly. He'd do what he had to.

At the same time, he'd be giving folks a new bone to chew on. Something to take the focus away from those old cases. The sheriff would be too busy to help Dana and the newspapers would have something new to feed on. Something that would provide misdirection.

He hadn't been caught before and he wouldn't be now. He was damned good at that—not getting caught. And he already had his first victim chosen. But he'd better get moving before things fell apart right before his eyes.

Today. He'd start today. He could feel the sexual

excitement the violence stimulated coursing through his body. Throwing some bills on the table, he settled his Stetson on his head, smiled at everyone, and walked slowly out of the diner.

****

He watched Leanne Pritchard stop at her truck, both hands filled with plastic sacks of soda, and stare at the flat tire. Even at this distance, he could see the frown on her face. She looked around, as if seeking someone to help her, but the parking lot was fairly empty of people. Besides, she'd parked way down at the end of a row, on the side, where hardly anyone ever went. He'd never let his own kids park so far away. But she was driving her daddy's truck and probably worried about scratching it.

She set her sacks down and patted her pockets, obviously looking for her cell phone. Kids never went anywhere without them these days. She finally pulled it out and stared at it. This was the chance he'd taken, that she'd be able to call for help. But it was a risk he was willing to take. He could just help her with her tire and be on his way. Wait for a more appropriate time.

But like so many kids these days—and adults— she'd apparently forgotten to recharge it. She jabbed it back into her pocket in disgust.

Okay. Good.

She started back toward the store, but he only let her get a few steps before calling her name. "Looks like you got a little problem, Leanne."

She looked up and recognized him at once. Of course. He was a friend of her father's. Tucking strands of her long, blonde hair behind her ears, she flashed a smile.

"Yeah. My tire's flat. Lordy, but Daddy's going to kill me."

"Over a flat tire? I don't think so. Where were you headed?"

"Back to…my friends. I made a soda run."

"They're waiting at the park?" he asked, chuckling as she gasped in surprise. "Honey, some things aren't too secret after all. Kids have been sneaking into the park as long as I can remember."

She dropped her gaze and nodded. "I-I was going to call one of my friends to come and get me, but my cell died. I guess I forgot to charge it." She perked up a little. "Say. Do you have one? Maybe I could use yours."

He held out his hands, palms up. "Left it at home, dang it. Charging on the counter. Need to get myself one of those car chargers, I guess."

"Oh." Her smiled disappeared as she frowned.

He reached down and picked up her bags. "Why don't we do this? I'll give you a ride back to the park. Then you can get a couple of those strong young boys to come back here and change your tire."

She sighed with relief. "Oh, would you? That was my plan, anyway."

"Sure. Come on. Just hop into my truck, and I'll have you there in no time. Lock up your vehicle."

But they hadn't driven for five minutes before she turned to him, puzzled. "Wait. We should be heading out toward the interstate."

"I know a short cut. Just relax, honey. I'll have you there before you know it."

Leanne nibbled her lower lip, obviously uneasy. "Listen, maybe you could just drop me off someplace where there's a phone."

"Now, now, Leanne. I'll have you there in short order. Just relax. How about I put in a CD. Music makes everyone feel better." He lifted the lid on the center console, fumbling inside.

She slid as close to the door as she could get, and he sensed the tension in her body. Okay, he couldn't wait any longer. Flipping up the console cover with his right hand, he pulled out the saturated cloth he'd stashed there, reached over, and clamped it over her face.

Panicked, she grabbed his wrist with both hands and tried to pull it away, but even one-handed he was stronger than she was. She wriggled frantically, trying to pull her head back, but his hand stayed clamped against her face until finally her hands fell away.

He smiled as he thought of the excitement ahead. His cock hardened, and his blood pulsed. Oh, yes. He was looking forward to this. The killing would just be a bonus.

Chapter Eight

The shower helped ease the tension of the day for Dana. The tea and brandy did even more. Pulling on shorts and an old Tampa Bay Buccaneers T-shirt, she settled at the dining room table with a sandwich, a drink, and her briefcase. Her laptop sat open in front of her, ready for input.

She tried to clear her mind of everything except the project at hand, but Cole Landry's ruggedly severe face kept flashing across her internal television screen. Thoughts that she'd never had—never *wanted* to have—about any other man kept poking at her.

What would it be like to have a man's hands on her that she desired and didn't fear? Holding her breasts. Chafing her nipples. Taking those nipples into the wet heat of his mouth. Laving them with his tongue.

Dana shivered. It wasn't that she didn't know how things were done. God knows enough men had tried to coax her into it, had tried their best, like Grant, to make it work. But none of them had ever reached her icy core, frozen away all these years.

Until Cole Landry.

What would she do if she found herself alone with him and the unfamiliar sensations buzzed up through her? How would she react? How would *he* react? She was at once apprehensive and wanting.

And stupid.

She crossed her forearms on the table and rested her head on them. Maybe if she closed her eyes for just a minute, she could gather her scattered thoughts.

****

She knelt on her bed, unselfconsciously naked, and held out her arms to him. He'd just kicked off his worn western boots and stripped off his clothes—jeans and a chambray shirt. He smelled of man and hay and horseflesh, a scent guaranteed to charge her pheromones. Her eyes feasted on his incredible body. Solid. Muscular. Broad shoulders tapering to a narrow waist and lean hips. Muscles carefully sculpted beneath the taut skin. Dark curls scattered over the hard wall of his chest, arrowing down to the thick nest at his groin.

And jutting directly at her, a magnificent cock, the head dark and swollen.

"You in a hurry, darlin'?" His sexy grin was positively lethal.

"Only to get you over here."

He bore her down to the mattress under his weight, her breasts pressing against his chest, the matte of hair tickling and abrading her nipples. Every nerve under the surface of her skin vibrated with anticipation, and the walls of her pussy fluttered, waiting for his cock.

"Miss me?" he asked in his low drawl.

"Always. You work too many hours."

"Well, tonight you're gonna relax me."

His tongue outlined her mouth before brushing across her lips and gliding inside. Every place it touched, heat burst forth and scorched its way through her body.

His mouth was everywhere, brushing against her cheeks, the line of her jaw, her neck. Sucking that very tender spot behind her ear. Biting it gently. Then the hollow of her throat where her pulse beat like the wings of a trapped bird.

His head dipped, and he captured one nipple with his lips, pulling and nibbling at it until it stiffened and peaked. Then the other one. His hand rhythmically squeezed her breast. Electricity sparked through her, straight to her center where she pulsed with unremitting need.

Her hands smoothed over the taut flesh of his back, feeling the powerful play of muscles beneath. The hot length of his cock against her thigh. The sensuous strength of his body between her thighs.

His mouth worked its way down her body to her navel, stopping to probe the furled flesh with the tip of his tongue. Then a hot, wet line to the curls covering her mound. And then... Oh, God! His fingers opening her, and his tongue doing a wicked dance on her clit. Her hips jerked, and her fingers clutched the thick pelt of his hair as sizzling sensations rocketed through her.

"Delicious," he murmured against the slickness of her labia. "I'll never get enough of your taste."

"I want to taste you, too," she gasped.

"Later." He looked up, her cream glistening on his mouth. "When I come this time, I want to be inside you."

His tongue continued to stroke her clit, two long, lean fingers sliding into her wet, hungry pussy, stroking her sweet spot until she was nearly mad with desire.

"Please," she begged.

"Please what?" he teased.

"Please...fuck me."

She couldn't keep her body still, thrusting her hips

at him, moaning, crying out.

"All right, then, darlin'. Get ready."

The crinkle of foil. The snap of latex. The press of the head of his cock against the opening of her passage.

He shifted on the bed, slid his hands beneath her ass to lift her to him, and drove home with one fierce roll of his hips. There! Oh, God, she felt so full, the long, thick length of him stretching her.

She lifted to meet him and the rhythm began. In and out. Thrust and retreat. Slow, hot, his cock dragging over every nerve ending in the walls of her pussy. Each time a little harder, deeper than the time before. He bent over her so he could lick her nipples, and shards of lightning shot straight to her center, gripping and clutching at his rigid length.

In and out, in and out.

She wrapped her legs around him, locking their bodies together and rocking her hips. As if that was a signal, he rammed into her harder, his balls slapping against her as he pummeled her faster and faster.

The coil of lust wound tightly inside her unwound and reached into every part of her as her climax built and built. As if sensing her thoughts, he drove into her harder one last time, tumbling them both into a black velvet space filled with fireworks.

She was mindless, shuddering with the force of the spasms rocking her, the beat of her heart so fierce she was sure it would burst from her chest. His cock pulsed inside her as he shattered with the force of his release, shouting her name.

Dana unwound her arms from his neck and—

Ouch!

Her arms fell away, bouncing her head against the

hard wood of the table. Dana sat up, rubbing her forehead, and realized she was panting and covered with sweat. And the dream smacked her brain.

Cole Landry. Sex. Damn, damn, damn.

Now, it came back to her in every vivid detail, awareness still thundering through her body. For her entire adult life, she'd tried her best to achieve sexual satisfaction. In any form. Anything that would melt the terrible wall of ice she'd been trapped behind all these years. She'd read everything from how-to manuals to erotic romances. Talked to more therapists than most people ever knew. But all to no avail. The wall remained immutable. So why now? And why with Cole Landry? She hardly knew him, for god's sake, and she was having erotic dreams about him?

That's what you get for daydreaming. He's beyond your reach, and even if he wasn't, he wouldn't waste his time with someone with so many sexual hang-ups. He probably just has to crook his finger and women fall into his bed.

Enough!

She hurried on unsteady legs to the kitchen for a glass of water, drank it standing at the sink, refilled the glass, and stumbled back into the dining room on legs still unsteady. Opening her briefcase, she pulled out her research material—copies from the newspaper records, the note pad she'd used at the sheriff's office, the...

Wait! Where was her phone? Although she took copious notes by hand, she always entered key facts on it. This afternoon, those included a list of things to follow up on—names, phone numbers, and addresses of people who might be able to provide her with some insight.

Her cell was her Holy Grail. It kept her organized and connected to her stray thoughts, her impressions, and everything that might otherwise seem trivial. Not to mention that it also contained every important number and name in her small but exclusive inner circle. She was never, ever without it.

Feeling the edges of panic creeping in, she searched again through her briefcase, her purse, her coat pocket and again came up empty. Frustrated, she dumped everything out of her briefcase and purse, scattering the contents on the table and shoving objects this way and that.

She bit her lip in frustration, hard as she dug through the mound of papers and junk. Still nothing. Again she checked the pockets of the slacks she'd been wearing. Nothing. Forcing herself to be calm, she went through every room in the house, trying to think where she might have put it down, a tiny thread of alarm skittering through her.

Thirty minutes later, she was still empty-handed and fighting another full-blown panic attack. What the hell had she done with it? When was the last time she'd seen it?

The table in the sheriff's department popped across her mental television screen. The small digital device lying on the table, peeking out from beneath the folders. She was always so meticulous about things like this, aware of the nature of the info it contained.

But today, she'd been too anxious to escape the good sheriff. That was pretty damn stupid. She'd let Cole Landry throw her off balance, and it had screwed her up. She rubbed her forehead, the headache nudging its way back to the forefront again.

All right. So she'd have to give in and admit that it was at the sheriff's office. Had he looked through it? Pried through her personal information? Although it required a password, she knew police departments had electronic wizards who could bypass such things.

And what the hell did she do now? Wait until tomorrow? Go back there tonight and do battle with some night dispatcher who might not even know what she was talking about?

Well, damn it all anyway.

The jangling sound of the doorbell startled her. Dana frowned. She didn't think the few people she made contact with since arriving in High Ridge would be coming around to pay her a social visit. Grant had once urged her to get a gun, telling her anyone who traveled alone to the weird places she ventured ought to have some protection. Now, she wished she'd taken his advice.

The bell rang again. This time the sound was a little longer, as if someone was holding a thumb down on the button.

She looked through the peephole in the door and nearly passed out. Cole Landry, macho sheriff, all around pain in the ass, and the object of her unexpected erotic daydream stood on her doorstep. Wiping her suddenly damp palms on her shorts, she undid both locks and cracked the door open.

Chapter Nine

Cole Landry's huge presence filled Dana's tiny porch and crowded her doorway. His Stetson was still perched on his head, but he'd changed into jeans and a T-shirt. His feet were shod in worn western boots, so similar to those in her dream, she wondered if he'd somehow been in her mind. The black T-shirt clung like a glove to his broad shoulders and narrow waist, and the well-worn jeans did little to conceal his long legs and muscular thighs.

Or the erection that was visibly pressing against his fly. What was that all about?

She didn't know what terrified her more—his presence, his arousal, or her reaction to both. Heat grabbed her like a fist, and every bit of saliva in her mouth dried up. She had to swallow twice before she could make a sound.

"Uh...hi." Well, it wasn't poetry, but at least she got the words out. "What can I do for you?"

His eyes burned into hers like smoldering coals. "I have something of yours and figured you might want it. Is it all right if I come in?" One corner of his mouth turned up in a semi-grin. "I promise not to attack you."

Dana felt the heat of embarrassment flush her body. She backed up and swung the door wide, and Cole removed his hat and stepped into the house. As he brushed past her, she caught his scent again, the same blend of male and horses from her dream, and again she shivered. She'd never reacted to a man this way, not even those she'd forced herself to go to bed with. Cole Landry should have *danger* painted on his forehead, in flashing red letters.

Digging for a calm she didn't feel, she waved him into the tiny living room, closed the door and stood as far away from him as the limited space allowed. Being this close to a man she'd just imagined having sex with totally unnerved her.

She watched his gaze roam lazily around her space, and she sensed his brain registering every detail. Not that there was much to see in the small cottage. A living room and dining area with a view into a small but well-equipped kitchen. A narrow hall that led to the two bedrooms and bathrooms.

She cleared her throat. "You said you had something for me? I don't mean to be rude, but I'm in the middle of doing some work."

He turned back to her, his mouth turning up in a smile that made her knees knock. Reaching into his pocket, he extracted her phone.

"This was under some stuff on the table where you were working today." He held it out to her. "You probably missed it, being in such a big hurry to leave and all. I figured it was important enough not to leave it there until tomorrow."

"Yes." She gave a small sigh of relief. "I realized when I started to work tonight that it was missing. Thank you for bringing it by."

She reached for it. Their hands touched, and a bolt of something akin to lightning shot up her arm and impaled her smack in the center of her chest. That traitorous pulse in her pussy was pounding hard enough to play in a rock band. She yanked her hand back at once, but he reached for it and gently placed her cell onto her palm. The flare of light in his eyes was the only indication that he'd felt the electricity, too. And he didn't seem to be in any hurry to move away from it.

She swallowed past the panic that flooded through her and backed farther into the room. She couldn't let him get any ideas about her or do anything that might force her to leave High Ridge before she finished what she'd come here to do.

"You know," he drawled. "It's only common courtesy to offer someone a cold drink or a cup of coffee in a situation like this. I'm good with either."

Coffee? A cold drink? Was she supposed to make casual conversation with him, too? "I know this sounds rude, but I really do have a lot of work to do."

He shook his head, almost dismissively. "Those cases are older than dirt, Miss Moretti. Another half hour won't make a difference one way or another. Besides, you look like someone who could use a break."

Her chin lifted automatically. "And what is that supposed to mean?"

He moved closer until he was only inches away from her. "It means, you're so uptight, if I flicked my fingernail against you, you'd vibrate like piano wire. I've seen people teetering on the edge of a nervous collapse before, and you give a pretty good imitation. So how about that cold drink and a little conversation about the real reason you chose the High Ridge crimes to write about?"

Dana nearly dropped her phone. She curled her

fingers tightly around it and schooled her features into as blank an expression as possible. But not blank enough. Because Cole was looking at her as if he could see right into her center, right into the workings of her mind.

Dana shivered. This was *so* not good. Not to mention the dream…

"I can offer you a cold drink," she said, giving herself a mental shake. "I don't know about the conversation."

With an effort of will, she made her feet move toward the kitchen, dropping her cell into her briefcase as she passed it. Yanking two bottles of soda from the fridge, she turned to head back into the living room, only to find a solid wall of muscle in her way.

Dana froze. She suddenly felt as if all the air had been sucked out of her kitchen and replaced by this man and images from the dream. Tiny drops of perspiration beaded her forehead, and her heartbeat felt like a bass drum against her ribs.

She had no idea how to handle the unexpected feelings running riot in her body. She certainly couldn't let him know how he affected her. Literally shoving one of the bottles at him, she slid sideways past him into the living room.

"Thanks." His deep voice resonated through her as he followed close behind.

She deliberately took the big armchair, leaving him the couch. As if he read her mind, one corner of his mouth quirked, but he folded his body into one end of the couch, stretched out his long legs, and tilted the bottle to his lips.

Dana could barely tear her eyes off him as the

muscles in his throat worked to swallow the soda. The pulse in her pussy beat heavily, a totally foreign sensation. Her nerves felt as if someone had removed all the protective coverings and exposed them to the sensuality of this man. Could he see the thudding of the pulse beat at her throat? Was her face unnaturally flushed? She had a feeling that somehow, in those eyes that revealed nothing, he knew her darkest secrets.

If this was all a deliberate attempt to put her off balance, she didn't dare let him know how well it was working.

He locked gazes with her again.

"So how about it, Miss Moretti? I'm not looking for social discourse, just an explanation. What's your real angle here?"

****

Cole wanted to slap his head and kick his brain back into gear. Coming here had to be the dumbest fucking thing he'd done all year. But the shock of seeing his water nymph from the night before—the vision of his intensely erotic dream—walk boldly into his office this morning, as if he'd conjured her from his dream, still hadn't worn off. Maintaining his composure had been hard.

It wasn't enough that she'd popped up out of nowhere to rake open the muck of a case everyone had buried as deep as they could. The hard-on he got the minute he laid eyes on her today was killing his concentration.

There was nothing sexy about the way she dressed, and her personality could freeze Hell. But he'd taken one look at her slender, shapely body, her soft mouth and thick, shining blonde hair that reflected the lights, and his dick had stood up and whacked him. Just like last night.

Wonderful. Just what he needed. A stiff dick for a nosy, uptight, and from what he could tell, slightly frigid writer. What the hell was he thinking? He'd given himself a mental shake and dismissed all possibility of her from his mind for about half a heartbeat.

Then he'd stupidly taken another look and seen hazel eyes flecked with green but so bruised he couldn't imagine what hell they'd seen. Looking at her now, so obviously trying to hide the fear she was feeling, he sent his dick a stern message to assume parade rest. This was not a woman who gave out sexual signals at all, although he sensed something buried deep inside her was fighting hard to get out. And that something was scaring her to death. Something was off kilter here, and he planned to find out what it was.

He watched her, curled into the big armchair she'd chosen, the too-large T-shirt hanging slightly off one shoulder, bare legs tucked firmly against her tempting ass. She'd poured her soft drink into a glass she clutched with a death grip, her eyes focused on the bubbles dancing in the liquid. She was ignoring his question, as if the longer she waited to answer, the sooner he'd lose interest. She'd soon learn he never lost interest when something mattered to him.

"Miss Moretti?" he prompted.

"Dana." She lifted her gaze to meet his. "Miss Moretti sounds too confrontational."

He swallowed a grin. Confrontational seemed to be her middle name, but apparently, she was holding out an olive branch. To pick his brain? Coerce him into…what…helping her?

"Dana it is," he nodded. "Will that get me an answer to my question?"

She frowned. "I'm sorry. What was it you asked?"

He leaned forward, resting his elbows on his knees, the soft drink bottle dangling from his hands. "I asked what this plan of yours is really all about. I get a sense here this is more than a writing project for you."

She lowered her eyes again, shielding whatever expression they held. "You know what I do, Sheriff. I select an unsolved crime that interests me, do the research, and write the book. That's not very complicated."

He pulled out what he'd been told was his knock-your-socks-off smile, hoping to lighten the tension filling the air. "Cole."

"Excuse me?"

"If you're Dana, I'm Cole." He leaned back, making his posture less threatening, and he could see her shoulders relax minimally. "So, Dana, what's the deal? Writers researching a story don't usually rent a house and put down roots, no matter how temporary they might be. They rent a motel or hotel with maid service, so they don't have to think about anything but the book."

One corner of her mouth lifted. "Have you ever seen the fake cowhide bedspreads at the High Ridge Motel? Or tried relaxing in one of their rooms? I need to feel comfortable when I work."

"Let's say I buy that. There's still something in your attitude that tells me this is more than a story to you. So give it up. What's the deal?"

She was silent for so long he wasn't sure she planned to answer him. Then she sighed, took a long swallow of her drink, and set the glass on the little table next to the chair.

"I think the worst crimes committed are those against children," she said at last, speaking slowly and deliberately. "They're the most defenseless people. The most vulnerable. And the most trusting. People who…injure them betray that trust. I think whoever did this to the children of High Ridge has been able to hide long enough. If I can find answers, maybe everyone can finally get some peace."

"All right. If that's your story." He lifted his bottle to his lips, looking at her over the length of it. "But remember, when you start to dig up secrets, sooner or later, all of them come to the surface. Even the ones you want to hide."

Did her face pale a little? Was that a tightening of her body?

He wished she'd put on something a little different to wear. Like body armor or chain mail. The soft fabric of her T-shirt, even as big as it was, draped lovingly against her breasts. The outline of her nipples, which he could see without any problem at all, told him she wasn't wearing a bra underneath it. Her shorts came down to the midpoint of her thighs, but they were loose, and even in her tightly curled position he could get a tiny glimpse of the tempting bits of flesh they covered.

Suddenly, an image of her naked flashed across his brain. Temptingly spread-eagled on cool, crisp sheets. Breasts full and pointing. Pubic curls covering a pussy that he wanted to plunge his cock right into. Inner thighs glistening with the juices of her arousal.

He squeezed his eyes shut, then opened them. Thank God her voice interrupted his X-rated reverie.

"I don't know what ulterior motives you think I have," she told him, straightening in her chair. "I just want to do a thorough job." She tucked her hair behind her ears. "By the way, I noticed something today when I was looking at those old reports. All of the...bodies were found somewhere near where they were originally taken. Don't you wonder how he could have managed that if he was just some itinerant? He'd have to know how and when to get in without being seen."

Cole frowned. Maybe he should have read the reports himself. "You're very thorough."

"I was hoping, after I've had a chance to analyze my notes, I could steal some of your time to ask you questions."

Okay. He'd play along.

"I think that can be arranged, although I'm not sure what I can tell you." He took a long swallow of his drink. "I assume you're planning to talk to the parents?"

She nodded. "The ones that are still around here." Her eyes challenged him. "Don't worry, I know how to be sensitive and circumspect."

"I'm sure you do."

She pushed herself up from her chair. "I appreciate you bringing my phone to me, but I do need to get to work."

"No problem." He unfolded himself from the couch. "I'll just stick this bottle in the kitchen."

"That's all right. I'll take it."

She reached for it at the same time he moved to hand it to her, and the skin to skin contact nearly fried him. Again, she startled him by jerking away and moving back two steps. Her hands shook as she opened the door.

When he moved aside, he was standing so close he felt her breath on his skin. An idiotic impulse seized him, and before he knew it, he did the dumbest thing ever. He lifted his hands to cup her face, thumbs stroking her high cheekbones, and very gently lowered his mouth to hers.

She was stiffer than a board, her mouth unresponsive. The hand holding the bottle popped up, and for a moment, he was afraid she'd hit him with it. But he didn't retreat nor did he increase the pressure on her lips. One of his hands slid easily down her back and cupped her ass, firm beneath the thin material of her shorts. She relaxed under his touch, her lips softened, her body hummed with silent vibration, and his erection gained a mind of its own.

Then, without warning, she tensed again, shoved hard at his chest, and jumped back. Her face was pale as snow, and her gaze flitted to everything in the room but him. It took him a second to realize she was frightened. Panicky. What the hell was going on here?

"I'm sorry," he apologized, taking a step onto the porch. "I had no right to do that. I was way out of line. It won't happen again. But Dana, there's something—"

"No." She clutched the bottle to her like a security blanket. Or a weapon. "There's nothing. It's best if we just forget all about this. Good night, Sheriff."

So it was back to formality. Okay. He'd have to figure out how to regroup here. More than his hormones were stirred. Miss Dana Moretti had secrets, and he meant to find out what they were. Because in a tiny space of time she'd crawled under his skin and sparked something deep inside him. He couldn't remember the last time a woman had done that, and he wasn't about to let this thing go without figuring out why that was.

"Good night, Dana. Call me when you want to talk. I'll make time. And Guardian Security might be able to help with some of your research. Our resources are extensive."

For a man who'd been more than circumspect in his love life since taking this job, he suddenly seemed to be losing his mind. And over a woman who had what looked to be a bad case of Post Traumatic Stress Disorder. He'd seen enough of it in the service to easily spot it.

So what was her story? What had traumatized her to such a degree? And what, if anything, did it have to do with the child murders now twenty-five years old? He'd really have to watch himself with her. He might be irritated that she was digging into those old cases, but they were sure to be spending a lot of time together. The last thing he wanted to do was send her over the edge, which was always possible when flying blind.

He sat in his truck for a long while, watching the house, seeing her shadow behind the living room curtains standing totally still. Was she watching, too?

Grinding his teeth, he cranked over the engine and backed out of the driveway. He had the feeling his life was about to get way more complicated than he wanted. Maybe he needed to have breakfast with Tate again. Or take him up on the invite to dinner.

****

Dana stood like a statue in the living room, staring at the curtains as if she could see through them to the man still sitting in her driveway. His empty soda bottle hung limply from her hand. The thunderous beating of her heart banging against her ribs and the pulses throbbing hard in all her private places sounded so loud she was afraid he'd hear them outside. Her entire body felt as if she'd been zapped with a hotwire, then dumped in a freezer.

Slowly, she brought one hand to her mouth and touched her fingertips to her lips. She could still feel the imprint of him there, like the mark of a branding iron. That had been a huge mistake, but the remnants of the dream had still clung to her. She'd nearly put herself in a bad place with him.

Then the panic had clawed its way up, freezing her insides. Gripping her. She knew she was frightened of her reaction to him. It wasn't just the lightning bolts of awareness that shot through her every time they touched. It was something more. For the first time in her adult life, her body was giving her the kind of signals she'd always hoped to have. Signals that meant she desired a man. Even though it petrified her, she wanted to respond to it.

Because he makes me feel safe.

How ridiculous was that?

Still, she knew that even if she was brave enough to let herself see where those feelings took her, she'd never be able to deliver. She was a fraud. But she could hardly tell that to sexy Cole Landry. And he'd ask questions she didn't want to answer.

God, she was such a mess.

She wondered what his real motivation had been for coming here tonight. He could have had one of his deputies deliver her phone, but he was curious. She saw it in his eyes. And determined to sidetrack her if he could. Was his kiss meant to throw her off balance, or was it something else? And if it was something else, then what?

Jesus. She was driving herself crazy with all this double think.

With a sigh, she stuck the empty soda bottle in the recycle container, pulled out a chair, and sat at the dining room table. It was time to stop thinking about Cole Landry and the unsettling way he made her feel. She had more important things to do, like analyzing the information she'd gathered so far.

Maybe she'd find the answers she so desperately sought, and in discovering them, she'd turn into the real human being she'd always wanted to be. A woman who didn't suffer from an endless string of nightmares. One who suddenly really wanted to find out if Cole Landry could be more to her than just the resident sheriff of Salado County.

****

Cole clenched his fists on the steering wheel as he drove along the highway heading home, the memory of the kiss still sharp and vivid. He could still feel the silken softness of her honey-blonde hair beneath his hands. Worse than that, the dream was still so clear in his mind, the image of her naked body playing hell with his testosterone level. The vein in his neck throbbed, and his cock was trying to break free of its restraint in his jeans. He should wear a sign that said Stupid. He should...what? Apologize? Damn it, he already had, but he wanted to do it again anyway. And more.

He was still about three miles from home when his radio crackled to life. He keyed the mic and lifted it to his mouth.

"Landry."

"Sheriff, this is Grace." Grace Hathaway had been

working night dispatch since long before Cole became sheriff. There was little she couldn't handle, but tonight her voice had an edge to it. "We've got some trouble."

Cole sighed. "Howdy McMann picking a fight in the Raccoon Saloon again? Frank Nolan's cattle breaking through the fence to the Silver Spur?"

Just what he wanted tonight. But Grace's next words put every part of his brain on alert.

"We've got a DB in High Ridge Park."

DB. Dead body.

A sour taste rose up from Cole's stomach. He couldn't remember the last time they'd had a body in High Ridge. There certainly hadn't been one since he'd taken office.

"Identified?" he asked.

"It's Leanne Pritchard." Grace's voice was tight, laced with a mixture of sadness and anger. "Cole, it looks as if she was beaten and raped before she was killed."

"Shit." Bile rose up in his mouth, sudden and unbidden.

Leanne Pritchard was just sixteen years old, with her entire life ahead of her. She was a sweet, friendly girl who loved life. Who the hell could do something like this to someone like her?

"Who's on the spot?" he asked.

"Mickey Garcia and Andi Lowell."

Cole relaxed a fraction. Mickey and Andi were pros. They wouldn't panic like some of his rookies might. They could handle whatever came up until he got there.

"All right, Grace. Get the coroner and the crime scene folks down there. I'm on the way."

"Already done," she told him. "Call back when you're on site."

Cole thanked God Grace was an old, experienced hand who'd seen just about everything. Including the gruesome attacks on the children Dana Moretti was determined to write about. Grace would keep her head no matter what. But she and Leanne's mother were good friends, so this was personal to her, and he knew it.

Hell, what wasn't personal in a town of five thousand souls?

Chapter Ten

The scene, not more than a quarter mile from the park's entrance gate, was easy to spot from the road, but only because of the portable spotlights. Everything seemed to be located within a thick copse of trees. When Cole pulled his truck into the park, he saw the coroner's wagon parked to one side, the crime scene van next to it, and two cruisers pulled in at an angle to them. Yellow crime scene tape had been strung around the entire area.

Off to the left, beyond the taped off area, a group of teenagers crowded against a large pickup. Partygoers. He was forever chasing kids out of the park. Now, one of them had gone and gotten herself killed.

The girls were jumbled against each other, crying, and the boys were doing their teenage best to both comfort them and look invisible. Other cars had pulled up beside the truck and adults with worried faces strained to see what was happening.

He spotted the Pritchards huddled together against a tree, surrounded by some of their friends. In a minute, he'd have to talk to them, an unpleasant burden that always fell to the man in charge. He could feel their pain spreading through the air. The loss of a child was one of the most difficult to deal with. He ought to know.

Scanning the area again, Cole saw his two deputies

quietly keeping the crowd under control. He climbed out of his truck and ducked under the tape, threaded his way through the trees, and came up next to Andi and Mickey. His eyes were drawn at once to the body of the young girl sprawled under the merciless glare of the portable spotlights.

She was lying in an open space in a small copse of trees, hidden from casual view. Cole was struck by the awkward angle of her body, legs bent, arms flung to either side of her head, as if someone had just dropped her carelessly in that spot. Her head was bent at an unnatural angle, and the muscles of her face were frozen in an expression of pain and fear. She still wore her blouse and her sandals, but Cole saw her shorts lying beside her, a pile of shredded material.

Nita Sanchez, the coroner, was working with the body. Having attended to the most necessary areas first, she'd tactfully covered the exposed area with a protective sheet. Bad enough for him to have to see this. He didn't want the parents having this image stuck in their heads.

"Got anything for me yet, Nita?"

She looked up as he moved closer, rage flashing in her eyes. "You mean besides the fact that she was brutally raped?" She shook her head. "It's a mess, Cole. You can tell she fought like a tiger. This didn't go down easy. She's got scratches and scrapes on her thighs and a fair amount of blood." Her hands tightened involuntarily. "It's obvious she was a virgin."

The coroner lifted the small canvas sheet to let the sheriff see the blood smeared on Leanne's thighs. When she gently rolled Leanne's body to the side, she exposed more blood between the cheeks of her buttocks, a sign of more damage to the young body. The surrounding area and her lower back were also covered in little marks, which, if he had to guess, looked like pinch marks.

He scrubbed a hand down his face, whether to erase the images from his mind or to give himself time to think, he couldn't say. "Shit. Anything else?"

"I can tell you she was strangled, her neck was broken, and her mouth was taped shut." She drew a line around the girl's lips with a gloved finger. "See the lines where the tape was, the reddening of the skin where it was ripped off postmortem?"

"Damn. I hate knowing we've got some kind of monster out there."

"Don't we all?" Nita's sigh was heavy with grief.

He scrubbed a hand against his cheek. "Yeah, well, the sooner you get the post done the better. You know that."

"I'll get her back to Drowdy's as quick as I can and get to work."

Elvin Drowdy owned the largest funeral home in the county. Because there was so little crime requiring a morgue, he had set aside a space in his prep room for the coroner to work when necessary, which until tonight she'd only used for accident victims.

Cole moved away to let her get on with her job, backing up to where his lead deputies stood. Andi looked up at Cole as soon as she sensed his presence.

"She wasn't killed here," the deputy told him. "The ground isn't disturbed anywhere, and she was arranged too carefully."

Arranged? He'd thought she looked dumped. Could be either. It wasn't like he'd spent a lot of time looking at murder scenes. War was different; that was survival. This…this was just sick.

Unexpectedly, bile rose in his throat, and he had to fight the urge to lose the contents of his stomach. "Do any of those kids have an idea what happened?"

Andi shook her head. "They were having a little after-hours picnic here…"

"Which they know is against the rules," Mickey pointed out.

"Yeah, yeah, yeah. But you and I did it," she reminded him. "Hell, every kid in High Ridge has done it. That gate at the entrance is a joke."

"All right," Cole broke in. "Details please."

Andi blew out a breath. "They were running low on soft drinks. No beer, everyone's underage, and they know what happens if you catch them. Anyway, Leanne had driven here in her truck so she volunteered to go to the store for supplies."

"No one saw her come back." Mickey picked up the thread. "They were all over at the opposite side of the park, away from the road. But after a while, they got worried about her. When she didn't answer her cell, they decided to fan out and start looking. See if maybe she was playing some weird game with them. You know, the way teenagers take it into their heads to do. When they got to this spot, two of the kids found her and yelled for the others. Someone called us on their cell."

"Jesus." Cole swiped his hand over his hair. "What a thing for them to see. Okay. We need to find her truck. Then we need it swept for evidence. Maybe it will give us an idea of where she might have been taken. I don't think we need both deputies on crowd control. Mickey, go tell one of them to get going."

Mickey pulled one of the deputies aside, gesturing and giving him orders before rejoining Andi and Cole. "It's been a long time since we had a violent crime here," he commented, anger scoring lines in his face. "Hell, there're only twenty-five thousand damn people in the whole county."

"The last time we had anything," Andi pointed out, "was twenty-five years ago. Remember those two years we had that pedophile running amuck? You were spending summers at your aunt and uncle's ranch, remember?"

Cole's stomach cramped. He'd been so young then, but details had stuck with him. Impossible not to. Surely, this wouldn't turn out to be the first of a series, like the pedophile killer. That's all he'd need, with Dana Moretti kicking up dust on the old cases and now, maybe, lured by this new one. How bad could his luck get?

"Cole?" Andi prodded him. "Doesn't it seem odd to you that Dana Moretti shows up asking questions about the pedophile cases and then this happens? You don't think there's a connection, do you? Maybe she rattled someone's cage?"

Cole shook his head, pushing back the dread clawing at his throat. No way did he want to think Andi's off the wall question had any real credence to it. "I don't see how one has anything to do with the other. For one thing, this girl's too old for our last killer. For another, he's long gone from this area. If we're lucky, this will be a one-time thing. We'll catch the guy, and that will be the end of it."

Mickey took off his hat, wiped his forehead on his

arm, and clapped his hat back on his head. "Jesus, this will make waves all the way to San Antonio."

Cole's lips thinned. "Yeah, we can expect a full court press from the media once they get hold of this. Everything's so much more immediate today than it used to be. Let's keep a lid on it as long as we can. Pass the word." He narrowed his eyes at the two people in front of him. "When that happens, no one—and I mean not one person—talks to the press except me. Okay, then. I'm calling a meeting first thing in the morning. Make sure everyone knows that. I'll meet you two back in my office when you're done here." He sighed. "I guess I'd better go speak to the parents."

****

Hidden in the trees at the top of a hill, he had a good view of the action. The spotlights the sheriff's deputies had rigged lit up the place like it was high noon. The coroner was still kneeling by the body, but he could see they'd covered her with a sheet.

Pity. He did so enjoy looking at her, even in death. She'd been such a luscious armful. Even when she'd come awake and tried to fight him. He'd loved the look of fear he created, the terror, the knowledge that things were beyond her control. That had always been part of the excitement, seeing the knowledge of their impending death in their eyes. His little flowers had looked so beautiful. And this little plum, she'd been easy pickings.

Oh, how grateful she'd been at his offer to rescue her from her little dilemma. Coaxing her into his truck had taken little effort on his part. Why not? He was a trustworthy soul. Everyone knew that about him.

She'd been a feisty one, but he'd taken the wind

out of her sails easily enough. The pain he inflicted was so satisfying, keeping him in a constant state of arousal.

He laughed silently to himself.

He'd thought long and hard about doing this. His other hobby was so much safer and nearly as fulfilling. But he needed to get rid of Carrie, and he couldn't make it too obvious.

This was only the beginning. He needed to have his next victim picked out and be ready to act quickly. And the ones after that as well, all of them leading him to the biggest prize of all.

Yes, sir. Before he sent Carrie to permanent hell, he'd show her what hell was like here on Earth. And he'd enjoy every minute of it.

He sighed, put his truck in gear, and let it roll silently down the incline and out of sight of the park. He really wanted to hang around until they took the body out. Maybe get another look. But that was flirting with danger, and he hadn't quite reached that stage again yet.

Except, of course, with his other little hobby.

Chapter Eleven

"I wanted you the minute I saw you, jogging in the rain, that T-shirt plastered to your breasts." Cole *traced her jawline with the tip of his tongue.*

"You should have been looking where you were driving instead of at my breasts," she teased, running her fingers through the curls of hair on his hard chest.

They were lying side by side, one of his hands idly rubbing through the curls on her mound, his fingers unerringly finding the wet flesh of her pussy. It seemed to her she was always wet when he was around.

"At least now I get to look at them all I want." His voiced was husky with need.

Bending his head, he captured one nipple in his mouth and pulled on it, swirling his tongue around it. Heat speared through her body, sending fresh cream into her pussy. Her pulse beat fiercely, driving up the hunger for him.

"Beautiful breasts," he murmured as he turned his attention to the other one.

Tugging the nipple with his teeth, he slipped two fingers into her waiting channel, chuckling against her breast when her inner muscles clamped down on him.

The hard thickness of his cock pressed against her thigh, and she wriggled a hand between them to close her fingers around it.

"Ah, God," he groaned when she squeezed gently.

"Careful, or I'll come in your hand."

"Maybe I want you to." She heard the desire in her own voice. "Maybe I—"

The ringing of her cell phone cut through the fog and jerked Dana from the dream. She was gasping for breath, and her skin was covered with a fine sheen of perspiration.

Holy crap!

Another dream about Cole Landry.

The phone continued to make noise, the annoying ringer she'd chosen stabbing at her senses. She fumbled for it on the nightstand.

"H'lo?" She ran her fingers through her sleep-mussed hair.

"Hey." Grant's voice was the last one she expected to hear.

"I'm surprised you called," she told him. "We didn't exactly part on the best terms."

"And that's exactly why I'm talking to you now," he told her. "I feel badly about the way things ended between us." He paused. "I don't hate you, Dana. I guess I was just hurt that, well…"

"That you weren't the one to break through the wall?" she snapped. Then she softened her tone. "Sorry. I didn't mean it to come out like that."

"I guess I'm sorry about everything, kiddo. I just wanted to make sure you're all right. I went by the house, but it was locked up tight."

"I…decided to take your advice." She twisted a strand of hair as she talked, a long-time habit, the only thing that ever betrayed the state of her nerves.

"About confronting the past?"

"Uh-huh."

"Good. That's good." Silence. "Maybe when you get back—"

"I don't think so," she interrupted, shaking her head, even though he couldn't see her. "I'm more grateful than you know for pushing me to do this, but I think what we had was all we were meant to have. Anyway, this may take a lot longer than I expected."

"Oh? Problems?"

"This seems to be the proverbial let's-sweep-it-under-the-rug situation. Everyone wants it to go away and me with it." She twisted the curl tighter, then pulled it out, letting it spring back like a coil of wire.

"I heard what you said before, but if things are tense would you like me to come down there?"

Dana could visualize Grant stretched out on his leather couch, phone propped to his ear, frowning at the thought he might get sucked into something beyond his comfort zone.

She burst out laughing. "I don't think this place is exactly your cup of tea. And you'd hate getting caught up in something so convoluted. But thanks, anyway."

"You *will* call me if things get too hairy, right?"

"Of course. Don't worry. I'll be fine."

Would she? In any event, one of the last people she needed tagging behind her was Grant, who, despite what she was thinking was a conscience call, had all but told her to go to hell.

Not that she probably hadn't needed to hear it. It gave her the shove she needed to dig back into her past. It also pointed out very clearly to her how shallow all her relationships had been, Grant being just a carbon copy of the others.

She said good-bye, ended the call, and leaned back

in her chair, rubbing her forehead. No way could she tell him she had such conflicting emotions about the whole thing. She wanted answers. She didn't want them. She wanted to reconnect with the place she was born. She wanted to get as far from it as possible.

And, of course, there was Sheriff Cole Landry, damn him. All her life she'd retreated from men, the horrific memories she'd pushed away freezing everyone out. Killing any desire she might ever have for a real sexual relationship. Yet now, when she was least prepared to deal with it, this arrogant, wildly sexy man had pierced the veil and stirred up feelings she had no idea she was even capable of, never mind how to deal with them.

Damn it all, anyway. Just for once, could things please go her way?

She studied the screen on her laptop. The notes she'd transferred from her study of the case files stared back at her. There was nothing dressed up about the facts. They were brutal. Gruesome, even, and very explicit. The deputies who'd found the bodies had left nothing to the imagination. The pictures they conjured were like something out of a torture chamber.

A shiver skittered over her spine as she felt the ghost touch of those calloused fingers probing her body, heard Kylie's high-pitched little screams. Remembered the terrible pain. Felt the tape ripped from her mouth and strange hands trying to be gentle with her.

When she'd seen Kylie's body, she'd thrown her head back and screamed so long and hard her throat ended up raw for days. She'd fought to get to her sister, but other hands restrained her, voices tried to soothe her, and finally, the sting of a needle had plunged her into blackness.

Now, with each case she examined, she relived it over and over again. Her stomach convulsed, and once more, she felt like throwing up. She was going to need a lot of hot tea and antacids before this was over.

The idea of tea sounded good right now. Something to settle her nerves, so she could be objective about all this. Getting up from the table, she headed into the kitchen.

But even as she heated the water, she knew tea wasn't the solution to what ailed her. She wondered if she'd really be able to go through with this whole project. If she had the stomach and the strength to push forward, searching through all the mental rubble for the tiniest clue that would tell her who the monster was.

Then she realized there was no wavering on this. Armageddon had arrived for her, and she couldn't run away any longer.

****

Cole leaned back in the desk chair in his office and rubbed a hand over his face, trying to wipe away his exhaustion. It was three in the morning, his eyes felt gritty and a dull ache had invaded the back of his head.

Mickey Garcia and Andi Lowell sat in two chairs facing him, looking just as weary as he did. Murder scenes were never pleasant, but those involving children and teenagers were the worst. Especially like the one they'd had to face tonight.

"This town's gonna be in an uproar come the morning," Mickey commented for the second time that night.

"Tell me something I don't know," Cole said.

"Sheriff." Andi cleared her throat, a dry-scratchy sound indicative of fatigue. "Do you think we're equipped to handle something like what happened tonight?" Andi asked. "And the fallout from it?"

Cole fixed his tired eyes on her, his body tense. "Are you questioning my ability to do the job, Deputy?"

"No, sir." She shook her head definitively. "I have all the respect in the world for you. And Mickey and I are right there with you. I just don't know how the rest of the force will do."

"They'll do what they have to." Just what he needed. Deputies who had no confidence in themselves or others to work this case the way they should. "We all will."

Andi shifted uncomfortably in her chair. "I'm sorry. I didn't mean—"

The ringing of the phone on Cole's desk interrupted her. His gut tightened as he listened to the caller, gripping the pencil he was jotting notes with so hard it snapped in his fingers. When he put the phone down and looked back at his deputies they were staring at him, questions in their eyes.

"That was Nita Sanchez. I asked her to call me when she finished the prelim autopsy."

"What did she say?" Mickey asked finally, clearly unnerved by the look on his boss's face.

"Leanne Pritchard was raped multiple times. From what Nita says, it looks as if he raped and sodomized her using some sort of device, possibly made of glass."

He could tell from the looks on their faces, they got the message.

"Jesus." The word popped out of Mickey's mouth.

"Holy shit, boss." Andi looked sick.

"There are bruises on her thighs and in various places on her body. He also pulled out clumps of her pubic hair by the roots."

Andi swallowed and clenched her jaw tight, no doubt to keep from vomiting. Mickey looked green in the light of the desk lamp.

"Nita swabbed for DNA, but she's not hopeful. The guy apparently used a condom, and possibly even wore latex gloves. But maybe we'll get lucky."

"We took statements from the kids," Andi told him. "How would you like us to proceed from here?"

Again, Cole dry-washed his face. He needed caffeine, badly.

"I say we talk to the kids one on one. We can't keep their parents out of it since they're all minors, so let's try it in their homes."

Mickey hunched forward. "You know their folks will want to stop us."

Cole held up a hand. "I woke up the county attorney and requested a blanket warrant. I'll make sure you each get a copy. Grab a couple hours of sleep before you start setting up your appointments. But do it fast before anyone has time to change their story."

Andi's eyebrows lifted to her hairline. "You think one of them may have done this?"

"No, but someone may have seen something and not want to come forward for reasons of their own. Don't forget, they were having their party in a facility that's supposed to be locked at night. I want to know whose idea it was and how they got through the gate. Anyone check the gate?"

"I... Sorry." A red flush crept up Andi's face. "We

didn't even think to look."

Cole looked from one to the other. "My guess is this town is so used to people breaking into the park at night no one even thinks twice if the gate is open. Right?" When neither of them answered, he repeated his question. "I said, am I right?"

"Yes, Sheriff," Mickey finally mumbled. "We'll be a lot sharper from now on. You can count on it. You have our word."

Cole rubbed his neck. "You'd think in three years I'd have realized how lax security is at the park. Once the attendant closes the gate at night, no one bothers to check anything." He grunted. "Shit. You guys don't need to apologize. I'm probably one of my own worst liabilities. But you can bet starting tomorrow the access won't be quite so easy."

"We'll get on the kids real early," Andi told him. "And we won't screw it up."

After his deputies left, Cole leaned back in his chair again. He needed to go home and catch a couple hours of sleep. Feed the horses and his dog. Shower, put on a fresh uniform. But he couldn't get the image of Leanne's body out of his mind.

He hoped this turned out to be a case of misplaced jealousy and teenage desire, although from Nita's description of the body, it didn't sound like it. He wondered, like Andi had asked, if Dana Moretti's determination to reopen the old cases had anything to do with this? Could it really be a coincidence that she showed up in town making noises and the first murder in twenty-five years took place? Did that mean she was in danger, too? He didn't even want to consider the possibilities.

Chapter Twelve

Without a newspaper to glance over, Dana flicked on the television on the kitchen counter to get her morning news fix. Switching to the local channel, she began to fill the reservoir of the coffee pot with tap water and measure coffee grounds into the basket.

She paid scant attention to what was being said until she heard the words High Ridge. When she turned to look at the screen, a reporter was doing a standup next to the entrance to High Ridge Municipal Park.

"…body of the teenager was found by her friends. Little is known at this time, although sources said she had left the park to go on a soft drink run. When she didn't return, her friends began searching for her. We hope to have more on this later today. For now, this is Jerry Macatee from KSAT 12 in San Antonio."

Dana's hands shook as she poured coffee into a mug. She had to sit down at the table before she could lift the mug to her lips without spilling any. She swallowed half of it and tossed the rest. Her appetite had suddenly disappeared.

A body. A female body. She knew, from her research, High Ridge hadn't seen a violent death since the pedophile spree. But this victim wasn't a child. So it surely wasn't the monster starting up again, right?

Quickly, she closed her laptop and shoved it, along with her files, into her computer case. She'd keep it locked in her trunk while she was out and set the alarm on the car. Considering the reception she'd gotten everywhere yesterday, she wouldn't put it past someone to break into her house in an effort to send her a message.

Her hands stilled. *Send her a message.*

Surely, this girl wasn't killed in some weird way to warn her off. Or divert everyone's attention. That was far too big a stretch of the imagination. Her stomach clenched, and she had to swallow hard to beat back what seemed to be the ever-present nausea. No. That would be just too far-fetched. She was being paranoid.

But she definitely would find out every detail she could.

She showered, dressed in slacks and a blouse, and shoved her phone into her purse. Before she started off to see the parents of the dead children, she planned to stop at Sheriff Cole Landry's office. He'd said if she wanted to talk, he'd listen. She was sure, though, this wasn't what he'd meant.

****

He sat in Harry's Café, enjoying his usual breakfast with his friends and keeping his ears tuned to the conversation around him. People speculated on everything from drug dealers to bikers to kids too high on alcohol. All of them reasonable guesses but enough to make him laugh.

He'd slept well the night before, his lust satisfied and step one of his plan successfully completed. Soon, he'd have to identify another victim. And he'd have to do it carefully, so no one would know that Carrie/Dana was his final target. He hoped.

Get busy. You want that sheriff so occupied he

won't know which day of the week it is. The good people of High Ridge could blame Dana Moretti for bringing evil with her. No one would shed a tear when it was her turn.

He wondered what people would think if they knew what went on behind the warm, friendly face they saw when they looked at him.

He just loved his delicious little secret.

****

Three hours of sleep hadn't helped Cole's fatigue or his disposition. He was at his office early to meet with all his deputies before they headed off with their assignments. But the first thing he fielded was an unpleasant call from John Garrett.

"People want information, Cole," John said. "When can I give them some?"

Right on the heels of that, the calls had started coming in from the outside media. So much for keeping a lid on things. People talked. As he had headed to the conference room, Grace handed him a pile of pink message slips.

"If you return all these calls, you'll never get any work done," she told him.

"Can you keep them off my back for a while?"

"Sure." She took the slips back. "No problem."

Now, he stood at the head of the table in the conference room, looking at expressions that ranged from puzzled to shocked to angry. Everyone was there except the two deputies guarding the crime scene. Kay Shore, the county attorney, showed up with a signed blanket warrant allowing his people to enter the homes of the kids who'd been with Leanne, to search, and ask questions.

"Search?" Andi's eyebrows lifted as she read her copy. "Search for what?"

"Nita said the perp used different instruments to violate Leanne," Cole answered. "Maybe whoever it is has a little bag of goodies he keeps tucked away."

Mickey stared at him. "In High Ridge? Sheriff, you've only been here three years. Maybe you don't know people in High Ridge, but they don't...don't..."

"Have kinky sex?" Cole finished for him. "I hate to disillusion you, Mick, but even in High Ridge, I'll bet I'd find a lot of people who like to spice up their sex lives. They just keep it in their own bedrooms. And they aren't usually brutal about it. Besides, don't forget. I spent my summers here for a lot of years. And people aren't often what they seem."

He let everyone know about the calls from the media and told them he'd be setting up a press conference.

"Grace will set it up, and I'll have a prepared statement to make," he said. "You've all got your assignments. Let's get to it."

He was shuffling through a new batch of messages when a knock sounded at his open door. He looked up to see Tate in the doorway.

He gave his uncle a tired smile. "A sight for sore eyes. Come on in, and I'll try not to poison you with our coffee."

Tate dropped into the chair opposite him and balanced his hat on his knee. "No coffee, thanks. I about drank the diner dry. I figured you'd need a kind face about now."

Cole snorted. "No kidding. It hasn't even been twenty-four hours, and I think everyone wants a piece of my hide."

"You know this county is very low key. Malicious mischief and the occasional domestic violence call are about all you've had to handle. Nothing like this." Tate shook his head. "Damn nasty business."

"Bad scene, Tate." Cole shook his head. "What someone did to that sweet girl…"

"You'll need to assure people you're on top of this, you know. I'm sure it was just some vagrant wandering through here. Stumbled on her and thought she'd be a nice treat. But people will want answers."

"I know, I know." Cole took a swallow of the liquid in his mug and made a face. "We can't rule anything or anyone out yet."

"You're smart, and you've got a good staff. If there's anything to be found, you'll uncover it. The operative word being *if*." He pushed himself out of the chair and gave Cole a tired smile. "You know you've always been more like a son than a nephew to us. Adele and I, we're here for you."

"Thanks, Tate." Cole raked his fingers through his hair. "You don't know what that means to me. Okay, work to be done. I've been pushed into making a statement to the press. Can you hang around for that? It would help to have friendly faces in the crowd."

"Sure. No problem. I'll just make myself scarce until then, so you can get some work done."

Barely an hour later, he stepped outside the front doors of the building to face the hordes waiting for him. This was, after all, a major event and the media would be drooling after details. He delivered a short statement, shorter than they would have liked, but he couldn't tell them what he didn't know.

"I'll issue bulletins as more information becomes available," he said. "If you really want to help, you can put out a plea for anyone who saw Leanne Pritchard last night and noticed her with anyone else outside the park. That's it. Thank you."

Tate, hanging out at the back of the crowd, nodded at him before climbing into his truck.

Cole had barely sat down behind his desk again when the mayor and the chair of the city council barged in.

Margene Hollis, who ran a large ranch with her husband, had been re-elected mayor four times. She managed the council and the town the same way she managed the Hollis cattle operation. At barely five-five, with fiery red curls that seemed to glow with energy, she had a sharp mind and an iron will that usually got things done the way she wanted them.

Max Willis had been chairman of the council almost as long as Margene had been in office. Together, they were a one-two punch. When most people saw them coming, they simply threw up their hands and gave them what they wanted. And so far, what they'd wanted was the good life for High Ridge.

But violence couldn't simply be bullied away.

Margene waved away an offer of coffee. "Listen, Cole. You're fairly new to High Ridge, so you may not know yet how things are around here."

Cole carefully arranged a look of patience on his face. "Actually, Margene, if you recall I've been sheriff for three years." He kept his tone mild. "As I'm sure you know, since y'all were the ones who appointed me. Before that, I visited my aunt and uncle here since I was ten."

"But you weren't *born* here," she insisted.

"Neither were a lot of other people, but they seem to fit in just fine." He deliberately kept his tone mild. Losing his temper with these people would get him nowhere.

Max popped a piece of his ever-present chewing gum in his mouth, his jaws working in a steady rhythm as he spoke.

"No need to take offense, Cole." His voice took on a placating note. "We just need you to understand how important it is to clean this up before a full-blown panic takes over."

Cole leaned forward on his elbows. "I can assure you both that this is the only thing on my agenda. And you can pass that along to the members of the council. In fact, you might want to make an announcement in Harry's. That's better than an article in the newspaper."

"Don't get testy," Margene snapped. "Remember, you're an appointed official. You can be unappointed, too, you know."

"That's enough, Margene." Max threw his gum wrapper in the wastebasket. "Don't let your mouth run off with your brain. All we're doing, Cole, is letting you know people are nervous and jittery. They want to make sure nothing happens to their kids."

"Me, too, Max. Me, too."

"Have you thought about calling in some help?" Margene asked. "Maybe from the Department of Public Safety?"

Cole ground his teeth so hard he thought the enamel would crack. He knew DPS was the parent organization not only for the state police and the highly respected forensics lab in Austin but also for the legendary Texas Rangers. They could be a big help if he needed them, but he wasn't about to yell 'uncle' when less than twenty-four hours had passed.

"That's the first thing I'll do if I see there's a need for it," he assured the woman. "For right now, we've got things under control."

"They'll be under control when you catch whoever did this." She stuck her purse under her arm. "And just so you know, we expect that to happen soon."

"We can tap into the resources of Guardian Security," Cole said. "My partners would be happy to sink their teeth into something like this."

By the time he got rid of them, Cole thought the acid in his system would burn a hole in his stomach. Or maybe it was Grace Hathaway's coffee. He had just gotten up to refill his mug when Grace herself came barreling through his door, carrying a Styrofoam cup filled with the bilious liquid.

"Grace, I told you. You don't have to wait on me. And I've got my mug, remember?"

"You'll need this." Her gravelly voice had dropped to a stage whisper. She set the cup on his desk. "If I had something stronger, I would have added it."

Cole opened his mouth to ask her what the hell was going on when he looked over her shoulder and saw the answer.

"Don't blame Grace." Dana was right behind the dispatcher with a hopeful look on her face. "I snuck by when she wasn't looking."

Cole nodded at his dispatcher. "It's okay. Miss Moretti doesn't look too dangerous. I think I can defend my honor."

"You just let me know if you want me to toss her,"

Grace grumbled, heading back to her desk.

Dana forced her mouth into a smile. "I promise not to attack you."

He wondered how much of her tension had to do with what she wanted today and how much with last night's kiss. "I'm not being rude, but I'm sure you heard the news. This isn't the best time for conversation."

"It's the lead story on the morning news on television."

Without waiting for an invitation, she sat down in the chair Tate had vacated earlier.

"Yeah, so I heard." Cole shook his head. "I really wanted to keep a lid on things, but bad news travels fast."

"News like this has a way of leaking no matter what you do," she pointed out. "Especially these days when everyone is overdosed on electronics." She cleared her throat. "As a matter of fact, I was hoping you could give me a little information about it."

"What for? It has nothing to do with your book. No relationship to the cases you're looking into."

She fiddled nervously with the bracelet on her wrist.

Even as tired and harassed as he was, Cole still managed to appreciate the silken fall of her hair that brushed her shoulders and the bright blue of her eyes that almost matched the color of her shirt. Out of nowhere, the dream from the other morning smacked him again, reminding him of the feel of her breasts in his hands, the taste of her nipples. Of sliding his fingers into her waiting cunt, teasing her sweet spot to bring her to full arousal. Even though none of it had been real.

Jesus! He couldn't believe himself. A nasty murder, and he was thinking about sexual fantasies. He was either too stressed out or losing his mind. And he didn't have time to be embarrassed by the hardness of his cock pressing against his pants, eager to get out and slip into Dana Moretti's warm, welcoming core.

Welcoming? She'd probably squeeze his balls with a wrench if she knew what he was thinking. Mentally, he shook himself and tried to focus on what she was saying.

When she spoke, he could tell she chose her words carefully.

"I think whatever happens in this town is important to my book. Even this many years later. I've learned not to pick and choose what's significant because I might miss something. Call me an idiot. I'm sure everyone else will. But I have this gut feeling that this is connected to those old child murders."

Cole studied her, frowning. He'd had the same unwelcome thought, without any rhyme or reason. "I'm not sure what you want from me, Dana. You of all people should know I can't discuss any of this."

"I was hoping you'd at least tell me what you told the media. I know you made a statement earlier. The vultures are still clustering outside."

"Sure. I can give you this." He plucked a sheet of paper from the In Box on his desk and handed it to her.

She scanned it quickly. "Was the victim…molested in anyway?"

He raked his fingers through his hair. "I really can't discuss any details with you. I have to get back to work."

As if he'd willed it, the phone on his desk chose that moment to ring.

"Nita Sanchez is here and wants to discuss the post with you," Grace told him.

"Five minutes," he said and dropped the receiver into the cradle.

Dana rose from her chair. "The other thing I came to tell you is I've written about horrific cases like this before. If you need to pick my brain, I'm available. And don't close your mind to the possibility this is related to those old cases. Maybe my looking into them has stirred somebody up."

"Shit. I hope not."

"Me, too." She hitched the strap to her purse over her shoulder "I'll get out of your hair now."

Then she was gone, leaving behind a delicate trace of a floral perfume. Cole wondered what was in the heavy load of baggage she carried around with her. Something had fucked up her mind. Last night, for a brief moment, she'd been into the kiss. The next second, she'd been terrified.

Dana was a puzzle he'd have to set aside, at least for now.

****

Dana tossed her purse onto the passenger seat of her car and leaned back in hers. What stupidity had prompted her to come here? She wasn't a novice in these situations. But all she could think of was a murder had been committed in a town where the last violent death was Kylie's. She just couldn't get rid of the sick feeling that her appearance in High Ridge had somehow triggered this latest crime.

The look on Cole's face when she asked about the

molestation had told her more than words could.

It was *him*. She just knew it.

She closed her eyes and waited for the racing of her heart to slow. Already nervous about seeing Cole again after last night, she'd acted like a rank amateur, asking him for information she knew he couldn't release.

Stupid, stupid, stupid.

She sighed and pushed her hair back from her face. Maybe she'd stop at Harry's for coffee and toast…and a little eavesdropping. She might pick up a nugget or two. That was, if the people gathering there wouldn't be too bothered by a stranger in their midst.

Which was a fifty-fifty chance at best, but one she couldn't pass up.

****

He ran his eyes over her in an unhurried fashion, taking in every inch as she entered the diner. She couldn't be more than five-four, her trim figure looking smart in navy slacks and a blue shirt. Her thick, dark golden hair swung easily across her shoulders, tempting his touch.

She was so much older than he preferred, but she still had a fresh look that appealed to him. Oh, yes. He would enjoy it when he finally had his time with her.

He wondered how she responded to pain these days. He'd never realized, until the first time, how creating it could be such an intoxicating aphrodisiac. One that made his dick swell to enormous size. Oh, how he loved it. He could hardly wait to have to his next victim.

A chance snippet of conversation this morning had planted the seed for who that would be. Now, he just had to scope her out and make his plans.

He watched Carrie choose a counter stool rather than a booth, putting herself right out there for people to see. Guts. She'd be a fighter. God, he could hardly wait.

He'd have her. And then it would be done, his need satisfied, and he could fade back into the woodwork.

****

Dana could feel eyes boring holes into her back as she hitched herself onto the counter stool. Conversation had dropped a decibel or two when she walked in. Not enough to make her center stage. Just enough to let her know they'd seen her and she wasn't winning any popularity contests.

She was certain John Garrett had passed the word about her. And that Jane Milburn had huddled with her friends about it. Yup. She was certain everyone in High Ridge knew by now she was the bitch who was going to dig into something they'd spent twenty-five years covering up and trying to forget.

The air was redolent with the aroma of bacon and eggs, pancakes, and strong coffee. Even the faint scent of horseflesh, probably from the ranchers in town for business and breakfast after the morning chores at the ranch.

"Coffee?"

Dana looked up, startled at the woman standing in front of her holding a coffee carafe. The look on her face would have rivaled Cole's for hostility.

"Yes, please. And some toast if I could."

The woman dragged a mug out from beneath the counter and filled it. "White or rye."

"Rye. Thank you."

"You ought to eat a good breakfast," the woman told her. "Give you energy when you get on the road."

"Thanks, but I'm not going anywhere."

"Pity. Oh, well. I'll get that toast." She put the carafe back on the warmer and pushed through the swinging doors to the kitchen. In a few minutes, she was back, slamming the plate on the counter.

So much for small town hospitality.

Then out of nowhere, Dana felt the thrust of evil blanketing her like a cloak. Threatening to suffocate her. Choking her. Her coffee threatened to surge back up in her throat. She picked up a piece of toast and nibbled on it, hoping to control the convulsive nausea. As casually as she could, toast in hand, she swiveled on the stool and let her eyes roam over the customers.

Everyone was drinking their coffee, eating their breakfast, chatting with their neighbors. No one seemed to be paying any particular attention to her. No one even looked familiar. Of course, after all these years, people changed physically, so whoever she sensed the feeling from could be anyone.

But she knew he was here, just the same. He was still in his hunting ground. In High Ridge, right here in Harry's Diner.

Stalking her.

He'd lost her all those years ago. Now, he was going to finish the job. Last night had just been a prelude. She felt that inevitable truth straight to the core of her body. But if she said it out loud, no one would believe her.

"I see you're still here."

Dana turned her head to see John Garrett sliding onto the stool next to her. "I am. Despite the fact that

I'm turning into the town's Typhoid Mary."

"You look like a smart person, Dana. I've read a couple of your books, and you're an excellent writer. Intuitive. Sensitive."

A hot blush bloomed in her cheeks. In this town, she'd take compliments wherever she could find them. "Thank you."

"Oh, I'm not here to give you strokes. I'm trying to figure out why someone like you hasn't gotten the message that High Ridge doesn't want you to open old wounds. Surely, there must be another crime you could chase after. Somewhere else."

She tightened her hands on her mug. "Let me ask you a question, John. Professional to professional."

Garrett signaled for the waitress to bring him a full mug. "Lay it on me."

"Doesn't anyone think it would arouse my suspicions if they just shut me out? That I might think they have something to hide? Aren't there people who want to know what really happened? To find out who committed these dreadful crimes?"

He nodded his thanks for the coffee. "It's like this. The families whose children were victims are still dealing with the shock and grief after all these years. It tore people apart. Destroyed marriages. You think they want to bleed all over again?"

"Maybe it would be good for them. They could finally have some closure."

"How would you feel if you were in their situation?"

"How do you think they feel after last night?" she asked. "Everyone here operates on the theory that if you don't acknowledge something, it will go away. But

117

now, here's this new murder. It opens up the possibility that another predator has decided to make High Ridge his feeding ground."

John blew on the hot coffee, then took a sip. "Jesus, I hope not. It's bad enough as it is."

"Or maybe," she said quietly, "it's the same killer hunting again."

He nearly dropped his mug. "You'd be wise not to go around voicing that theory. Everyone knows whoever it was is long gone."

"That's what everyone wants to believe," she corrected.

"It's the truth," he said stubbornly.

"So what will you be putting in the paper?" She sipped at the hot coffee.

"Not much. There's not much to tell. But we sure won't be digging up the past."

Dana frowned. "Sheriff Landry gave me a copy of the release. If she was taken in the convenience store parking lot, I'm surprised someone didn't see her."

"She was parked way over to the side, not too visible, I guess."

Dana watched his face as she asked the next question. "I assume she was raped?"

"Yeah." Garrett sighed. "Sheriff's not giving out any details on that, but scuttlebutt says it was pretty brutal."

It's him. I know it's him.

She had to get out of here. Dropping the half-eaten toast back on her plate, she fished some singles from her purse and dropped them on the counter.

"Thanks, John. I think." She made a show of looking at her watch. "I need to get going."

"Leave the people alone, Dana," he repeated.

"We'll see."

She escaped before anyone else could add their two cents and locked herself in her car, shaking, watching through her sunglasses to see who came out of Harry's after she did. But no one seemed particularly interested in her or where she'd gone. And the feeling of evil didn't reach out to grip her again.

Did he know who she was? Had he somehow, after all these years, recognized her? For a minute there, she had been back in that barn, consumed with fear and pain.

No. This was ridiculous.

Yet somehow, she'd picked up on his thoughts and they related to her. *Dana. Not Carrie.* That was even scarier.

She sat for a full five minutes, deep breathing and pulling herself together. She hadn't felt this much fear since she was seven years old and made the worst decision of her life.

Finally, she checked her makeup in the mirror on her sun visor and, applied fresh lipstick, and looked at her phone. By the time she got to the first family on her list, she'd better be in full control of herself.

Chapter Thirteen

He could tell by the sudden paleness of Dana's face and the way she'd tried to sweep her eyes casually over the room that she'd sensed him. He'd been thinking about her, planning for their eventual meeting. Somehow, he must have sent off unconscious vibrations she'd picked up on.

Careful. Don't want to spook her.

He'd have to learn to keep his thoughts to himself when she was around. But who knew she'd be so sensitive to him? So susceptible?

Susceptible. That was a good word. She'd make an excellent victim with her susceptibility.

He'd been so hard this morning just remembering Leanne. He'd had to take a cold shower before he could leave the house. Tonight, he'd meet Tony and pluck one of the delightful little flowers from the big van.

And tomorrow, victim number two. He already had her picked out and a plan in place. This, too, took some careful maneuvering. And if it didn't work tomorrow, there was always the next day. But he had a time limit. If one plan failed, he'd have to figure out another.

****

Cole was sure the coffee had eaten a hole in his stomach by now, yet here he was, sipping at yet another mug of the venomous brew. But Nita Sanchez sat in front of him with her completed autopsy report, a copy of which he held in his hands, and he needed all the fortification he could get to deal with it.

"I've seen vicious," Nita told him, "and I've seen sadistic. I won't say you get used to it, but you learn to protect your emotions after a while. But to see what someone's done to a young girl like this…" She rubbed her eyes. "There's a terrible evil out there, Cole. You've got to find him before he does this again."

"Don't I know it."

"I cannot imagine the pain Leanne went through. This attack was…depraved."

"Jesus. God." Cole had to force himself to keep reading. "He bit her?"

Nita nodded, gripping the arms of her chair to control her obvious rage.

Cole had to swallow hard against the vitriol rising in his throat. "Were you able to get any impressions?"

She shook her head. "No. I think he used something over his teeth, too. He was well prepared."

"And the massive bruising on her thighs and buttocks?"

"That's where he pinched her."

"What about DNA?"

"I doubt we'll get any. I found traces of latex, which means he wore gloves."

Cole dropped the report back on his desk and forked his fingers through his hair. "It also means he was prepared. This was a premeditated act."

Nita's eyes were filled with a volatile combination of misery and rage. Most of the bodies she worked on died of natural causes or were accident victims of some kind. Salado was a fairly quiet county, which was why he'd taken the job in the first place. While the latter could be badly injured and often mangled, he knew nothing compared to what had been done to sixteen-year-old Leanne Pritchard.

Meeting with her parents had been the worst hour of his day. He had no answers for them, no explanation. No assurance that this man would be caught in a hurry. But catch him he would. That was for damn sure. This was his town now, his county, and he wasn't about to allow this evil to linger.

His only problem was, he had no idea how to get rid of it. This was one smart son of a bitch. He left no clues, no traces, nothing. Absolutely nothing.

And to add to his shitty day, sickened by the crime and dreading the visit with the parents, he'd been more abrupt than he needed to be with Dana Moretti. Sure, she should know better than to try to extract information out of him with a case this fresh, but he could have been a little nicer about showing her the door, especially when she volunteered to help. God knows, he could use every bit he could get.

Especially with that crazy theory she floated.

Damn.

"Earth to Cole." Nita's voice broke into his reverie.

"What? Sorry."

"I said the tox screen should be back later today. There was a faint odor of something on her face. I'm assuming it's whatever he used to subdue her. Maybe that will help us."

"God, I hope so." He studied her for a moment. "Nita, you've lived here a long time. Got a sense for the rhythm of this place. Do you think there's a remote chance that this could be in any way connected to those child murders from twenty-five years ago?"

"What?" She glared at him. "No, and I don't think you should be passing that around, either."

"Just do me a favor. Please? Check your report against the old autopsies and see if anything compares."

She pushed her chair back and reared to her feet. "I'll do it, but it's a waste of my time. Whoever did those killings twenty-five years ago is long gone."

And isn't that what everyone wants us to believe? Even the killer.

****

Stan and Lois Kelly lived in a small house near High Ridge Middle School. Dana sat in her car for a moment, studying the area. All the houses were small but well-maintained, most of them made of the familiar Texas stone and adobe. The lawns in front were neat, some with an abundance of flowers, others with neatly trimmed shrubs.

A family neighborhood. Only some of the families had been ripped apart.

She hadn't called in advance, unwilling to give the Kellys a chance to refuse to see her. Gathering her purse and her courage, she headed up the narrow walk and pressed the doorbell.

At first, there was no answer, although she could hear movement inside the house. She waited a little longer, then pressed the bell again, this time more insistently. The door cracked open the length of the chain inside, and a pair of haunted eyes peered out at her.

"Go away," a woman said. "I know who you are. Just go away."

Dana made her voice as even as possible. "Mrs. Kelly, I just want a few minutes of your time. That's all. If you could just spare me that little bit."

"I have nothing to say to you. I don't want to talk about it."

The door closed. Dana sighed and pressed the bell again.

"I'm trying to give all of you here some closure," she called. "Don't you want to find out who did this to your child? That person has been running around free all this time."

Silence.

"Mrs. Kelly?" She lowered her voice slightly. "Just give me ten minutes. That's all. Please."

She was about to leave and try the next address when the door slid open, the loose chain rattling against its hard wood, and a hand motioned her inside.

"I don't want you standing out there where all the neighbors can hear you," Lois Kelly told her. "But I don't have anything to say to you."

Dana hurried inside before the woman changed her mind.

The house was immaculate, so neat it was almost inhumanly clean. Dana had seen this before, the compulsive cleaning, over and over, as if by doing so the stain of what happened could be washed away. And it kept one from thinking. Repetitive motion could be wonderful for blanking the mind. She should know, she harbored many of the same habits.

Lois Kelly was thin almost to the point of emaciation. Her straight dark hair was cut short—less upkeep—and she wore no makeup. She was dressed in black slacks and a black blouse. Dana wondered if she'd worn mourning clothes all these years.

"Jane Milburn told everyone what you're after."

Her voice was high and thin. She stood in front of Dana, twisting her hands tightly as if they were the only thing holding her together. "You want to dig it all up again and bring back the nightmares just so you can make money. We won't let you do it."

"Lois." Dana pulled out her best professional voice. "May I call you Lois? I think Jane misunderstood what I said to her. That's not my intention at all."

As she talked, she moved to a narrow wing chair by the window and casually lowered herself into it.

"Yes. Yes, it is." Lois Kelly's face took on a pinched, demanding look. "Why are you doing this?"

Dana looked around the small room. Nearly every surface was covered with framed photos of a smiling, chubby redhead with dimples and snapping eyes. She wasn't older than five in any of them, the age the little girl had been when she was raped and murdered.

"Every one of you has mourned your children all these years, yet you've had no real closure. That's what I'm hoping to do. Find some answers that will give you closure."

Lois untwisted her hands and shoved them in her pockets. "What makes you think you can do what the sheriff couldn't? Besides, whoever it was has moved on. There's been nothing in High Ridge since then."

"Until today," Dana pointed out.

Lois's face turned rice paper white. "Are you saying it's the same man? That he's come back?"

Dana couldn't shake the feeling that somewhere there was a connection, but she didn't want to give voice to it just yet. People would think she was nuts.

"No, not at all. I'm just hoping this doesn't turn out to be an unsolved case like your Bonnie's." She shifted slightly in her chair. "What I've found with all of my books is that I bring a fresh eye to an old situation. Often I can see things that other people overlooked because they were too familiar with them. And many times that leads to answers that hadn't been available or even imagined when the original crime took place."

"Familiar?" Lois's eyes widened. "Do you think it was someone we know?" She shook her head violently, disabusing both of them of the idiocy of the statement. "No, no, no. That's just not possible."

"Why don't you come sit down with me?" Dana suggested. "Just for a few minutes. Tell me about Bonnie. I'd really love to hear about her. Come on. I'll bet you don't get to talk about her too often."

Dana had found time and again that people buried their grief along with their loved ones, then dealt with it by banishing the subject from all conversation. But once she got them to talk, it was like opening the floodgates of a dam. And all too often, the tiny missing nugget spilled out in the flow of words.

Lois barely noticed that her unwanted guest had taken a seat and was carefully guiding the conversation. Dana was sure she was the first person outside a small circle of friends who had even been in this house since the death of their child. Very often she found herself the catalyst that opened all the locked doors.

"Stan says it hurts too much to talk about her." One tear slid down her cheek. "And he blames me for what happened. Says it was all my fault." She dropped into the chair at the other side of the window like a rag doll, tears flowing in earnest now. "But it wasn't," she protested. "He was there, too. He was right there. Why didn't he watch her better?"

Dana's heart pinched. These people had locked themselves in this obsessively neat house, all these years living with sorrow and blame, barely existing. Maybe even hating each other. Dana had seen that, too. How many others would she talk to who were frozen in time like this?

She reached into her pocket to turn on the voice-activated recorder, then leaned over and touched Lois's hand very gently. "Why don't you just tell me about Bonnie? I'd love to hear about her."

"She was such a sweet thing." Lois pulled a tissue from her pocket and mopped at her eyes. "So cheerful all the time. Laughed at everything. Stan would come home and toss her up in his arms, and she'd just laugh and laugh. He said it was the one thing he looked forward to all day."

Dana nodded at the photos. "She looks like a very bright little girl."

"Oh, yes. She was smart all right. Maybe too smart. She wanted to know about everything. That's why…" The tears welled again.

"I don't understand. Are you saying that had something to do with what happened? I thought you were all at a picnic?"

"Yes." Her dark head nodded. "We were at the big Fourth of July picnic out at the park. Bonnie was having such a good time. Stan pushed her on the swings, and they had rides for the little kids."

"What happened? Can you tell me?"

"She was fascinated by the clowns. She wanted to know all about them."

Dana felt every drop of blood in her body chill. Clowns. Oh, God. "Were there a lot of clowns at the picnic, Lois?"

"Four or five of them. Making those balloon figures and doing tricks for the children." She balled the tissue up in her fist. "She was right next to me, sitting with her balloon animal. But she wanted another one. And she wanted the clown to show her how they were made. She kept asking one of us to take her."

"But you didn't," Dana guessed.

She shook her head. "Stan had come back from the softball game and wanted a cold drink, and I was fussing around, getting it poured for him. He wanted a cup with ice, you see. And a snack. Two of the men on his team walked up and were talking to him. And I just turned my back for a minute. Only a minute."

There was such pain on Lois's face that Dana could hardly bear to look at her. "Are you saying she wandered away?"

Lois nodded. "There were so many people there. Almost the whole town attended that day. And when I turned around, she was gone and no one could find her." She hiccupped. "I ran around calling her name. Stan did, too. And pretty soon other people helped. We even thought maybe she'd wandered into the woods. The park is pretty thick with trees."

An ideal place for a predator. All he had to do was lure the child close, subdue her, and carry her to a car hidden from sight. "But you think she went looking for one of the clowns?"

Lois nodded. "That's all she talked about. She kept repeating the word over and over." She frowned. "But you know, the sheriff questioned every one of those clowns for a long time, and they all swore they hadn't seen her after the balloon show."

"All of them? You said there were four or five?"

"You know, now that I think of it, there was something funny about that." Lois rubbed her cheek, a faint tremor in her hand, and frowned. "But I can't remember exactly what. I think it had to do with the number of clowns. Even the chamber of commerce who hired them wasn't sure if four or five showed up."

Dana's chest tightened, and she had to force herself to breathe. What better disguise than that of a clown? He could conceal every aspect of his identity, blend in with his surroundings and at the same time be an attractive lure for children. Her unstable stomach roiled.

"Listen, I've talked way too much." Lois stood up, their little chat finished. "Stan will have a fit if he even finds out I let you in here. You'll have to leave right now. Please."

Dana rose, gathering her purse. "No problem. I appreciate the time you've given me. And Stan won't find out from me that I was here." Impulsively, she hugged the sad, nervous woman. "Maybe when I put everything together, something good will come out of this, and you can all have some peace. Thank you for your time."

Lois practically shoved her out the door, and the chain snapped into place the moment the door closed.

Clowns. Damn. Of course. Just like the one who lived in her nightmares. She needed to go home and scan through her notes. Any place in public and she'd be dogged by people asking questions or throwing sarcastic remarks.

Chapter Fourteen

Dana had planned to visit one other set of parents that afternoon, but after her session with Lois Kelly, she didn't think she could handle another one so soon. Being personally involved made a whole lot of difference in how a case affected her. Listening to Lois was like reliving her own nightmare.

As soon as she got back to the house, she changed into jeans and an old shirt and began pulling up all the notes she'd made from the reports, looking for clues. She took her time, not wanting to miss anything in her haste to search for similarities. Her eyes were gritty from studying the small screen, and her stomach reminded her to feed it as the doorbell rang.

Distracted, she didn't bother to do her usual check through the peephole and just yanked the door open. She was shocked to see Cole standing there, holding a pizza box. He was obviously freshly showered and shaved and dressed in clean jeans and T-shirt.

"I already apologized for bothering you this morning," she told him. "I thought you'd be done with me." She started to close the door, needing to get him out of her space.

He stuck his booted foot into the opening. "I actually came to apologize." He pointed to the box he was holding. "And I brought a peace offering."

Dana sniffed. The delicious scent of cheese and

pepperoni drifted past her nose.

"So can I come in while the pizza's still hot?"

Before she could stop herself, she'd swung the door wide and waved him in.

In the kitchen, he put the box on the counter while she got out plates, napkins, and drinks and put them in a stack. She didn't know which shocked her more— finding Cole on her doorstep or letting him into her house. After the emotional day she'd had, she wasn't sure she was ready to cope with him and his overpowering masculinity.

"Here, let me help." His voice was right at her ear, a low rumble that warmed her in the oddest way.

She pressed her hands against her thighs to keep them from trembling and turned right into a wall of hard, male muscle. "I, um, need a little space here."

He stared down at her, the color of his eyes darkening to hot chocolate. His hands on her shoulders felt like hot coals, but strangely enough, that too seemed comforting.

"I can almost hear your mind buzzing." His voice was a raspy whisper. "That kiss last night was no mistake."

"I… You…" Her heart was beating triple time, and she knew the pulse at the hollow of her throat gave away the sensations rocketing through her.

"Admit it." His hands cupped her face. "You felt it, too."

Dana couldn't move. She stood there, feet cemented to the floor as his mouth came slowly down on hers and his lips brushed hers in a soft caress. She managed to move her hands up on his chest, but rather than use them to push him away, she kept them there feeling the heat of his skin through his T-shirt.

What was wrong here? Men terrified her. Scared her so badly she was unable to have a normal sexual relationship. So why wasn't she freezing up inside? Running away? Where was the familiar feeling of panic? How did she go from traumatized to aroused without taking a breath? Who was this woman who had taken her place?

The moment stretched on and on, and still, she didn't move. The kiss intensified. His tongue traced the seam of her lips, and without thinking, she opened for him, letting him inside, feeling his tongue like the sweep of a flame. Feeling her nerves dance in response and liquid soak her panties.

He never increased the pressure on her mouth, kept it light as he tasted every bit. She heard a soft moan and was shocked to realize it came from her.

And then it happened. The panic. The fear. She wrestled her way out of his arms, heart racing, and took a step back. Then two.

Cole stood perfectly still, watching her. "I don't know what's got you spooked, Dana, but I promise you, I'll never do anything to hurt you."

"Cole—"

His thumb caressed her cheekbone, and she wondered why she didn't move away.

"And I don't know what's happening here," he said in a low, even voice. "I want to say I can't ever remember a connection this instant with anyone. I know you feel it, too. But I don't want to frighten you, so we'll go slow. Very slow." The smile widened. "At least, we'll eat the pizza first."

Her brain was totally frazzled, her vision hazy as

he dropped his hands and took a step backward.

"Pizza," she repeated.

"First," he reminded her and nodded at the utensils on the counter. "Can I help with anything?"

Somehow, she pulled herself out of her daze. "Oh. Yes. Sure." She was babbling like an idiot. "Beer. In the fridge."

In a flurry of nerves, she finished putting the dishes and pizza on the table and took the chair across from him, doing her best to gather her scattered wits. Why was this happening now? How could it happen so suddenly after all these years? And why with this man?

When the time is right, you'll know it. She heard the voice of her therapist, Dr. Summers. *The barricades will fall, Dana.*

But Dana hadn't been prepared for them to fall so quickly. All she could think about was that damn dream and how much she suddenly wanted it to be a reality. For so long she'd felt certain those dreams were out of her reach but now…

Now, at the worst possible time, when what she was doing required every ounce of inner strength to keep it together, when she'd brought herself back to the birthplace of her nightmares, here was Cole Landry turning her emotions upside down. Unexpected hunger and her familiar companion, panic, battled within her.

She looked at Cole and saw the lines of fatigue etched across his face and the shadows under his eyes. "How about another beer? You look like you could use it."

He gave her a lopsided smile. "I won't turn it down."

"Go on into the living room. I'll bring it to you."

He was half-lying on the couch, looking as if he could use a week's sleep, when she handed him the opened bottle.

"Thanks." He sat up, raked his fingers through his hair and took a long swallow of the beer.

Standing in front of him, Dana fiddled with her own drink. "I never should have barged into your office the way I did today. That was idiotic of me, and I'm sorry." She chewed her bottom lip. "I was shaken by Leanne's murder happening the moment I get here to do research for my book. I mean, nothing happens here for twenty-five years, then I show up, and boom!"

"Don't you think that's kind of a stretch?" He took a long pull at the bottle. "I know the people in this county. It's got to be a stranger."

"Just like it was twenty-five years ago?" she demanded with a sudden burst of anger.

"Listen—"

She held up a hand, the anger dissipating as quickly as it had surged. "Sorry. I know it sounds farfetched, but I'm…nervous."

"Scared?"

"No. Yes." She tossed her head. "Whatever."

"But not enough to shut down this crazy project."

"I can't Cole." She dropped into the armchair. "I have to do this."

He sat up straighter. "Can you at least tell me why?"

She shook her head. "I have my reasons. Leave it at that. Okay?" She tucked her hair behind her ear. "Let's say the pedophile wasn't from around here. That he moved on. Someone that sick doesn't just stop what he's doing. Believe me, I've been researching these kinds of psychos for years, and if there's one thing that's true, it's that they don't quit. They *can't* quit. So where did he go? Where did he set up shop next? Did they find out? Did anyone even look? Check the national databases? Maybe find a pattern?"

Cole took another swallow of beer before answering her. "Jesus, Dana. It was a cold case—very cold—by the time I took office here, so I had no reason even to look at it. But I'd like to think that was done. Maybe whoever it was is already dead. Auto accident. Almost anything."

"Wouldn't that be a nice, neat package. Then everyone could close the books and forget about the whole thing." She smacked her forehead. "Oh, I forgot! Everyone in High Ridge *has* forgotten about it."

She looked away before he could see the tears in her eyes. Lowering her head, she began to peel the label from the beer bottle and drop bits of paper in a little dish on the table next to her.

It didn't matter what anyone thought or said. She knew the truth. He wasn't dead. He was here, in High Ridge. She'd sensed him today. But how could she tell that to Cole? He'd think she was crazy for sure.

He cleared his throat. "Okay, I hear you. But right now, I've got every single body focused on the Pritchard case. Truth to tell, though, I came over here tonight because I needed to get away from the gore and misery, and I thought…"

"Yes?" She sat up straighter, her body tightening. "You thought what?"

"I thought it would be nice to hang out and talk about something besides crime and murder."

She stared at him. "Because we have such a great

relationship?"

He laughed at that. "Not yet, but I'm hoping."

Hoping? Hoping for what? For a normal relationship with a normal woman? *Big laugh on you, Cole Landry.*

But her pulse skipped slightly, and her words stuck in her throat. "Cole, there's something you need to know about me."

One eyebrow cocked, and a grin teased at his solemn mouth. "You're an escaped convict? A hooker looking to retire? A black widow who kills men for money?"

She shook her head. She couldn't even smile at his attempted humor. "I'm not very good with relationships. I don't want you to think—"

"Dana, I don't think anything. And I'm not asking you for anything. Just your friendship. All right?"

"That's all? Because…"

Cole swung his legs around and leaned his elbows on his knees. "No worries. For right now, friendship is a good thing. And Dana?"

"Yes?"

His voice softened. "You don't have to be afraid of me."

"I-I don't know why you feel the need to tell me that."

"Because every time I get close to you or touch you, you react as if I'm about to strangle you."

"I just… Forget it. Forget I said anything. I'd like to be friends. Just like you said." She gripped the bottle a little too tightly. "We'll see. Meanwhile, why don't you tell me how you ended up in High Ridge, Texas. It's not exactly the center of the universe."

He lounged back into the couch again, balancing his beer bottle on his stomach. "Well, let's see. Ten years in the Marines took a lot out of me. I wouldn't change a day of it, but I reached a point where I couldn't deal anymore with death and destruction." His eyes took on a faraway look. "Too many good men died right next to me. I needed something for my own peace of mind."

"But you knew about this place?"

"My aunt and uncle live here. Adele and Tate Bishop. They own that big Santa Gertrudis ranch west of town. I used to visit during the summers." He drank the last of his beer. "The sheriff here was having some arthritis problems and wanted to retire. Tate suggested I might like to apply to the county commission for the job. Bought myself a few acres outside of town. A few horses. And here I am."

Dana cocked a brow as she reached for his empty bottle, silently asking if he wanted another.

"One more. That's my limit for tonight." When she handed him a fresh one from the kitchen, he took a long swallow. "I actually have an associate's degree in criminal justice. One of these days, I'd like to get my bachelor's. I guess I should have started it before the roof fell in here."

"You'll find who did this. You don't seem like the kind of person who'll quit pushing until he has all the answers."

"Right now, I feel like a person who's in over his head."

"The television reporter tonight said she was raped and sodomized." Dana realized she was clenching the bottle again and forcibly relaxed her grip. Images smacked her of what the woman had gone through.

Cole made a face. "Television reporters. They're like pimples popping up when you least need them. Yes. Raped and sodomized and tortured. Then tossed away like some piece of garbage. Makes me want to throttle whoever this is."

Dana took a sip of her drink. "Her parents must be devastated."

"Mrs. Pritchard's in the hospital. She collapsed after I spoke with them yesterday. And her husband isn't leaving her side. They're an older couple. Leanne came along when they'd least expected to have kids. She was their world, a bright, sweet girl who was the light of their lives. I worry they might die of grief."

"I'm sorry." She shifted in her chair. "You said you came here to get away from the gore and mayhem for a few hours, and I've made you fall right back into it. Let's change the subject."

Dana was surprised at how easily she and Cole fell into a conversation. She' d expected him to bombard her with questions, but maybe he was saving them. Cole was the last person in the world she expected to have things in common. But by the time ten o'clock rolled around, the hesitancy and stiffness between them had morphed into genuine liking. She even felt comfortable with him.

When she walked him to the door, they were close enough that if she stood on tiptoe, their lips would meet, but one kiss tonight from this man was enough. For now. He rested his hands on her shoulders and studied her eyes, as if he was trying to look inside her.

"Tonight has been really great," he told her. "I needed this. Thank you."

"I enjoyed it, too."

"I'd like to do it again if I can get this case under control. Would that be all right?"

She nodded. "You don't have to wait. Stop by anytime you want to talk. I mean, if you need to. About the case. Or anything." She studied the lines of strain on his face. "I know what it's like, the need to unload the tension."

"You said before you don't have good luck with relationships."

"Cole, listen—"

He touched one finger to her lips, his eyes holding hers. "Are the demons chasing you the reason for that? Because something's got a death grip on you. I could tell the first time I met you. I saw it in your eyes." He let one finger trail softly along her cheek. "At first, I thought you were just a hard-ass, but that's not it at all, is it? You're frightened to death of something, so you hide behind a wall of steel."

"You're wrong," she protested half-heartedly. "Dead wrong."

It was a lie, and they both knew it, but she knew he wouldn't push her. At least not tonight.

He smiled, and there was so much understanding in his expression she didn't know what to say when he reached up and brushed a thumb across her cheek.

"I don't think I'm wrong. And whatever it is, I know it's what's got you on the hunt after this story. I don't know if you're trying to find answers or you're running away from the questions, but I know it's something."

Her body drawn taut as a bow, she tried to pull away,. "I'm fine. Really. Just fine."

He dropped his hands to her shoulders again. "No, you're not, darlin'. Far from it. I just wanted you to know this works both ways. I'm here if you need someone to talk to. Maybe help you with whatever it is."

But…what would it be like to actually dump it all out in the open? Tell him what happened? Tell him about the clowns and what she'd found out? Maybe even tell him about the sense of evil that had permeated the air at Harry's. No. She couldn't tell him anything. Not yet. She couldn't trust him enough. No matter how much she wanted to.

"I'm fine," she insisted once more. "You need to get home and catch some sleep or you won't be any good to anyone."

He studied her face for a long time, then stepped back and reached for the doorknob. "Right. I won't keep you. Thanks for letting me come by like this. As to your offer, don't be too surprised if I take you up on it sometime."

"Anytime," she assured him.

When he was gone and she made sure all the doors and windows were locked, Dana put on some water for tea and took a mug out of the cupboard. She was amazed and proud of the fact that she'd been able to get through Cole's unexpected visit with some semblance of normalcy. Today had been one emotional collision after another. She'd held herself together all evening, but now, in the quiet of night, the familiar shakes were taking over.

Filling her mug with hot tea, she carried it to the dining room table and booted up her laptop. Sleep was probably the smartest thing she could do, but the new information she'd discovered plagued her. And hovering at the back of her mind was the image of the grinning clown, enticing her and Kylie, then grabbing them and racing from the fairgrounds. What a mockery! That something so appealing to children had been used to destroy them.

She'd found three incidents so far in the crime reports that mentioned the clowns. How many more were there? Pulling up the file she'd transferred her notes into, she began again to study each case. If only she could find some way to do a better search.

Chewing at her bottom lip, she began to enter her search parameters and click on the links that came up.

****

The cabin was dark except for the lamp beside the bed. Thick black curtains sealed the interior from the outside, giving no indication that anyone was inside. No one ever used this place anymore except him, but he wasn't taking any chances. He'd set motion sensors around the perimeter, remembering the shock of nearly being found out all those years ago at the place he'd once used. The last thing he'd expected was kids stumbling on the location as an ideal place to smoke pot.

But here in the cabin, he was completely isolated. No one knew how to get here anymore except for him. With the precautions he'd taken, he felt secure that he had all the time in the world.

He looked at the girl lying on the bed, wrists manacled and fastened to the headboard, eyes wide with fear above the tape on her mouth. Probably no one could hear her out here, but again, he wasn't taking any chances. He didn't want to have to look for another hidey hole.

She was older than he liked, but Tony had told him to take it or leave it. The crop tonight had not included any of the real young ones that were so delicious to his taste. He'd have to speak to Tony about that.

They'd concluded their business at the usual spot, the others were turned over to his buyer, and he'd whisked this little darling off in his truck for some fun and games.

He hummed as he gathered his tools and toys, lining them up on the bedside table.

"There was a little girl, who had a little curl, right in the middle of her forehead. When she was bad, she was very, very bad, and when she was good she was…" He chuckled. "Just his cup of tea."

The mere thought of what he was about to do had his cock erect and throbbing. He'd have to work to maintain control. The older he got, the harder it was to hold back. He rose from the bed and slowly began to strip off his clothes. He enjoyed the struggles of each young girl as the understanding and fear in her eyes grew stronger. The screams muffled behind the duct tape drove him to new heights as he played his games.

First the toys. Oh, yes, he loved every kind of toy.

This one was little more than limp flesh by the time he wiped himself as best he could and pulled his clothes back on. Her eyes fluttered when he closed his hands around her throat, and the fear was stark as she realized what he was about to do. Her fear drove him as he snapped her tender neck.

After checking carefully to make sure no one had managed to pop up unexpectedly, he lifted her body and carried it out the back door. Five hundred yards into the trees was an old well. He'd already opened the padlock on the cover. Shifting it to the side with one foot, he heaved her slight body into the opening and heard it thud as it landed on the remains of those who had gone before her.

Finished, he slid the cover back in place, fastened the padlock, and strolled back to the cabin humming his favorite tune.

Chapter Fifteen

It was seven a.m. when Cole arrived at his office. As soon as he dropped into the chair at his desk, he received a call from Reno Sullivan, Guardian's senior partner.

"You know Susan Pritchard's in the hospital, right?" Of course, Reno would already be up to speed. "She's had a complete breakdown. Leanne was the sun and the moon to her."

Cole rubbed his face. "Yeah, this has to be hell for them."

Grace inched her way into the office quietly and deposited a cup of coffee on his desk.

He mouthed, "Thank you." To Reno, he said, "Nobody's resting until this is over, but we could use Guardian as advisors on the case. I'm sure I can get the county to pay."

"This one's a little too close to home, Cole. We'll help all we can and cover the cost," Reno offered. "But what about the Rangers. They work murder cases. Or the FBI?"

"It's barely been thirty-six hours since we found the body," Cole pointed out. "And this isn't the kind of case the FBI will jump in on. At least not yet."

"Then tell me what you've got."

Cole picked up his cup, blew on the hot brew, and sipped at it, trying his best not to make a face at the taste. "Someone slashed one of her tires while she was in the Supermart. Probably waited for her to come out, so he could offer her a ride. We have to consider the possibility it might be someone from around here. Leanne would never get into a car with a stranger. Her daddy would have tanned her hide, and she knew it."

"I agree."

"Her truck was way off to the side. Someone could have grabbed her and knocked her out before she could scream."

"The town won't want to think about that as a possibility."

Neither did Cole, but Dana's words kept haunting him. As a conscientious lawman, he had to consider every aspect of the situation. He'd found himself staring out the windows of his truck on the way to work, wondering if any of the men he passed could be the one he was looking for and hating himself for thinking it.

"Just to fill you in, I've got deputies checking everyone we can pinpoint as being at Supermart around that time. The manager pulled all the slips with charge or debit card numbers, and the names we don't have, the bank's getting for us. We're talking to everyone who was working, hoping they'll remember if they saw some of their neighbors there or others we can talk to."

Reno grunted. "What else have you got?"

"No evidence of anything where Leanne's body was left, which indicates she was killed somewhere else. I'm damned if I can figure out, though, how he got her there without leaving any tracks. Every possible route to the park is being checked and rechecked in case someone might have noticed something."

"If another young girl turns up like this…"

"That could indicate a serial killer, and we'd be calling the FBI first thing," he said, not wanting to think about the hell that would bring to High Ridge. "I won't sit on my hands, waiting to see what develops."

As soon as he got off the phone with Reno, Cole sifted through the reports his deputies had left for him, checked to see who was out doing what and where, and decided his stomach was too touchy for Grace's coffee without something in it to soak it up.

"I'm going over to Harry's for a breakfast roll," he told the dispatcher, clapping his hat on his head.

Maybe Uncle Tate would be there and he could bounce some ideas off of him again. Tate always had a good head for analyzing things. And he always stopped at Harry's when he came into the city.

****

She dreamed again about Cole Landry.

"You said I could taste you this time," she told him.

"I'm counting on it." His voice was husky, edged with lust. His very masculine face was darkened with need, his whiskey-brown eyes now the color of rich coffee.

She dropped to her knees on the carpet in front of him, one hand cupping the heavy sac of his balls, the other sliding up and down the swollen thickness of his cock. She ran her tongue over the broad, flat head, catching the bead of fluid that sat like a pearl on the slit.

Looking up at him, holding his gaze, she slowly lowered her mouth over him and took him inside her mouth. He was so large there was little room left to move her tongue, but she managed to twist it around his shaft slightly, pressing it against the throbbing vein that wound around it.

His fingers threaded through her hair, holding her head, moving it to a better angle. Her fingers continued to play with his balls while she hollowed her cheeks and sucked his cock as hard as she could. He rocked back and forth on his heels, a low moan rolling up from his throat, the sound urging her to move her head faster, squeeze his sac harder.

"Oh, Jesus. Oh, shit. Oh, hell."

She felt the tightening of his sac, the tensing of his body, and then he erupted, spurting thick semen into her mouth. It glided down her tongue and against the back of her throat. She clutched his erection convulsively, tightening her fingers around the base as she sucked him dry.

When the tension finally left his body, she smiled, knowing she'd made him feel good.

"Your turn," he told her in a low voice, cupping her elbows to help her to her feet. "Time to pay attention to that sweet, little pussy." He placed her on the bed so her legs were spread wide. "Tonight, I'm going to lick every inch of you. Make you come with my hand and my tongue before I finally fuck you senseless."

Heat blasted through her like a furnace, the walls of her pussy already quivering with anticipation. She was so ready for him that when he touched the tip of a finger to her clit, she jerked, as if fire had whisked over her.

"Aah." The sound was one of pure male satisfaction. "Someone's very horny tonight."

He spread her lips and bent his head, flicking his tongue back and forth against that swollen bundle of nerves. Dana shook with the intensity of the sensation consuming her. Stiffened nipples ached for his touch, and the muscles low in her tummy tightened.

He took his time, teasing her clit first with his tongue and then with his finger until she came just from his focus on that one part of her body. Spasms rocked her while he held her still, his body preventing her from squeezing her thighs together. Then he began again, this time with his mouth on that bundle of nerves and his fingers stroking in and out of her wet folds.

She planted her feet on the mattress and lifted herself to him, pushing down on his hand. He teased and tormented, adding a third finger then pulling his hand away completely.

"Noooo," she wailed. "Please, please, please."

"I love it when you're hot like this," he purred and thrust his fingers inside her again.

She rode them hard, pushing against them, pushing, pushing...

She woke up, yanked back to reality, her hand between her legs. Holy hell! What was happening to her? This whole thing was screwing with her mind.

Extricating herself from the twisted, sweaty covers, she stumbled into the bathroom for one of the mild tranquilizers she rarely took. The sight that met her eyes when she looked in the mirror was almost as frightening as her dream.

"I look like a scarecrow," she said out loud. "Sleep, Dana. You have people to see tomorrow."

But the tranquilizer made her fuzzy and when her alarm went off, she struggled to wake up. She stood longer than usual in the shower, trying to wash away the cobwebs and the memories of the dream that disturbed her sleep. All these years, it had been the darkness that intruded, the scent of the wood shavings and of the man doing terrible things to her body. The taste of fear never left her mouth, asleep or awake.

Now, with the onrushing force of an avalanche, images of Cole were invading her dreams and wrapping themselves around her. She was doing things to him in her dreams—and enjoying the hell out of them—that she'd never been able to even contemplate with other men. Hell, she'd only managed straight sex a couple times and struggled to even finish that. And forget pleasure.

She finally turned the shower to ice cold and shivered under it until her skin was covered with goose bumps. At least, she managed to wake up her brain. Unfortunately, her body was still hot and demanding.

Had coming back here unlocked something inside her? Made her subconsciously try to break out of her self-imposed emotional prison? Maybe she was condemned to have a sex life only in her dreams. She snorted at that and pushed everything to the back of her mind to focus on the day ahead.

She drank one cup of coffee while she toasted bread and buttered it, then filled her travel mug with the rest of the hot liquid. Checking to make sure she had her phone, she headed out to Ivy and Lee Winslow's small ranch on the north side of town.

As she turned onto a ranch-to-market road, she found herself stealing glances in her rear and sideview mirrors. She couldn't shake the feeling that somehow the killer was around, keeping a close eye on her. A shudder raced up her spine, and she gripped the wheel tighter. She was almost glad when traffic thinned out and she could check the cars behind her. When she turned onto the long driveway to the Winslow house and every car sped by at a normal pace, she let out a long breath.

She figured her best approach with Ivy Winslow was the same thing she'd used with Lois Kelly—just show up and hope for the best. A phone call might have gotten her an emphatic no. Especially since, by this time, she was aware her activities were a topic of local conversation. That was, when everyone wasn't talking about the horrific death of Leanne Pritchard. Advance warning would have been more polite, but Dana had found in the past it was harder to turn away someone already at your front door.

Twenty-six years ago, the Winslows had three children, two boys and a girl. Lily Winslow, the baby of the family, was only four years old when she disappeared from the picnic area of the annual rodeo. Dana wondered how the Winslows had put their life back together after their little girl's body was found. Were they like the Kellys, so wrapped in grief that all they had left was bitterness? Or had they managed to find a way to get on with their lives, especially with two other children to raise?

Dana pulled up in front of a big stone house surrounded by six acres of land. In a fenced pasture next to a barn, five horses grazed and swished their tails at flying insects.

After checking herself one last time in the mirror on the sun visor, she mounted the steps and rang the bell. The curtain covering the eyebrow window moved to one side, then the door opened. No chain this time, thank heavens.

Ivy Winslow was tall and just shy of being chubby. Her gray-streaked brown hair was pulled back into a ponytail and, like Lois, she wore not a smidge of makeup. But unlike Lois Kelly, Ivy's face was not pinched or bitter. Her hazel eyes were filled with long-standing sorrow, but she seemed in control of herself.

"You're Dana Moretti," she said.

"Yes." Dana blinked. "I am."

"Jane Milburn pointed you out to me in the grocery store the other day." Ivy reached out a hand. "Come in, come in. I figured you'd get around to us sooner or later."

Dana stepped into what was obviously the large central room of the house, with big windows, a rock fireplace and gleaming hardwood floors. Her heels tapped a rhythm on the wood as she followed Ivy Winslow into the kitchen where the woman gestured toward a granite table.

"Have a seat, please." Ivy busied herself at the counter. "I just made a fresh pot of coffee, and I have some cinnamon rolls left from yesterday. Let me just get things together here."

Dana sat at the end of the table, putting her purse on the chair next to her and activating the voice recorder app on her phone. She couldn't believe how gracious the woman was—a complete change from Lois Kelly—yet the air of tension around Ivy was almost palpable.

"Please don't fuss over me," Dana protested. "I was just hoping we could have some conversation."

Ivy turned to look at her, years of anguish lining

her face. "I know you want to talk about Lily. I'm much better at it if I have a cup of coffee and something to do with my hands."

A lump rose in Dana's throat. "Coffee and rolls would be just wonderful. Thanks."

Ivy placed mugs and plates on the table, then took a chair across from Dana. Taking a careful sip of her coffee, she set her mug carefully on the granite surface, folded her hands, and looked Dana straight in the eye.

"I believe in always getting right to the point," she said. "Jane tells me you're writing a book about what happened here in High Ridge. To our children."

"Yes, and I apologize." Dana broke off a tiny piece of roll, nibbling at it politely. "I know I should have called before just showing up. But to tell you the truth, I wasn't sure of the reception I'd get. Everyone seems to want me to take a hike, get out of town. Disappear. I thought maybe the surprise element would work better."

Ivy took a small bite of her roll and chewed it slowly. "Most of the parents will want to shut you out. Linc and I decided a long time ago that the only way to get past that awful horror and keep Lily alive in our hearts was to talk about it and try to live with it." She brushed an imaginary crumb from her lap.

"That has to be a difficult thing to do," Dana commented.

"You have no idea." Her eyes drifted to a point over Dana's shoulder. "At first, I wanted nothing more than to die and be buried with my baby." She shifted her gaze back to Dana. "They wouldn't let us see the body, you know. Jed Nickels—he was the sheriff then—absolutely refused. And our pastor, when they gave him the details, agreed. But I wanted to rip that coffin open, see the horror for myself, and then die with her."

Without thinking, Dana reached out a hand and laid it softly on Ivy's arm. The woman flicked her eyes down at the touch, and although she didn't flinch, Dana drew her hand back. Okay, she wasn't an enemy, but neither was she a friend. She got the message.

"I know how devastated you had to be," she said in a gentle tone.

Ivy let out a long, slow breath. "You can't even begin to imagine. And Lincoln. He was shattered, but he found strength somewhere to keep us all together."

"How did your boys handle it?"

"Josh and Nate were six and eight at the time. This kind of thing was beyond their ability to understand. Again, I give Linc all the credit for figuring out how to reach them and help them through it."

"He must be a very strong man," Dana pointed out.

"He's a rock." Ivy picked at a piece of frosting on her roll. "He was our strength and our refuge. And when we finally reached a place where we could function again, he allowed himself to fall apart. And we were there for him."

"You sound like you love him a lot."

"We love each other," Ivy told her. "None of us will ever forget Lily. She was a wonderful, beautiful child. But the boys have grown into terrific men. They've married really great women, and we're all very close. It was a struggle, but it's definitely been worth it."

"I probably shouldn't say this," Dana said carefully, "but so many times, in cases like this, it destroys the family."

"Ah." Ivy's look was sharp. "You've been talking to Lois Kelly. Or was it Mila Garza? Sonja Escobedo? Natalie Grimes?"

"Lois," Dana admitted. "But I hope to speak to the others, too."

"Tell me something, Miss Moretti."

"Dana. Please."

"Dana, then. What do you hope to achieve here? What have you accomplished with your other books? Help me to understand."

"As I tried to tell Lois, I bring a fresh pair of eyes and a research brain. Many times, I've spotted things investigators missed." She sipped at her coffee, taking time to choose her words carefully. "It doesn't always turn out this way, but in some of the cases, I've actually been able to point the police in directions they'd overlooked. Bring a resolution to the case and closure to the families."

"And you think that's what you can do here?" The hope in Ivy's voice was almost painful to hear.

"I don't know. I never know. But I plan to try."

Ivy studied Dana's face carefully. "Why this case? There must be thousands for you to choose from."

"I have a special hate for people who abuse, torture, and murder children," she explained, striving for the right mix of professionalism and sympathy. And trying desperately to leave her own anguish out of it. "The number of victims in this particular case is so overwhelming, along with the fact that no one was ever arrested. As far as I can tell, there weren't even any suspects."

Ivy snorted. "No kidding. By the time I managed to

pull myself together and understand that I had two sons who badly needed me, Linc was conducting a one-man campaign for the sheriff to bring in outside help. Any help. Anyone who could sift through the meager clues and interviews."

Dana raised a brow. "But he didn't? I thought maybe I'd just missed it in the reports I read."

"You have to understand," Ivy sighed. "Jed Nickels had been on the force for fifteen years at that time, starting as a rookie deputy. And he has deep roots here. His people go back four generations. When he was appointed sheriff, he saw this as his own little kingdom to rule. Anything from the outside was considered interference."

"But didn't other parents demand answers?" Dana asked, something she'd been wondering. "Weren't they anxious to find the killer?"

Ivy's chambray-clad shoulders lifted in a slight shrug. "Some did. Others were too busy blaming themselves and each other. And this was a closed community back then. Outsiders weren't welcomed, and bad news didn't breach the county limits. Jed's word was law. If he shut down information, it stayed that way. If he chose not to call in outside help, no one questioned him, either out of respect or fear."

The pain in the woman's voice cut clear to Dana's soul. Was that how her mother had felt, at least in the beginning? Later, when the initial agony passed, she'd retreated behind a wall Dana could never breach. She didn't even remember the last time she'd been hugged or told she was loved.

She pulled herself back from the well of memories. "What can you tell me about that day?"

Ivy refilled her coffee mug, and Dana could almost see her brain sorting through the details of that day.

"We'd gone to the annual rodeo. Josh was good enough by then to compete in the junior events, and we all cheered him on." Her gaze drifted again. "About one o'clock, Linc got hamburgers and drinks for all of us, and we went to sit at one of the picnic tables in a shaded area."

"Lily was right there with you?"

"Of course." There was a trace of indignation in the tone. "We were very careful about that."

"I'm sorry. I didn't mean to imply anything." Dana wet her lips. Now came the hard questions. "What happened next?"

"Nate had to go to the bathroom, and Linc was always leery of letting the boys go to public restrooms alone. Events like the rodeo, for example, were magnets for drifters, so he got up to go with him." Ivy rubbed her arms as if suddenly chilled. "Someone called to Josh, and when he turned around, he knocked his drink all over the table. I was busy mopping up the mess with the extra napkins. Lily was right on the bench next to me."

"Did she see something that caught her attention?"

"Only the clown." Ivy's chin wobbled, and her eyes clouded with tears. She brushed at them impatiently with the back of her hand. "Josh said she saw the clown."

The familiar cold feeling settled in Dana's stomach. "The clown? There was a clown there?"

"Yes. Besides the ones used in the ring to distract the bulls, the rodeo committee hired clowns to entertain the kids in the picnic area. You know, keep them from getting restless. Lily was fascinated by them. One of them gave her a balloon animal he made."

The balloon animal again.

This was one sick bastard.

Dana was certain she was on the right track. Capturing the kids' attention with his balloon tricks made it easy to entice them away from their parents. And somehow, he managed to choose each child carefully, making himself available when the parents were distracted by other events.

"They're a great lure for children." Dana hoped she kept the bitterness out of her voice.

"They certainly were for Lily. Josh said, afterward, the clown motioned for her to come to him because, when I turned around, she was just...gone." Ivy drew in a deep breath and let it out slowly, obviously making a great effort to center herself again. "A four-year-old has no fear of clowns. She probably thought he was going to give her another balloon."

Dana knew exactly how Lily felt. She'd been that child. She tried to find something to say, but Ivy seemed on a roll, and she didn't want to stop her.

"I yelled for her." Her voice was insistent, begging for Dana to believe her. "Josh yelled for her. By the time Linc and Nate returned, we were frantic, searching everyplace."

Dana frowned. "No one saw where she went? Where the clown went?"

Ivy shook her head. "The picnic tables were at the edge of the rodeo area, right next to the fairgrounds. There's a thick stand of trees and a road just beyond. It wouldn't have been any trouble for him to snatch her up and take off with her."

The fairgrounds again. Dana swallowed back the bile rising in her throat. She already knew the answer to the next question she asked. "Wouldn't she have screamed?"

"Lily was the tenth child taken. Sheriff Nickels said there were traces of chloroform in each of their systems, so I'm guessing he sedated them immediately."

Suddenly, the odor of chloroform was strong in Dana's nostrils, and she scrubbed her face with her hands, as if to wipe it away. "I assume all the clowns were questioned?"

Ivy tightened her grip on her mug. "Oh, yes. But no one could say exactly how many there were. Some said four, some said five. Even the clowns themselves weren't sure."

"Didn't people think that was strange? I mean, someone had to hire them."

"Afterward, I thought the same thing." She shook her head. "But everyone was being so defensive, no one wanted to even admit to their own names."

"I understand clowns were involved at some of the other events, too," Dana prodded. "Didn't anyone suggest it was time to stop using them?"

"The county changed companies, but most of the clowns were retired men who did this for fun. No one wanted to seriously think that one of them could be the killer. The pedophile." She spat the last word. "And clowns had been a staple of every county activity for generations."

"But—"

"I know, I know." Ivy held up her hand. "I guess it was a case of not wanting to believe it could be anyone we knew. Someone we considered harmless." She shrugged helplessly. "And then it stopped."

Dana's heart almost stopped, too, at the statement. She knew why it had ended, but she asked the question anyway. "Did something happen?"

"Two little girls, Kylie and Carrie Nolan, were taken at the fairgrounds. Apparently, whoever the man was, he'd either stumbled on or knew about an old, deserted barn almost ten miles from High Ridge. The land had been tied up in probate for years, so no one ever bothered about it. But some high school kids were looking for a place to smoke dope and the barn looked pretty good to them."

"Did they see who he was?" Her heart was beating erratically.

Ivy shook her head. "No. They must have scared him off. But they certainly got a shock when they swung their flashlights around inside the barn. Kylie was dead and Carrie just barely alive."

Dana dug her fingernails into her palms. "Does anyone know what happened to their family?"

"Only that they left town right away. I think they moved to another state, but we never heard where. They buried Kylie and just…disappeared."

Ivy Winslow managed to pull herself together again, but Dana needed to get out of there. She hadn't realized how emotionally she would be affected by Ivy's cooperation. Or how the mention of Kylie, the little sister she hadn't been able to save, would be her undoing.

She gathered her purse and pushed back from the table. "I've taken more of your time than I intended. You've been very gracious, and I appreciate it."

"It isn't graciousness," Ivy denied. "Don't be fooled. A lot of people in this town, me included, have read a couple of your books. That display in the bookstore window really draws people."

Dana's laugh was humorless. "The truth is, my publisher pays for that kind of prominent space. I'm glad to hear it isn't wasted."

"You have a good eye for things. If you can find even some little thing that will get this bastard, after all this time, I'll do anything I can to help you."

"Thank you. A lot." As Dana headed toward the door, Ivy's words jangled an idea loose in her mind, and she turned to the woman. "As a matter of fact, there is one thing if you wouldn't mind."

"Name it."

"Maybe you could get a few of the other women together. Ease the way for them to meet with me, answer some of my questions. I know the men won't talk to me."

Ivy thought a moment, then nodded her agreement, determination setting in on her face. "I'll do it. Where are you staying? I'll set it up and call you."

"I've rented a house for however long I'll be here. One night at the High Ridge Motel was about all I could handle." She pulled out one of her business cards and wrote on the back of it. "This is my cell number. You can reach me twenty-four/seven. And thank you."

Dana's entire body was tight with the tears she'd choked back, and the pain in her chest threatened to overwhelm her. She was about three miles from the Winslow house when she found a place to pull off the road, away from traffic. Turning off the engine, she put her head on the steering wheel and cried harder than she had in years.

Chapter Sixteen

Shannon Fowler kicked a stone in front of her as she trudged down the dusty road from the bus stop to her house. She hated living out here in the middle of nowhere. Surrounded by pastures and hay fields, the Fowler house was the only one for miles. Her parents thought it was great. Her dad worked for the people who owned all the property. They gave him the use of the house for practically nothing, just for taking care of the hay and watching the cattle when they moved them into the closer pastures.

It also gave him a place to fix cars and trucks for people without having to rent a shop and worry about what he called "idiotic things like licenses." People just brought him their junkers, and he fixed them up and pocketed the money.

Her mother spent her days baking cakes and cookies that she sold to Patty's Pastries. As the woman said so often, they weren't ever going to get rich, but they didn't starve.

But Shannon hated it. None of her friends lived within walking distance and none of them had a driver's license yet. That meant someone's parents had to cart them, and that was often a problem. She daydreamed a lot about the day she'd graduate high school. A handsome man would ride into town in a brand-new truck and carry her off to a beautiful life on a big fancy ranch.

That's what Shannon wanted. A ranch, where she could have her own horse and ride him any time she wanted. But at fifteen that possibility seemed a long ways away.

She heard the truck before she saw it, rumbling down the dirt road, kicking up stones around it. Who would be driving down this road at this time of day? Visitors were almost nonexistent. She stepped to the side to move out of the way, then smiled when it stopped and she recognized the driver.

"Hi," she called and gave a little wave.

"Hi, Shannon. Early finish with school?"

"Yeah. They didn't finish all the state testing yesterday. Those of us who did got out early."

He nodded. "Used to love those days myself. So, you walking home?"

"Have to. Dad's not gonna pick me up, and mom's usually in town this time of day making deliveries."

"Well, if you don't think your folks would mind, I don't have a problem dropping you off at your place."

Shannon chewed her bottom lip. She knew not to get in a car or truck with a stranger, but this was no stranger. Everyone knew him and her folks would probably be grateful he'd offered her the ride. Besides, walking down this road was such a pain in the butt.

Making up her mind, she grinned. "Sure. That would really be great. Thanks."

She tossed her book bag into the cab and climbed up to the seat, carefully fastening her seat belt.

"I'm sure glad you came along," she said, tightening the belt. "What are you doing way out here in Noplace, anyway? Hardly anyone ever comes down this road."

He chuckled. "Just taking a short cut to the Nobles' ranch. Your road goes straight through and cuts off about five miles from the highway."

"Then I'm real happy you decided to do it today."

He grinned. "The pleasure is all mine."

While she was still settling herself in her seat, he pulled off on the side of the road, put the truck in park, and fumbled in the center console.

Shannon frowned. "What's the matter? Is something wrong?"

"No, little girl. Something's very right."

In seconds, he'd pulled a damp cloth out of a plastic bag and clamped it over her nose.

Shannon gripped his forearm as hard as she could and tugged, kicking at him with her feet, a scream rising in the back of her throat. The stuff on the cloth smelled terrible and made her dizzy. She tried to keep fighting, but whatever she was inhaling made her weak and sleepy.

"That's right," she heard him say. "Just go to sleep, little girl. We'll be there soon, and then we'll have a lot of fun."

As the darkness took her, Shannon's last thought was she'd never been more scared in her life.

Chapter Seventeen

Dana thought about going to Harry's for a quick lunch, but she was so disturbed by her visit with Ivy Winslow that she drove straight home. In the dining room, she booted up her laptop again and, while it was loading, made herself a cup of Tension Tamer tea. By the time it was ready, she had the book file open and began scrolling through it very slowly.

She sipped at the tea, hoping it would calm the jittery feeling in her stomach, feeling disorganized and hating it. With every other book, she had a pattern she followed. First the outline, filled in as she did her research. Then the list of questions, varied slightly with each person she interviewed. A spreadsheet she filled in as she acquired each new piece of information.

Being personally involved was throwing her off her game, and she hated it. Hated what had happened back then and what was happening now. Clowns. How could some sick freak use something so innocent and so appealing to lure kids to their death? It made her sick just to think about it. Especially, since she knew how effective he'd been, how easily she and Kylie had been lured to danger.

Kylie. Oh, God. All these years, she'd managed to put the image of her sister's body at the back of her mind. Remembering the touch and feel of the man was bad enough. But last night, Kylie had been front and center in her nightmares, her adorable little face blending with the image of her body and thighs smeared with blood.

Yesterday, she'd found three other cases online besides the Kellys' where clowns had been mentioned. Today, Ivy Winslow had added a fourth. Now, she went through the information she'd copied from each incident report looking for more. By the time she finished, she found the mention of clowns nine times.

Nine times!

Dana leaned back in her chair, running her fingers through her hair. Idly, she slipped the scrunchee off her wrist and pulled her hair into a somewhat messy ponytail to keep it out of her face.

Why hadn't anyone ever put this all together? Why hadn't the old sheriff—what was his name? Nickels?—seen some kind of connection here? If he was any kind of cop, he should have picked up on it. How much did he remember now?

She'd track him down and arrange to see him. The article she read about his retirement said he'd sold his house in town and lived on a few acres not too far from the Winslows. Pulling up the internet, she searched for his address and phone number and made the call.

"Hello?" The voice of the woman who answered was slightly breathless, as if she'd run to pick up the phone.

"My name is Dana Moretti," she began. "I wonder if I might speak with Sheriff Nickels?"

"Whew! Let me catch my breath a second. I was just out in the yard when I heard the phone ring." Pause. "My husband hasn't been sheriff for several years now. If you call the office, they'll get you to the new one, Cole Landry."

"I know your husband is retired, Mrs. Nickels. I understand. But he's the one I'd really like to speak with. Is he home?"

A longer pause. When the woman spoke again, her tone changed. "You're the person who's wanting to write a book about what happened to those kids all those years ago. Right?"

"Yes, that's correct. I've written a number of books about unsolved crimes, and I've had success working with the people involved."

"You need to leave this one alone," the woman snapped.

Dana sighed. She should have known nothing about this would be easy. "Mrs. Nickels. I'm going to write the book whether I talk to the folks of High Ridge or not. But I want it to be as accurate as possible so for that purpose, I need to interview people who were involved in the case, like the former sheriff. I'd just like a few minutes of his time. Is he available?"

"No, he's not. He won't be home until this afternoon, but I know he won't want to talk to you. Just leave him alone. It was a terrible thing he went through, not being able to find that killer. It still haunts him."

"I'm sure it does," Dana said smoothly. "And I'll bet he has a message he'd like to send to those parents after all these years. This would be a wonderful way for him to do it."

"I don't know." The woman's voice dropped a tone. "This business with Leanne Pritchard has him upset all over again."

"Would you just tell him I called? I'll try again this afternoon to reach him. If he's home, I'd like to come by for a little while."

The woman was silent for so long Dana thought she might have hung up on her. Finally, she said, "I'll give him your message. Then it's up to him."

Dana ended the call and reached for her tea but found it cold. Making a face at the bitter taste, she dumped it in the sink and made a fresh cup. Then she sat back down at the table.

Two of the reports hadn't contained any mention of clowns. Was that because there weren't any around or because they had been overlooked? Or hadn't anyone seen either of those children run after a clown? Dana wrote down the names of the families and did a search for their telephone numbers. Maybe she could talk to one of them before speaking with the sheriff.

The sheriff. That conjured up the image of the most recent one, Cole Landry. Her physical reaction to him frightened her. She was such an emotional cripple that, up until now, just the thought of a man touching her made her stiffen with fear. But Cole stirred unfamiliar feelings and inspired dreams more erotic than she could imagine. Their very promise of pleasure confused her even more.

She wanted a truly loving relationship. She wanted to get married someday. To have children. Things Kylie would never be able to do. Ever. That's why she'd started this journey to hell. Finding the pedophile and finally being able to move on with her life was her way to honor Kylie's memory. She should be living for both of them. Thus far, she'd been doing a really lousy job.

Sighing, she jotted down the addresses for the Garzas and Escobedos, the two families whose case reports made no mention of a clown. After stuffing down a peanut butter sandwich and a glass of milk, she combed her hair and freshened her makeup. The Garzas lived the closest. She'd try them first.

****

Cole had been all over the place interviewing the kids who'd been at the park one more time. Exhausted, he decided to stop at the Bishop ranch and bounce ideas off Tate. His uncle was just coming from the barn when Cole pulled into the driveway.

"Decide to take me up on dinner?"

"Maybe." Cole gave him a tired smile. "At least a drink. I think I could use that first."

A sympathetic look washed over the older man's face. "Let's get to it, then. Come on." He led the way into the house.

"Tate?" a voice floated out from the kitchen. "That you?"

"It's me. And with a surprise," he answered.

Adele Bishop hurried from the kitchen, wiping her hands on her jeans. When she saw Cole, her face lit up and she turned her cheek for his kiss.

"What a nice surprise. We hardly get to see you these days."

"My bad." He pulled out a grin and gave her a hug. "But I'm here now."

She looked at Tate. "I didn't even hear you drive up. Did you get all your errands finished?"

"Most all. Cole and I are going to hide in the den and have a drink. Then I'll twist his arm to stay for dinner."

"Wonderful." She smiled at him. "Your favorite. Smothered pork chops. I'll yell when it's ready."

"So how's it going?" Tate asked when they were

settled in big chairs with aged bourbon.

"Not great." Cole set his Stetson on a small table and ran his fingers through his hair. "I've been out talking to the high school kids again but didn't get one more thing out of them. I'm telling you, Tate, this whole thing is making me sick."

"I know, son. I'm just hoping you'll catch a break." He took a healthy sip of his drink. "But if it's just some transient passing through, you may never get him."

Cole made a fist and smacked his thigh. "Damn it. This time, I'll find the bastard. We won't have another one of these things hanging over the county."

"You need to do something about that writer, too." Tate took another sip of his drink. "People are upset that she's raking all that old stuff up again."

Cole tensed, a surge of protectiveness for Dana blindsiding him. He knew those kisses would come back to haunt him. "You know I can't run her out of town. She hasn't broken any laws. And maybe she'll find something Nickels missed all those years ago."

"She's trouble, Cole," he muttered over coffee. "Jed Nickels was a good lawman. We don't need anyone stirring up old memories best left buried. Who knows if all this gave some other nut job ideas and Leanne's just the first victim."

"I'd hate to think that. And I know Dana would be distraught if she thought that was the case."

"Dana, is it?" Tate looked at him with shrewd eyes. "Not getting into bed with the wrong people, are you, son?"

Cole grunted. "Not anywhere near getting into bed."

Except that was exactly what he wanted…if he

could just slay her demons. He had a gut feeling it had to do with the old child murders. But what? What was the answer to the riddle of Dana Moretti? He was determined to find the key to unlock her secrets. But at the moment, he was ass over tea kettle in this horrendous murder, and she had a wall around her ten feet high.

Except those kisses…

She could be right. That there was something everyone was trying to keep swept under the rug. That was a hard concept for him to wrap his mind around. He knew these people. None of them fit the profile of a vicious killer, nor did he think it likely the parents who still mourned their children would be willing to hide that killer.

"Cole? Am I losing you?" Tate stirred his ice cubes with a finger, the clinking sound snapping Cole out of his mental wandering. "Maybe this new homicide will scare her away."

"Not her. She's seen worse than this, I'm sure. Anyway, she's fresh eyes and been through this before. She just might see something everyone else missed."

"I'm just telling you—"

Whatever he started to say was interrupted by the ringing of Cole's cell. "Yeah, Grace. What it is?"

"Sheriff, you better get back here right away. We got ourselves another big problem."

Cole felt as if a stone had just dropped into his stomach. "What kind of problem?"

"Shannon Fowler's mama, Bootsie, just called in." Grace's voice was with filled with tension. "The girl's three hours late getting back from school."

Cole knew all the parents were skittish after what

happened to Leanne. "Let's hope she's just gone off with one of her friends. Anyway, school doesn't get out until three, right?"

"Not today. They were supposed to be off all day, but they didn't finish the testing yesterday, so the principal made them all come in for two hours this morning. She should have been home long before this."

"Has Bootsie called the school?" He knew that was a stupid question. Of course, Shannon's mother had called. Still, he had to ask it.

"Of course, she has. The buses left with all the kids more than three hours ago. Andi was in the office and called some of her friends, and they haven't seen her, either, except to watch her get on the bus."

"All right. I'm on my way. Round up everyone you can and have them meet me in the conference room."

He clicked off and pushed himself out of the chair. "I'll have to miss Adele's smothered pork chops. We've got ourselves a missing teenager."

"Damn it to hell." Tate set his glass down and stood up. "Who is it?"

"Shannon Fowler. I'm praying she's just off doing some stupid thing and didn't call home."

"You let me know what's going on," Tate said, clapping him on the shoulder. "And if I can help in any way, just holler."

"I will. Thanks. Make my excuses to Adele, okay?"

He covered the distance to his office in record time, making a call to Guardian and filling in Reno along the way, though he hoped the extra help would turn out to be unnecessary. Five of his deputies were waiting for him, all of them wearing sick expressions.

"What? Did someone find her?"

Andi spoke first. "No. No body. But Sheriff, I tracked down the bus driver and he swears he dropped Shannon off at the head of her road. She has to hike more than a mile to her house and there isn't another living soul on that whole stretch. Only thing out that way is pastures and the Fowlers' house."

"Anyone could have come along and taken her," Mickey pointed out. "And if, like Leanne, it was someone she knew offering her a ride, she'd hop right in."

Cole's stomach roiled, and a headache began at the back of his head. He looked at his deputies. "I'm assuming someone's driven that road end to end and stopped to see Bootsie?"

Gaylen Kleist, his senior deputy, nodded. "I did, boss. I was out that way, and as soon as I got the call, I went right over."

Cole dropped into the chair at the head of the table. "And?"

"And nothing." Kleist shrugged. "I drove the whole length of the road, both ways, real slow. Twice. Nada. Not a sign of her."

"If the bus driver dropped her off at the head of the road, she disappeared somewhere between there and her house."

Andi cleared her throat. "Sheriff?"

"Yeah, Andi."

"If this is the same man, he could have taken her anywhere. How the hell do we know where to look?"

Cole was feeling sicker by the minute. Salado County covered a big area, and there were a lot of uninhabited acres. Much of it was ranchland, and he didn't think the perp would risk going onto land under the watchful eyes of cowboys. But there were huge pastures of coastal hay and other grasses, not to mention wooded areas.

"All right." He looked around the room. "The first thing we need to do is call in Search and Rescue. We've already lost enough time as it is. Tina Solize is the best there is. And besides the dogs, they recently got funding for a helicopter, so they can search by air." He shoved his chair back from the table. "Mickey, get a map of the county and divide it into five sectors. We'll start with the area where the Fowlers live. I have a feeling he'll dump her close to home, just like he left Leanne near her friends."

"He wants us to find her, doesn't he?" Andi commented.

"Yes. I think he does. He's sending a message. The bastard's so arrogant he thinks he can pull this off right under our noses and get away with it. He's done it once already. Maybe more if he's connected to the other disappearances."

"You know, once word gets out, we'll be flooded with people," Gaylen pointed out. "Everyone will want to help, and they'll be trampling all over the place."

"You're right." Cole rubbed his jaw. "Okay, here's what we'll do. Gaylen, where are those two rookies I've got appointed to night shift?"

"Probably home sleeping."

"Wake 'em up. Get 'em down here. Have them report to me, and I'll get them set up taking calls and giving people instructions on what to do. Find out from Grace who's worked with SAR looking for lost kids before. We'll need someone with some smarts in each area."

"Got it. I'll go call right now," Gaylen headed toward his desk with a long stride.

Cole turned to look at the others. "Mickey, make copies of that map after you draw out the sectors. Give one to Gaylen and the others to me."

"I'm on it."

"The rest of you get your assignments from Gaylen." Cole slid his chair back, his frustration mounting with each ticking of the clock. He headed to his office to contact Tina Solize.

"I'm just back from a trip to South Texas, Cole." Tina sounded a little ragged when she answered the phone.

"I hate to pull you out again with practically no rest," Cole told her. "I wouldn't do it if it wasn't an emergency."

She gave him a rusty laugh. "Cole, everything for me is an emergency. If it wasn't, no one would need me."

"I guess you're right." He explained how he was setting up the search sectors and what Gaylen would do with the volunteers. "If you can come by, we'll give you the maps and the other information. Whatever we've got."

"Good. Very good. Okay, give me an hour, and I'll meet you with my team. We're racing the clock here so let's start with the sector containing her house."

"Right. I think this bastard wants us to find her so he probably dumped her close to home."

"Good thing I've got that new chopper. We'll need air support to cover the entire county. My pilot can also fly a grid pattern over each search area, but using it ups the cost. I'll find the money to pay for it somewhere."

"Guardian has offered to pick up the cost on this. Just give us the full ride."

"I'll call my pilot and get him going."

By the time Cole hung up, Grace was at his door with a mug of her poison. "I don't care how bad you think this is," she told him. "You're gonna need it. The word's out. We're flooded with people who want to look for Shannon, and they're all pissed off."

"Where's Gaylen?" Cole asked.

"Trying to get everyone organized," Grace told him. "He's got the two rookies on their way in. He told them come as you are as long as they got here ASAP. And the phone's ringing off the hook."

"All right. Let's get organized."

He fortified himself with the thick brew in the mug, found Mickey with the maps, grabbed one, and then hurried to the front of the building. As he'd expected, the news had spread faster than measles. This was not working out quite the way he envisioned. The lobby was jammed with people, clustered around Andi, who was trying to organize them. He spotted Gaylen on the front steps, trying to get everyone's attention in the front parking lot.

Cole opened the door and eased out beside his deputy. "Go on inside and take the phones from Grace until the rookies get here. I'll talk to the mob. I'll deputize the Guardian agents as soon as they arrive."

He was immediately assaulted with questions.

"Where's Shannon?" someone shouted, the minute Gaylen moved inside.

"Why can't you catch whoever's doing this?" came from another direction.

"Are you letting our county go to hell?" a third

person yelled.

Cole held up his hands. "Hold it, hold it. If everyone will give me a minute, I'll give you a heads up on where we are." He waited until the noise level dropped to steady mumble. "Here's the deal. We don't know if anything has even happened to Shannon Fowler. She could be off with one of her friends some place not even aware of the uproar she's causing."

"Shannon's a good girl," someone protested. "She'd never do anything like this. Cause her folks to worry and all that."

"I didn't say for sure that's what happened," Cole pointed out. "I'm just saying we have to look at every possibility. Now. I've called in Tina Solize's SAR team. She'll be here shortly, and we'll start searching closest to the Fowlers' home. That's the last place she was seen. I know you want to help, and we can certainly use you. We just need to do this in an organized fashion, so we don't miss anything."

"What do you want us to do?" a man at the front of the crowd asked.

Cole knew these were basically good people, and he really needed their help. "Find your neighbors here in the crowd. Then go back to where you live and start searching your area. Work in groups of two and three."

"Are we looking for a body or a live person?" someone wanted to know.

"I'm hoping a live person, but I'm preparing for any eventuality."

"Hey, Sheriff."

Cole turned at the shout. A man he vaguely recognized as a friend of Tate's was waving a hand at him. "Yes?"

"How come it's taking so long to find out who's running loose in our neighborhood?"

Cole swallowed the retort that bubbled up in his throat. "It's been less than forty-eight hours. Please keep that in mind. This is our only priority, and you can rest assured I'm prepared to call in the Rangers at a moment's notice."

"What can we do to help?" someone shouted.

"Hold on just a few minutes. Someone will come out and organize you into groups and tell you which sectors to hit. Thanks for coming." He ducked back inside and spotted the rookies who had obviously come in through the back entrance.

"We're flooded with calls," he told them. "And I want to keep dispatch free. I'll have Grace set up the phones so all incoming calls go directly to these phones. If one line is busy, it will roll over to the other. If you get anything at all, pass it along to Grace to put it on the radios."

He left them to it and checked in with Gaylen.

"I need to go meet Tina. Are you set here?"

Gaylen nodded. "I'm good."

"You know we'll have a media mob here at any minute. I don't want any of the press inside this building."

Gaylen nodded. "Believe me, they won't get in. Go on. I'll take care of things here."

****

Dana heard the news when she stopped for gas at and overheard two women talking about it at the next pump. When she finished, she approached them. "Excuse me, I couldn't help but overhear what you were saying. Is there a young girl missing?"

The women stared at her. Finally, one of them said, "You're that writer stirring up all the mess from those old cases, aren't you?"

Dana pasted on a smile and held out a hand. "Not stirring up, just investigating. But you're right. I'm Dana Moretti, the author."

Their stares were unblinking. Then one woman gave her a limp handshake. "I suppose you want all the gory details about what's going on."

Dana shook her head. She was getting used to the hateful attitude that kept following her around. "I'm just really concerned there's another victim. Can you tell me who it is?"

The women looked at each other.

"Shannon Fowler," the handshake woman said. "Lives at the edge of town. She got off the school bus, and no one's seen her since."

Sentence by sentence, Dana pried the details out of them, trying not to show how upset she was. It was *him*. All her intuition told her it was. But why now? He was safe. Had been for twenty-five years. So why had he started again? What was driving him now? God, she hoped people were wrong, and her showing up hadn't triggered it.

And why was he after older girls now? Was it too dangerous to go after the little ones? And how was he choosing his victims?

Temporarily placing the Garzas on the back burner, she headed for Cole's office. Maybe she could help in the search. Use her volunteer SAR experience. Nausea bubbled up in her throat. Maybe by now Shannon had been found safe and sound. Alive. Not a body.

Not again. Please, God, don't let it be happening again.

Chapter Eighteen

The lot at the sheriff's office was filled with news crews and a variety of vehicles parked every which way so Dana had to find space more than a block away.

Cole must be having fits.

She didn't even know what she was doing here. He'd be much too busy to see her. Still, she was pulled by an invisible string and wanted to help if she could. Realizing the back door would be her best option, she skirted the building and was almost at the side when a woman yelled out.

"Hey, isn't that Dana Moretti over there? What's she doing here?"

A reporter blocked her path, shoving a microphone at her. "Miss Moretti? Deandra Billings, NBC news. Can you tell me why you're here?"

"Sorry. I really have nothing to say." She forced herself to be polite. She hated newshounds.

"Just a few words. Please." The woman moved closer, signaling to her cameraman to follow. "Are you working on a new book? Does the murder and disappearance have anything to do with it? Give us your take on what's happening here."

"I don't have a take. Sorry."

She moved up one more step, trying to edge away, but the woman was actually blocking her path. Suddenly, hard fingers closed around one arm.

"This way," a strange masculine voice said.

She looked up to see one of Cole's deputies holding onto her.

"Back off," he told the reporter. "All of you. When we have something to tell you, we will. Meanwhile, don't make things worse by harassing people." He literally dragged Dana inside and pushed the door shut. "Sorry I had to grab you like that." He gave her a tired smile and held out his hand. "Gaylen Kleist. Grace, our dispatcher, recognized you from the other day."

"No apology necessary," she breathed. "I really appreciate your help. These people don't need me to be the focus of what's going on."

He gave her a curious glance. "Just exactly why are you here?"

"I heard about Shannon's disappearance, and I wanted to volunteer to help search." She brushed her hair back from her face. "I've worked with a lot of SAR teams while researching my books. Things the teams and the police might miss because I search differently."

"You get no special treatment and no information," he told her. "And anything you learn has to be cleared with Sheriff Landry. If it turns out all you want is to dig for information, I personally will take you back to your house, help you pack, and show you the edge of town."

And he'd have every right to do just that.

"Of course. I completely agree. Just tell me where I'm needed the most."

He studied her for an endless moment, as if debating with himself. "All right," he said at last. "Sheriff Landry's out at the staging area at Hancock Road. This county's more than six hundred square miles so we had to pick a starting place."

"Is that close to where Shannon lives?"

"Yes. Sheriff's thinking whoever took her might have dropped her close to home. There's nothing out there for miles but hay fields, pasture, and trees. And the Fowler house is smack in the middle. Hardly anyone ever goes down that road except on purpose, so there wouldn't be much danger of whoever this is being seen."

"You think she's already dead," Dana guessed.

Gaylen looked at her. "Yes, and so do you. Come on. I'm just heading out there. I'll take you with me. And hope Cole doesn't take my head off for bringing you." He looked at the deputies manning the phones. "You guys good? I'm heading out to Hancock Road."

They both nodded, giving Dana a look of curiosity.

"Okay, then. Grace can get me on the radio if there's a problem."

"We may be rookies, but we're not dumb," one of the men told him. "We can handle this. And we'll keep the media out of here."

Gaylen's mouth twitched with an involuntary smile as he hustled Dana out the back door and into his SUV.

"Hang on," he told her. "I'm taking a short cut to avoid the vultures."

In a minute, she realized what he meant. Instead of pulling out onto the highway, he drove across the field behind the building, jouncing across bumps and holes until he reached the road running parallel to the street the office was on.

"Now, I see why all of you drive SUVs," she commented when they were back on pavement again.

"Lots of places in this county with bad roads or sometimes no roads at all. Only a four-wheel drive will do you any good if you have to reach someplace over rough terrain." He reached for the microphone on his radio and pressed the transmit button. "Grace, patch me through to the sheriff, will you?"

In a moment, Dana heard Cole's voice, rough-sounding through the static. "Where are you, Gaylen?"

"On my way to you. I, um, have a passenger with me who stopped in to see you. I thought you'd want me to get her away from the news vultures cluttering up your parking lot. The television folks you predicted all showed up."

There was a crackling moment of silence before Cole spoke again. "I assume she can hear me?"

Gaylen held the microphone in front of Dana's mouth.

"Hello, Cole. I don't want you to think I have an ulterior motive here, but I've worked with SAR teams before."

Another pause. "You told me you often see things with a different eye. Pick up things someone else might miss."

"That's right. Not always. I'm not a trained investigator, but I've learned a lot while researching my books." She cleared her throat. "And unfortunately, I've found more than my share of bodies."

"Fine. But anything you learn out here stays locked down until this case is over. Are we clear?"

"I understand."

"All right. Gaylen, bring her right to me as soon as you get here. Tina's arrived, and we're about to get things organized."

Chapter Nineteen

He chuckled at the chaotic scene on television. He was alone at home, sucking on a beer and amusing himself with the media circus. They'd find Shannon soon enough. He'd made sure to leave her where it wasn't too obvious but easily discovered. Just like with Leanne. After all, what was the fun of doing it if he couldn't show off?

He laughed to see the young sheriff spinning his wheels, trying to cope with a situation far beyond anything he'd expected when he took the job.

He leaned back in his recliner, popped the lever, and put up his feet. He'd give them another day. Maybe two. Then he'd be after his next victim. He couldn't move too slowly. He had to get to Dana Moretti before she dug too deeply into the past and found information better left buried. Or worse yet, found a thread somewhere that led to his current activities.

No, he needed to keep his focus and finish the job he left undone twenty-five years ago.

Chapter Twenty

He had finally decided to drive to the sheriff's office and scope things out. He was always so visible people would think it strange if he didn't show up. But by the time he got there, most of the crowd had left. Even the news vans were gone, probably chasing after the sheriff.

"Hey." Wanda from Harry's diner came jogging down the steps from the building. "I figured you'd show up down here sooner or later. Work or play, you never miss a chance to help out."

"Glad to do whatever I can," he smiled. "Terrible thing, you know. Just terrible."

"That poor girl," Wanda agreed, her voice filled with sadness. "I just hope we find her alive."

He dropped his eyes to hide the salacious glee that gripped him. "Yes, so do I. So where is everyone?"

"Sent off by the deputies to search the areas around where they live. This is a big county. We don't need everyone searching in the same place."

"Have they finished looking close to her home?" He tried to make the question as casual as possible.

"Beats me. I heard Cole called in Search and Rescue, so maybe he's got them covering that area. Gaylen took that writer woman out there, too, though I sure don't know what anyone thinks she can do. She needs to get out of here."

Oh, no, I have plans for her.

"Maybe so."

Wanda pushed up the sleeves of her blouse. "Well, I'm heading back to the restaurant. Harry's making extra coffee and setting up donuts and stuff to take out to the volunteers. See you later."

He watched her go, trying to decide what his course of action should be. He looked at his watch. Best to go on home and monitor things from there. He didn't want to do anything that would call unusual attention to him.

Still, he wished he could be there when the body was found.

Meanwhile, he could make a little more mischief.

****

As they approached their destination, Dana saw two SUVs from the sheriff's department set up as roadblocks. A deputy recognizing Gaylen waved them on, and they bumped along on the shoulder for about a hundred yards.

Dana spotted Cole next to his vehicle. He was talking to a tall blonde in jeans and a black T-shirt with some kind of logo on it. Several more cars were parked on the shoulder and a large group stood silently waiting. Behind them in the field were two four-door cab trucks with Solize SAR painted on the doors. Next to them were three men wearing the same black T-shirts as the woman, all looking as if they were carved from granite, faces included.

Dana followed Gaylen to where the group was gathered, waiting for Cole to spot her. He looked up and motioned Gaylen over, then shifted his gaze to her.

"Hang on," he mouthed.

She nodded and moved to the side. Shoving her hands in her pockets, she scanned the crowd and realized they weren't your average volunteers. At least half of them were wearing Solize T-shirts, which made them regulars. The others were talking quietly among themselves while awaiting instructions.

Dana wandered toward a car parked away from the others. One look at the weeping woman inside and the man with his arm around her was enough to tell her they were Shannon's parents. Another man sat in the back seat, leaning forward, obviously talking to them.

Dana's heart pinched. She knew full well the terrible place these people were in. Like the Kellys and her parents. She prayed that Shannon would be found alive, but the sick feeling she had inside told her it was already too late.

A hand tapped her shoulder, and she turned to see Cole standing beside her.

"Tina Solize is the best there is at Search and Rescue, but we're only surmising Shannon's…Shannon will be found here. We divided the county into five sectors, but we're starting here, closer to her home. This is where she was last seen. There are a lot of hiding places so we're hoping to get lucky. We've got air support coming shortly. You say you've done this before?"

She nodded. "Back at home I volunteered when I could. And I'm not telling you why. I'll help in any way I can."

"Come on then."

When Cole introduced her to Tina, the woman held out her hand. "I've read several of your books, Miss Moretti, and I've talked with teams you worked with before. They say you're an excellent spotter."

"Thank you. I told Cole I'm here to do whatever I can. Where and how are we searching?"

"Okay." On the hood of Cole's SUV, she smoothed out a large aerial map with a segment marked off. "The bus left Shannon right there at the head of the road. The driver says she started off toward home, and that's the last anyone saw of her. Cole and one of his deputies have gone up and down both sides of the road and haven't found a thing."

Dana studied the map. "Where was Leanne's body found?"

"At the park where the other kids were waiting for her to come back." She pointed with her finger. "Close enough so if her friends looked, they'd find her."

"That's probably what he did here." Dana said. "And having a helicopter will help identify likely areas. I've learned there's always a pattern. Each of the serial killers I've written about had a special pattern for disposing of the bodies. One guy always used pools, another flowerbeds. One had his own killing ground on a piece of land he owned. Usually related to whatever the trigger was from their past."

Cole frowned. "So…similar places?"

She nodded. "Just like in the child killings. He wants his victims found without too much trouble and makes it just enough of a challenge to prove how much smarter than us he is. So, he'll pick someplace close but not obvious. I'm pretty sure we'll find her somewhere in this area."

"I hope you aren't still trying to connect the two cases," Cole warned.

She shrugged. "You have to at least consider the

possibility."

"Let's find Shannon first, before we go off on any tangents."

"I just don't want you to write it off completely."

Tina shoved her phone in her pocket and rejoined them. "The helicopter will be here in less than five. I'll have them overfly this area first. I marked out a five-mile radius to start. No more. We can always widen it." She looked at Cole.

"Good." He turned to Dana. "Don't go anywhere. I still need you."

"I'm not leaving," she assured him.

"Smart lady," she heard Tina say to Cole as she turned back to the topographical map. "Not at all what I expected."

"Me, either," Cole said, and Dana swallowed a tiny grin.

Dana listened while Marty Ahern, the pilot, ran his finger over the five-mile area Cole had outlined on the map.

"I'll take one wide pass," he explained. "Then I'll fly an X pattern. Corner to corner. Tina, give your dogs a good sniff of something of the girl's. Then take them out to the corners of this space and work toward the middle. If she's not here, we'll move to the next section. Your regulars know what to do. They can instruct the others." He turned to Cole. "Sound okay to you?"

"Yes. Fine." He looked at Tina. "Whatever you all think best. I just want to get started. That's still a lot of ground to cover on foot."

"All right, then."

Tina trudged back to her van and took out a paper

bag just as the handlers walked up with the dogs. All four animals were German shepherds, straining at their leashes but tuned to the commands of their handlers.

"Listen up, everyone." Tina pulled a T-shirt from the bag. "We'll let the dogs sniff this then start at the corners and crisscross the area. Marty's getting ready to fly a pattern and see what he can spot from the air. Once the dogs are set, everyone load up. Jerry?" She looked at one of the handlers. "Divide up the group, okay? And head for the outer corners of this sector." She handed each of them a map.

"Where do you want me?" she asked Cole as the four groups loaded up and took off.

"I hope you don't get air sick, because I'd like you to go up with the helicopter."

Dana swallowed hard. "I'm okay. Not my favorite ride, but I've done it plenty of times before."

"Here." Cole shoved a large envelope into her hands. "Take this up with you."

Marty helped her climb into the helicopter. "I've read some of your books. Happy to have you aboard on this one."

"Thanks."

She buckled in, hoping as always she didn't disgrace herself by throwing up. Marty handed her a set of headphones with a lip mic attached.

"You'll be able to talk to me this way," he explained. "It gets pretty noisy up here."

"Been there, done that." She gave him her best smile. "I'm ready."

"So I gather. All right, then. You know the drill. If you see anything you think is a likely spot, tell me and I'll go in lower."

"Okay."

As the helo lifted off, Dana felt the familiar sensation of her stomach dropping. She swallowed hard several times, and as Marty leveled off so did her insides. Below, cars and trucks moved out to the corners of the sector and people climbed out and fell in behind the dog handlers.

First, they flew over the entire area Cole had marked out.

"I do this to fix the landscape in my mind," Marty said over the headsets. "Now, I'll start the pattern."

Dana kept her eyes glued to the ground, watching for the kind of places she knew men like this liked to leave their victims. In her hands, she gripped the photo from the envelope Cole had given her. It was taken where Leanne was found, and she tried to spot something similar.

She could see the four lines of searchers converging slowly from the distant corners of the area, spreading out like an army of ants. The land was mostly pasture, but trees lined one side of Hancock Road and in several places a heavy copse of sycamore and oak broke up the landscape.

Marty was starting the second leg of his pattern when something caught Dana's eye. Forgetting the comm system, she yelled his name.

The pilot touched his ear. "You can speak normally with the headphones, and I can hear you."

"Oh. Sorry. Look." She pointed to a dusty ribbon cutting in from a highway at the edge of the sector. "See how that road goes into that thick stand of live oaks? Right there? The really heavily forested one? Can you get any lower?"

"You bet."

He swooped down, and Dana ignored her stomach and concentrated on the ground below. It was hard to see through the trees, but she was sure she spotted something that didn't belong there.

"Can you talk to Tina?" When he nodded, she pointed again. "Tell them to move the searchers over to that area?"

"Will do." He picked up a satellite radio and held it so Dana could hear, too. "Tina, come in. Come in, Solize leader."

"I'm here, Marty. Got something for us?"

"I think so. Got a spot for you to check. I'll mark it for you." He hovered over it, giving her the coordinates.

Immediately, they saw the closest team begin to converge on the spot Dana indicated. Marty continued to hover until the searchers reached it and entered the thick stand of trees. It seemed like forever to Dana before the radio crackled again.

"Tell the lady she's got great eyesight and better instincts," Tina said. "We found her. And the dogs are going wild."

"How come?"

"Wait until you see what this bastard did to kill her scent." Even over the sat radio Tina's voice held barely contained fury.

"I'm taking my passenger back to Cole," Marty told her. "I'll pick him up and bring him to the site. Better radio him and tell him to call off all the other searches."

He clicked off the radio and turned to Dana. "Hope you don't mind, but we need to keep the scene uncontaminated."

"I'm not so sure I want to see it, anyway," Dana replied, nausea clutching at her.

****

Cole hoped he wouldn't embarrass himself by being sick. He'd seen some terrible things in Afghanistan and Iraq, but the sight of Shannon's body was enough to turn anyone's stomach. After the helicopter dropped him, he called Nita Sanchez, keeping his back to what was left of Shannon Fowler until the county van arrived.

"I'm going to have to transport her before I can tell you anything," she said, her voice taut with rage. "I'll need to clean her up to look for trace evidence and I can't do it here. If I ever get my hands on that bastard, I'll gut him like a wild animal."

Shannon was completely nude, lying in a position similar to Leanne's. But probably assuming dogs would be used to hunt for her, the killer had smeared her entire body with honey. It was getting on toward summer, and the Texas heat made her a ripe target for ants and other insects. At first, Cole thought her skin had a black substance all over it, until he saw the black moving and realized what it was.

"I think a lot of people will be standing in that line," he told the coroner. "Jesus. I can't believe this."

"I can't even tell what other damage was done to her until I get rid of the bugs," Nita told him.

The Crime Scene Unit photographed the scene from every angle. Then Shannon's body was loaded in Nita's big Ford Expedition, and she bumped along the field to the dirt road.

Cole turned to Tina. "Thanks for all your help."

"I wish it could have had a different ending." She

shook her head. "I can't believe another human being did something like that."

"Whoever he is, he isn't human." Cole tightened his lips. "When I get my hands on this animal, he'll wish he was never born."

"Just don't get yourself in trouble, Cole," she warned. "It isn't worth it."

"Yeah, I know. All right, tell your people thanks for me. CSU will go to work here now and see if they can get anything at all. I'm heading back to the office to handle things from there."

"Will do."

They shook hands, and she trudged off to round up her crew.

Mickey and Andi had stretched crime scene tape around the drop area, and the CSU techs were in the process of combing every inch for any stray bits of evidence. Anything at all that could be useful.

"This is probably a waste of time," Cole told them. "He was meticulous about not leaving any trace with Leanne, so I don't expect to find anything here. But it's got to be done."

"No problem," Mickey said. "I'll do whatever it takes to get this maniac."

"Me, too," Andi echoed.

"All right, then. Check in with me when you're done."

The helicopter was long gone, so Gaylen had someone pick Cole up and take him back to his SUV. He climbed into it, weary to his soul. He hoped someone had given Dana a ride back to her car, and she'd gone home as he suggested. He was glad she hadn't seen the scene close up.

Cole knew the media would be nipping at his heels for information. The deputies were still keeping them out of the area, but he'd have to tell them sooner rather than later. The Fowlers were at home with their pastor and friends from the church, but Cole had no such insulation.

Shit. Once the details got out, they'd have reporters converging from all over the country. What a fucking mess.

And Grace had radioed him that people were gathering at the office again. Word of the body's discovery had spread like wildfire, and the good citizens of Salado County were after his hide.

Double shit.

Well, at least people's attention had been turned away from Dana's project. Now, instead of being after her hide, they were after his.

But they'd have to wait. He had a few calls to make, first to Reno to give him an update, then to the FBI and anyone else who could offer help. This was definitely a serial killer.

Chapter Twenty-One

Dana stopped on the side of the road on her way home from the sheriff's office and vomited until her stomach was empty. She'd heard two people from Solize discussing the condition of the body. She knew the images in her mind would find their way into her nightmares.

Bastard!

That was all she could think when she finally stopped heaving. If she had a gun, she might hunt him down and kill him herself. Suddenly, the scene in the barn with Kylie and the man who'd taken them rose in the air and smacked her in the face. The scent of cedar and moldy air surrounded her, and she was afraid she'd heave again.

This killer was taking his victims close together. Years ago, the pedophile had gone days or even weeks between victims. It was barely two days since Leanne's death. If this was the same man, had he recognized her? She'd felt him the other day, felt his evil presence. He was here and he was the one. It was hard for her to look at anyone in town without staring, wondering if she was looking at him.

Was she the catalyst? Was he trying to divert attention or frighten her off? Was she his ultimate target?

All she wanted was to lock herself in her house and

bury her face in a pillow. But when she pulled into her driveway, she was ready to be sick all over again. Someone had liberally used red spray paint on the neat little adobe house she was renting. *"Bitch go home"* and *"You'll be next"* were sprayed in different locations across the front and someone had smashed the big living room window.

Who would do this? Who could be so vicious? Did they really think they could frighten her off? Maybe she did need to back out of this.

After all the emotional traumas she'd been body slammed with, after the unremitting tension and hostility since her arrival in High Ridge, it was just too much. This was the tipping point, the thing that snapped the control that defined her life.

Her hands were shaking so badly she could hardly get her cell phone out of her purse. Unable to even remember the number of Cole's office, she just dialed 911, knowing the dispatcher would answer.

"Sheriff's office. What's your emergency? Hello? Hello?"

Dana had to swallow twice before she could get the words out.

"Sheriff Landry."

"You need the sheriff?" The voice was calm and matter of fact. "He's very busy at the moment."

"Help. Need help." Dana could barely get the words out. "This is…Dana." She dragged in a breath. "Dana…Moretti."

Shivering, she gave her address and dropped the still-connected phone on the seat, completely undone for the first time in years. She hugged herself, rocking back and forth in the limited space between the back of the seat and the steering wheel. She heard a voice coming from the cell, but she had no idea what it was saying nor could she make herself answer.

She was still rocking when she heard sirens in the background and the squealing of tires as a car—maybe more than one—pulled up behind her. Then her door was yanked open and Cole was crouching beside her, unbuckling her seat belt, putting one arm around her and smoothing back her hair.

"It's okay." His voice was calm and reassuring. "It's okay, Dana. I'll take care of whatever it is."

He reached over her to pull the keys from the ignition. She was peripherally aware that he handed them over to someone behind him and was talking to him, swearing under his breath before he turned back to her.

"Dana? Listen to me. I'm here, and you're safe now. I'm going to help you out of this car, okay?"

She felt as if she were walking through water as she uncurled herself from the seat and let Cole help her stand. She leaned into him, drawing on his strength. The last time she'd fallen apart like this, she was seven years old. That's how old she felt right now.

"The house," she moaned into his chest. "It's not even mine. Cole, who would do something like this?"

He stroked her hair, his arms still around her. "I don't know, but I'm going to find out."

He kept his voice even, but Dana could hear the fine edge of anger running through it.

"I-I have to get someone to fix this." She sniffled and lifted her head. "Jane Milburn will kill me."

"Jane Milburn is the last person I'm worrying about right now. And I'll get this taken care of."

"Cole?"

She glanced sideways at the voice and saw a deputy walking up to them.

"What did you get?" Cole asked.

"We checked the house. Nothing's touched inside, but we found this rock in the living room." He held out a rock three times bigger than his gloved hand. A black X was painted on it.

"Shit. Okay, put it in an evidence bag. Can you ask Grace to call someone to come out here and board up the window for tonight? I'll worry about the rest tomorrow."

"Sure. Dan's still checking the back and around the sides of the house."

"Okay, thanks. Give me a minute here." He put his hand beneath Dana's chin and tilted up her faced. "You can't stay here tonight. It isn't safe."

She was having trouble processing everything and shook her head, as if to clear the fog.

Cole must have thought she was disagreeing with him. "Don't fight me on this. Please?"

"B-but my things are there. And where would I go? I—I don't want to go back to the motel." She shivered at the thought of being alone and exposed there.

He stroked his thumb across her cheekbone. "You're not. I'm going to take you to my place. Let's go inside so you can pack what you need. I'll send someone back for your car."

"What? I can't stay at your place." With a danger that had nothing to do with the killings.

"Why not?" His grin was almost real. "It's a great place, and it's even clean. How many single men can say that?"

She hiccupped a laugh. She ought to go to a motel, but she didn't seem to have the strength to make a decision for herself. She was falling apart like melting ice cream.

"I'd take you to stay with my aunt and uncle," he added, "but you don't know them, so you might feel uncomfortable."

That was certainly true. "I can't believe I'm such a mess," she told him in a weak voice. "This isn't me at all."

"You've been through a lot in a very short time. Stress will do that, you know."

"But I can usually handle—"

"This isn't usual." He released her from his arms and took her hand. "Come on. Let's go get your stuff."

In a fog, she let him lead her inside, vaguely aware that one of the deputies came in and talked to him while she gathered some things together and tossed them into her travel bag. She found her laptop, sleepwalked her way out to Cole's SUV, and let him help her into it.

She could barely concentrate during the drive to his place. He spoke on his cell phone and the radio, but nothing he said penetrated. When he pulled into his driveway, she had only a hazy impression of a neat ranch house with a barn behind it. Somewhere, she heard a horse whinny.

Cole unlocked the door and guided her inside, through a large great room and down a short hallway into a bedroom.

"I even have clean sheets on the bed," he joked.

She turned to him, frowning. "Is this your room?"

"Uh, no, this would be the guest room." He set her computer and suitcase down and gathered her to him.

She wanted to curl up next to him and never move. "If I get you in my bedroom, Dana, I'll have a lot more on my mind than just keeping you safe."

She leaned her head against him, trying to draw strength. He held her like that for two or three minutes before she finally drew in a deep breath, let it out, and somehow managed to draw in her frayed edges. "I think if I could have a cup of coffee, even instant, I could pull myself together and not be quite such a mess."

"One cup of coffee coming right up."

She sat at the table in the kitchen while Cole heated water and fixed the hot drink for her. But then he opened a cupboard and took down a bottle of whiskey, pouring some into the coffee.

"You need something to counteract shock," he told her. "Drink up."

Curling her hands around the mug, she took a sip, careful not to burn her tongue. The blend of hot coffee and whiskey flowed into her, and almost at once, she felt her edges smoothing out. After two more sips, she set the mug down and looked at Cole leaning against the counter, arms folded, watching her carefully.

"I'm better," she assured him. "And completely embarrassed."

"Don't be. Like I said, you've had more than your share of stress in a very short time." He studied her with those dark brown eyes. "But that's not all that's turned you upside down, is it, Dana? Something else has you by the throat. Something that's had hold of you for a very long time."

She lowered her gaze and picked up the coffee again, taking another swallow. "I don't know what you mean."

"Yes. You do." He pulled out the chair next to her and sat. "Don't worry. I'm not going to beat it out of you. But I have a gut feeling it's tied up with everything that's happening. I'd like you to tell me before you turn up as one of the victims."

She set the mug down again and wet her lips. "Cole, listen. I—"

"No. Not now. After you finish your coffee, I'm going to bundle you into a blanket and wrap you up on the couch. And I think another shot of whiskey would be good. Maybe you can nap a little."

"I think I'm afraid to close my eyes," she told him in a shaky voice.

"Hence the whiskey," he explained. "Come on."

When he urged her up from the chair, he stared at her for a long time, his eyes darker than melted chocolate. Then his mouth came down on hers.

Dana sighed.

All the coffee and whiskey and anything else couldn't compare with the effect of that kiss. Something tight inside her uncoiled, and some of the tension seeped from her. She opened her mouth, and his tongue swept inside, dancing over every surface. Licking. Tasting. His hands were warm on her back, up and down her spine. She could have kissed him forever.

When he finally lifted his head, Cole was breathing as unevenly as she was.

"Well," she said.

"Yes. Well." He smoothed her hair back from her face. "We have two problems right now. I have to get back to the office, and you're too vulnerable for me to do what I really want."

"But—"

He touched a finger to her lips. "Taking care of business is a priority." His expression turned serious. "The last thing I want to do is make a move that will frighten you, and I think that's what would happen. So go into the bedroom and put on something comfortable. Roy should be here any time now, and I need to go speak to him."

"Roy?"

"One of the rookies. I pulled him off the phones, and he'll be doing guard duty until I get home."

"No. Stop," she protested. "You need every person available on these murders."

"I won't be able to work knowing you're unprotected, and I have a bad feeling you aren't out of danger. Yet."

"It was probably just some of the people in town who want me to leave."

"Maybe yes, maybe no. I'm not taking any chances. Now, go change clothes."

Once in the privacy of the guest bedroom, she pulled on jeans and a long-sleeve T-shirt and went into the great room to wait for Cole.

Cole.

He had looked so weary, so defeated, when Marty dropped her back at the head of the road. When he climbed into the chopper, he'd moved like an old man. She'd had to resist the urge to wrap her arms around him and give him a quick hug. She was fiercely battling the unfamiliar sensations of physical desire where he was concerned. And the dreams weren't helping.

But Cole wasn't just incredibly sexy. He was strong and dependable, genuinely sensitive, deeply caring. Seeing him today, seeing the anguish on his face after finding Shannon's body... It had devastated him. She could tell what he felt had nothing to do with his job. He was simply the kind of man who cared, and cared deeply, about those he felt responsible for.

And she'd added another brick to his load.

By the time Cole was back in the house, she was curled up on the couch, hugging herself as if to chase away the internal chill.

He took a long look at her and in what seemed like seconds had a quilt folded around her and a tumbler of whiskey in her hands.

"Drink it slowly," he told her, "but drink it all."

"I'm s-sorry to be such a basket case." She hated being like this in front of him. In front of anyone, but especially Cole.

"Dana." He sat down beside her and cradled her chin in his palm. "Today would be enough to send anyone into shock so quit apologizing."

She swallowed a little of the whiskey, welcoming its burn. "Thank you."

"Have you eaten? I haven't checked my food supply lately, but I know there's stuff in the freezer you can nuke."

"Don't worry about me. I'm not the least bit hungry."

"You have to eat. Feel free to forage in the kitchen."

"The last thing you need to worry about is my food. You've done enough already."

He pulled her cell phone from his pocket where he'd stashed it and put it on the coffee table. "Leave this on, so I can call and check on you. I don't know what time I'll be home."

"Don't worry." She felt as if she'd already said it so many times, but it was important to make him understand she had to be low on his list of priorities right now. "I'm good. Really." She even sipped some more of the whiskey for him. "Why don't you tell your deputy to come inside where he can be more comfortable?"

"No. He'll be on the porch where he can see if anyone approaches the house."

Her eyes widened. "You think someone would come to *your* place? No one even knows I'm here. Well, except for your deputies."

"I'm not taking any chances. You just finish that drink and try to nap. Got it?"

She forced a smile. "Yes, sir."

He stared at her again with that burning gaze, then bent down, cupped her chin, and kissed her until her head swam. Then he stuck his Stetson back on his head. "I'll call you."

His boot heels clicked on the plank flooring as he headed toward the front door, leaving Dana sitting on the couch in a different kind of shock.

She sat, automatically sipping on the whiskey and willing herself to relax. When the glass was empty, she set it on the table and folded herself into a corner of the couch. She leaned back and closed her eyes, and in a moment, despite everything, the dream was there again, curling around her.

"You taste so good," he murmured, his mouth against her neck, his teeth nipping lightly. His tongue soothing the little bites.

"So do you."

She was bolder with him than she'd been with any

other man. Gripping his cock where it pressed against her body, she ran her thumb over the velvety head, feeling the pearl of fluid sitting there. Lifting her thumb to her mouth, she licked it slowly, turning her head so he could watch her.

"You like to tease, don't you," he growled.

"Uh huh. But so do you."

Wasn't that exactly what he was doing now? Rubbing his thumb lightly over her swollen clit? Letting just the tips of his fingers trail into her wet slit? He shifted, and his mouth closed over one stiff nipple.

"Ohhhhh." The sound slipped from her mouth like a soft caress. Heat shot through her, burning her from the inside out. Making the pulse in her core accelerate like the beat of a jungle drum.

"You like that?"

"You know I do." She returned her hand to his swollen erection, feeling his pubic hair against her hand as she gripped the thick root of his shaft. "But you like this, too."

"How about this?" He slid two fingers into her, finding her hot spot and rubbing it lightly.

She squeezed her thighs, trapping his hand as she rubbed up and down his cock.

"Oh, yeah. You definitely like that." He pulled his hand out and slipped his fingers back toward her buttocks, probing gently for the tiny, puckered hole there, using her cream on his fingertips to ease the way. His arm pressed against the lips of her pussy. "Like that, sugar?" He rubbed one finger around and around.

Lust shot through her, nearly choking her with its intensity. Her pussy throbbed, and she tried to slide back and forth on his arm. The more he pushed against that opening, the more aroused she became until she wanted nothing more than for him to fuck her. Hard. There. Everywhere.

He took her nipple between his lips again, grating his teeth over the sensitive surface. She was bombarded by so many sensations at once she wasn't sure she could stand it.

But he was bent on making this last as long as possible.

Her hand closed convulsively around his cock as the first climax roared through her. Her hips jerked, her body pressing into his touch as tremor after tremor shook her.

And when her breathing evened out and her racing heart slowed, he began all over again.

Stroke, stroke, rub, rub.

Everything was so extra sensitive now. She wanted—

Something startled her awake. Her body jerked, and she banged her foot into the coffee table. "Ouch!"

Her cell phone rang, and she realized that was what had woken her.

"You okay?" Cole asked.

She couldn't miss the stress in his voice and hated the fact she'd added to it.

"Yes. I'm good. Took a little nap."

"Okay. Just checking. I'll see you later."

When she disconnected the call, she hugged the phone to her chest. Just the sound of his voice soothed her. Not to mention making her pulse ramp up and her body throb with an unsatisfied need. An *unfamiliar* need.

For a woman who had never been able to enjoy

sex, she sure as hell was dreaming about it a lot. Despite the awful circumstances of the day, her body vibrated with unsatisfied need, a strange sensation for her. What was she going to do about this?

Work. That's what she always did. It would help her blunt the events of the day and the lingering effects of the dream. Gritting her teeth, she made her way to the guest room to get her laptop. Back on the couch, she booted up the computer and opened the document with the spreadsheet she'd created. Maybe there was something else she was missing. Something in addition to the clowns. Something to take her mind off everything that had happened. And…sex.

****

"Thanks for sending help for the search." Cole said to Reno after giving him a status update on the murders.

"You're welcome," he said. "You sound too tired even to think."

"It's bad." He blew out a breath. "I could be shooting in the dark but…" He explained about the old pedophile case and Dana's theory the two killers could somehow be tied together.

"Too bad the sheriff at that time didn't ask for help."

"I've been telling myself the same thing for the past forty-eight hours."

"Okay. Zak s still on a case, but this is a priority. And I'll send Scott Clayton, first thing in the morning. Nick and Zak will follow by noon."

"I appreciate it, Reno, more than you know."

"We're a family, Cole. Told you that when you came on board. Now, we'll need copies of everything. Autopsies. Crime scene reports. Witness interviews.

Whatever. I'll let you know if there's anything more we need. Then the three of us here will drive out to your place for a meeting. I don't think Dana should be left alone."

"Right. Hell," Cole snorted, "The county commission is probably ready to boot me off the investigation for not moving fast enough."

"Politicians can get rambunctious," Reno agreed. "But when you catch the perp, they'll forget how mad at you they were. Happens all the time."

Cole leaned back in his chair, rested his feet on his desk, and rubbed his forehead, hoping the headache would ease. "Well, I appreciate your help."

"We're in this until we catch the bastard."

He hung up and called Dana, just to check on her and make himself feel better. She sounded distracted but who could blame her? Then he checked in with Margene and Max to bring them up to date.

"And the deputies I've had looking for anyone who saw Shannon this afternoon haven't turned anything up. We'll regroup in the morning when Guardian adds their men to the ranks of the deputies."

"I'll bring the commission up to date," Margene told him.

He rubbed his forehead where a growing pain kept slashing across his brow. "Thanks."

His last call was to Tate, just to listen to someone telling him he was handling things okay. His uncle's opinion always meant a great deal to him, and the man was, after all, the one who had recommended him for this job.

"You're doing the right thing," Tate assured him. "Not just because you can use their expertise but because you know Margene and Max will roast your balls if you don't."

"Yeah." Cole sat back in his chair. "I love it when politics dictates law enforcement."

"Just remember, I'm here whenever you need me."

"And I appreciate that."

As always his uncle's voice settled him, allowed him to pull himself together and focus on what needed doing. He was tempted to tell him about Dana, maybe ask him to go by and check on her, but decided he'd have too much explaining to do. He wondered what she was doing. If she was able to get a little rest. He'd hated having to leave her, but he'd had no choice.

He thought back to last night, how easy it was being with her. He didn't remember relaxing like that with any woman. Of course, before the Marines, he was just a snot-nosed college kid who thought he had the world by the balls. Then he'd put so much of himself into being a Marine, he hadn't had much left over for anything except just getting laid between missions.

Now, Dana was in danger, and the chances were equal it was their latest serial killer or some of the angrier residents. To protect her as well as to really know her, he had to find a way to unlock the secret she kept tucked away in the deepest part of her. And that would be easier said than done.

A knock on the door jerked him out of his mental ramblings and brought him back to reality.

The door opened, and Gaylen stuck his head in. "Phone's ringing off the hook again."

Cole made a face. "Could have figured that. People wanting my head, no doubt. I know Roy being out leaves us a man short."

Gaylen held up a hand. "We'll manage. You're doing the right thing with Dana."

"Thanks. Hope the others agree. What else?"

"Everyone's back from questioning people. They got zip. And in case you've missed all the noise, the reporters are dogging it out in the parking lot again."

Cole looked at his watch. "It's eleven o'clock. Don't they ever go home?"

"Not when they smell blood."

He dropped his feet to the floor and stood up. "Okay. I'll go talk to them. Are Andi and Mickey back yet?"

"Just came in."

"Get everyone in the conference room. I'll be there as soon as I get this over with."

The reporters were clustered at his front door like vultures at roadkill. John Garrett stood at the back of the crowd and signaled him to go around to the side. John would keep whatever he was told to himself until Cole gave the go ahead to release it. Meanwhile, the editor was at least in a position to write something that would possibly help settle the county down.

He stuck his head back inside to tell Grace to let Garrett in the side door, then stepped out to face the yammering flock.

"I don't have much to tell you at this moment, but here's what we've got. Shannon Fowler disappeared today on her way home after the bus dropped her off at the head of Hancock Road. Her body was found just a little while ago with the help of the Solize Search and Rescue team. The autopsy hasn't been completed yet, so I don't have any details for you. I'm not going to speculate, so you'll just have to wait until I have something concrete to say."

"This is the same person who abducted and killed the other girl, right?" a tall, lanky man in front asked.

"I have no confirmation of that at this time."

"Oh, come on, Sheriff," someone else shouted. "Two killings in a sparsely populated county like Salado in three days? They have to be related."

Cole gritted his teeth. "As soon as we have evidence linking them, I'll be sure to let you know."

"We saw Dana Moretti here earlier," the lanky man said. "Then she was out at Hancock Road with you. What's the story with her?"

Cole held up his hand. "That's all I can tell you at this time and all the questions I'm going to answer. I'd really appreciate it if you'd move your vans out of my parking lot before I have to have my deputies move them for you. Thanks."

"We're only going as far as the High Ridge Motel," a woman informed him. "If we don't hear from you soon, we'll be back with more questions."

Wonderful. Just what I need.

"Fine. When I have something to share, you'll know about it."

Inside at last, he poured himself a cup of Grace's sludge, figuring he needed it to clear his brain, then headed for the conference room.

On the wall was the sketch Mickey had drawn of the scene where the body was found. Red marker outlined where the body was.

"I tell you, Sheriff," the deputy said, "that was one bad sight. That poor girl."

"The only consolation," Cole told him, "is she was dead before any of that was done to her. At least, I hope she was." He had a hard time getting the details of the autopsy out of his mind.

"Well, Andi and I covered every single inch of the area under and around where she was lying. Not a thing. Nothing."

"I'll say this," Andi chimed in. "I think whoever brought her there was wearing soft moccasins."

Cole lifted an eyebrow. "What makes you think that?"

"I went over my notes from where Leanne's body was found and tried to figure out how someone could have put her there without leaving a trace. Then I remembered my uncle always wears moccasins when hunts. He doesn't want to leave tracks for anyone to see where he puts his blinds."

"Maybe your uncle's getting in a little extra activity," someone joked.

"This isn't an occasion for humor," Cole snapped. "Andi, that's a good thought."

"You want me to check and see who sells those moccasins in the county?" Mickey asked.

"You can, but it's probably a waste of time. He could have bought them in San Antonio or online. And we don't know how long he's had them. Or how many pairs have been sold."

"And we can't exactly go around looking in every closet in Salado County without reasonable cause," Gaylen added.

"That's right," Cole agreed. "We'll have to try another tack."

"And what would that be?" Andi asked.

"I'll let you know as soon as I figure it out." He rubbed his forehead again, wondering if the headache would ever get any better. "Heads up, folks. I've called in Guardian Security, and we're meeting shortly." Seeing the frowns on the faces around the table, he added, "We could be looking at a serial killer here, much as I hate to think it. I'd rather have all the help I can before things get any worse."

"Aw, Sheriff," Mickey complained. "We can handle this."

"No, Mickey," Cole said quietly. "We can't. We don't have the first idea where to start. There hasn't been a murder here in almost three decades. All of you are excellent deputies, but this is way over everyone's head. Including mine. Guardian has far more experience in the private sector and much better resources. Next would be the FBI, but I'm not ready to go there yet."

"I suppose they'll want to take charge of everything," Andi grumped.

"Listen, all of you," Cole said pointedly. "This isn't about us. This is about those two girls. This is about all the other young girls out there that this sick freak can target if we don't get him first. Keep that in mind when our help arrives tomorrow. I'll expect everyone's cooperation. Right?"

Slowly, each of them nodded.

"All right, then. It's been a long day for everyone. The crime scene is under guard so go home and get some rest. Be back here early, so I can introduce you to the Guardian agents."

Gaylen held back until the others had all filed out of the room. "Sheriff, I just want you to know I think you did the smart thing. The younger deputies think they know it all, and they haven't even scratched the surface. Like you said, they're good, but this is deeper water than we're used to swimming in. I respect a man who knows when to ask for help. Whatever you need me to do, just holler."

Cole felt his throat tighten. Gaylen Kleist was the oldest of all the deputies. He'd been on the force for fifteen years and probably had every right to have expected promotion to the top spot when Nickels retired. But he accepted Cole without a fuss, did his job and watched to see how things shook out. His words meant a great deal to Cole.

"Thanks, Gaylen."

"You ought to get out of here, too. It's late, and I think you need to check on your house guest."

"Oh, yeah. My house guest."

Gaylen started to say something else but was interrupted by a knock on the doorjamb.

"Got a minute?" John Garrett asked. "I got the idea you wanted to talk to me privately."

He'd forgotten all about the fact that Garrett was waiting for him.

I really do need to get out of here.

He motioned the man into the conference room. "Yes. I'd like to ask for your help."

"Don't tell me you're giving the hometown paper an exclusive." Garrett's voice was laced with grim humor.

"Not exactly. What I'd really like is for you to write something to help keep the county under control. Like I just asked Max and Margene to do."

"You have to give me something to write, though," Garrett protested. "Your little press conferences might as well be nonexistent."

"There's a lot I don't want to release yet. The details are pretty gruesome, and the Pritchards and Fowlers don't need to see it splattered all over the press. But I'll give you the info and you can figure out how to spin it."

John sat down in one of the chairs opposite Cole, took his little tape recorder out of his pocket, and set it on the desk. "You okay with this?" he asked, indicating the instrument.

"As long as you shut it off if I tell you to."

"No problem. Let's get started."

It took Cole ten minutes to give the newspaper editor the bare bone details of both crimes. He left out the autopsy details, particularly the horrendous sexual abuse, but he gave the man enough for an informative article.

"Here's the important part," he said. "We may have a serial killer here, and I don't want to wait for more bodies."

"People will be happy to know you aren't too pigheaded to cry uncle when you have to." John's approval was obvious.

Cole held up his hands, palms outward. "I'd be very foolish if I was. This isn't about me. It's about catching a killer. Hopefully, before he takes another victim."

Garrett picked up the recorder, put it back in his pocket, and stood up. "I'll get started on this right away. The paper comes out again tomorrow, and I saved some front-page space, just in case. But if we want the presses to roll on time, I'd better git. As it is, we'll be working until the sun comes up."

Cole stood up, and the men shook hands. "Thanks

again, John. This will be a big help."

"I'll do a sidebar, too, kind of like an editorial," Garrett called over his shoulder as he turned toward the door.

"Everything helps. Everything."

****

Dana worked on the spreadsheet for more than two hours, but her mind kept wandering, thinking back to Kylie and that scene so many years ago. She didn't look up until the front door opened and she heard Cole talking to someone, then the door closed.

"Did you sleep at all?"

"Yes. Some." Her cheeks heated as the images from the dream danced in her head. Then she took a good look at Cole, at the fatigue and worry lining his face, and her heart ached for him.

Her heart? Ached? When had she felt *anything* for a man? "You look terrible."

He forced a weak grin. "Nice to see you, too."

She stared at him. "Oh, my God, Cole. Has something else happened?" She set aside her computer and scrambled to her feet.

"No." He sprawled on the couch and tugged her back down beside him. "I just hate to think anyone like that is living in our community. That it's someone I see every day."

"Just like no one wanted to think the pedophile lived here," she reminded him.

"I know." He scrubbed his hand over his face. "But it's obvious strangers stand out here. Plus neither those little kids nor Leanne or Shannon would be the type to get in a car with a stranger."

He draped his arm over Dana's shoulder, and at the

moment, she wasn't inclined to move it. "So you think they could all be related?"

"Let's say I'm willing to examine the options. I've got my associates at Guardian Security coming in the morning. I'll be anxious to get their take on it. I read the preliminary autopsy report on Shannon a little while ago. I can't even begin to tell you how awful it was."

Dana's stomach clenched. She didn't know if she could listen to this part. "That had to be hard for you."

"This whole thing is hard for me. I saw terrible things when I was with the Marines, but this tops my worst nightmares."

"Oh, Cole." She wanted to pull his head to her breast. Do something to soothe him. And where had that come from?

He gave her a tired smile. "By the way, thanks for what you did today. I appreciate it."

She shrugged. "I was glad I could help. I was surprised you even asked me."

"Hey, I'm not stupid enough to ignore an offer like that. You did good, Dana. It might have taken forever to find her otherwise, especially with her scent masked."

She lifted an eyebrow. "Masked?"

"Damn. Me and my big mouth." He told her about the condition of the body.

As brief as his description was, Dana could hardly bear to hear it.

"Did you eat?" she asked.

"No. How about you?"

She shook her head. "After...I didn't have any appetite. But I'll look for something to fix for you."

"No, thanks. I don't think my stomach would

welcome anything solid. But I could stand a cold drink. How about you?"

"I'll get it."

He held up his hand. "No, I'll do it. Sit."

He brought back two glasses filled with ice and soda and drank half of his before sitting down again.

"Thanks." She smiled at him. "That tastes good."

"I don't like the reason that brought you here," he told her, "but it feels…nice to have you here to talk to. You know, you aren't exactly the most relaxing person to be with—"

"Gee, thanks," she interrupted.

He continued as if she hadn't said anything. "But somehow, with you, I feel I don't have to pretend anything. I can be whatever I am at the moment. However I feel."

Dana's throat tightened. "Thank you. That's a real compliment. I'll try to be deserving of it."

"Oh, you may not think it's such an honor after a while," he teased. Then sadness clouded his eyes again. "Jesus. I can't imagine there's somebody out there, right in this county, capable of doing things like this." He took another long swallow of his drink.

She ran her finger around the rim of her glass, trying to decide if she should say what was on her mind. She could be all wrong—actually, hoped she was—but she needed to know if she was seeing shadows where there weren't any.

"Let me give you something different to sink your teeth into." She stared into her glass. "I talked to some of the parents of the children who were killed. Ivy Winslow mentioned something, so tonight, while I was trying to keep myself from thinking about today, I went back over all my notes. Cole, in all but two of the cases, clowns were involved."

He frowned. "Clowns? Like party clowns?"

Dana nodded. "Children are drawn to them. They're familiar. I'm wondering why no one tied it all together back then?" She had to ask the question banging around in the back of her mind. "Was the sheriff covering up for someone else?"

Chapter Twenty-Two

Cole's frown deepened. "I have no idea. It seems to me, if there's a common thread in a situation like this, it only makes sense to follow it." He stared at her. "God, what a terrible thing if it's true and they missed it completely."

"The only mention I could find was that either Jed Nickels or one of his deputies talked to the chamber and the rodeo association. They were the two organizations that dealt with the clowns. And that was only because they talked to everyone at each site. Not because they smelled something fishy."

"And?"

"And it's weird." Dana wet her lips. "People couldn't seem to agree if there were four clowns or five at any given event. Apparently, not even the clowns. Most of them said four, but a couple said five. But I guess no one figured clowns were likely suspects."

"Even though the easiest thing for a predator is to camouflage himself with a costume and makeup and blend into the activity?"

"Uh huh."

"What else?" Cole asked when she stopped suddenly.

"I probably should keep my mouth shut, but I have a lot of issues with the way Nickels handled the whole thing. Why clamp such a tight lid on it? Why not ask for outside help, like you're doing? I mean, after two deaths, you're looking for solutions, for help, for anything that will find this guy. So why, after two years of child rapes and murders, did Nickels do nothing?" She heard her voice rising and tried to temper it. "There's a lot of whys in this case, Cole."

Cole shrugged. "I think those are questions no one ever wanted to ask. Jed's family goes back four generations, and he was like the elder statesman of the county, you know."

Dana took a swallow of her soda. "I've seen that in other situations. One in Florida in particular. The sheriff ruled with a big smile and a heavy hand. No one ever thought to question him about his methods or why he handled that particular case the way he did. The killer turned out to be his own son."

"That wouldn't work here. Jed doesn't have a son. Only daughters. Even if he did, those kids were just babies when all that happened. But Jesus, Dana. What if you're right and he actually *did* cover up for someone?"

"Cole, what if it turns out this is the same man from twenty-five years ago? And now, for some reason, he's moved to older girls."

Cole blew out a long breath. "Hell, that makes just about every man in this county over the age of fifty a suspect." He narrowed his eyes at her. "And it means you being here and digging up those old cases really did start him up again. It puts you in even greater danger."

"Think about this," she went on. "With that kind of predatory personality, how likely is it he's just been dormant all this time? He's had to find some other place to blow off that steam. Has anyone ever checked surrounding counties?"

"Probably not, but I'm sure as hell going to."

"Leanne had problems with her truck at night and needed help," Dana went on. "Shannon would have accepted a ride rather than walk all the way down that road."

Cole raked his fingers through his hair. "You have no idea how much I hope you're wrong, Dana."

"Me, too."

"Being here with you does me a lot of good."

Her laugh was shaky. "Even if I did add to your bag of troubles?"

"Even if." Cole rose from the couch and reached a hand to Dana to help her up. "I think we could both use some sleep."

"You're right." She closed her laptop and stacked her papers.

Suddenly, it hit her fully she'd be sleeping under the same roof as this man. A man who pushed every one of her sexual hot buttons. Who starred in her erotic fantasies. She'd come to High Ridge hoping to get past her hang-ups. She just hadn't expected it to happen quite this way. When she straightened, Cole was right behind her.

"Everything okay in your room?"

"Uh, yes."

"Good. Well, I'm going to take a shower and get some sleep. Someone's dropping your car off. I'll probably be gone when you get up in the morning. I want to be at the office early."

"Then, I guess, um, good night." What was the matter with her that she was suddenly socially clumsy this way?

****

Cole stood under the shower, letting hot water wash away the stench and grime of the day. Dana puzzled him. There was something skittering beneath the taut professional surface.

Fear. Panic. Maybe both. Whatever it was, it wasn't from something recent. An old wound that was festering perhaps or maybe a recent scab that had been torn away.

He thought about the few kisses they'd shared. Not mild by any means. Incendiary. But there again, something wasn't right. Oh, she'd responded at first, but then quickly withdrew behind a wall he couldn't breach.

He let his mind wander as he dried off and toweled his hair. Had she been raped? Had an abusive relationship? He dismissed either option out of hand. Those signs were different. He'd seen enough of them to know what to look for. He was just damn glad he hadn't blurted out the details of his erotic dream.

He pulled on a pair of sweatpants, jerking them up over his hips, then grabbed his toothbrush and toothpaste. He stared at himself in the mirror while he brushed his teeth, but it wasn't his image he was seeing.

Dana.

She devoted herself to finding answers for other unsolved crimes, hoping to ease the pain of her own life. And after all this time, something had happened to push her to confront her past. A failed relationship? More than one?

Something about this case triggered whatever she was hiding. He was convinced that at some time she'd been a victim herself. Was that what drove her? Was that why she was so interested in the old cases? If that was true, he wondered how she could stand to be in the same room with a man at all.

Hadn't she had therapy of any kind to help her?

His last thought as he fell asleep was that, despite everything, Dana Moretti had gotten to him. Something was going on between them, and he wasn't going to just let her walk away before he figured out what it was. If this thing between them was to move forward, he needed to find the answer. He also knew it wouldn't be easy.

****

A scream woke Cole as abruptly as a flood of ice water. He sat straight up in bed, the hair standing up on his arms. Had he imagined it? No! There it was again.

Had someone broken in? Attacked Dana? He threw back the covers and ran to the room she was in, banging open the door. She was alone but sitting straight up in bed, her body rigid, head thrown back, the scream still echoing in the air.

Cole took a deep breath and tried to calm his out-of-control heartbeat as he approached the bed slowly. Her eyes were wild, unseeing, and the muscles in her neck stood out.

"Dana?" He lowered himself to the bed next to her, gently touching her shoulders. "Dana, honey? Wake up. You're dreaming."

When he touched her, she was clammy with sweat and ice cold. He wanted to pull her against his body, share his warmth, but he didn't want to frighten her, either. As a Marine, he'd seen nightmares before and knew he had to be cautious. He shook her very lightly, repeating her name over and over.

When she opened her mouth to scream again, he

was afraid he'd have to slap her to snap her out of it. He dug his fingers into her shoulders and shook her hard. Her head jerked forward then back again, and her eyes, unfocused, began to clear.

"Wha—Cole?" She blinked. "What happened? What are you doing here?"

"Darlin', you were screaming the roof down." He slid his hands over her exposed skin. "You're covered with sweat, cold as ice, and shaking like a leaf. Let's get you into a hot shower."

"No. Please. I'm okay. Really." She pushed against him weakly.

He pulled her to his body, stroking her back. "You are far from all right. Come on. You'll feel better. Then you can tell me what it was all about."

"I...I can do this myself." She swung her legs over the side of the bed, but when she tried to stand, she nearly crumpled to the floor.

Cole lifted her in his arms and carried her to the bathroom, holding her against him while he turned on the shower and adjusted the spray. He hesitated a moment, then shut his mind to everything but necessity and stripped off both her sleep shirt and his sweats. He took one moment to admire her slim body and full breasts before pulling her into the shower with him.

As soon as the hot spray hit her, she came alive in his arms, struggling. "Damn, Cole. That's hot. And I can shower by myself."

"Not this time," he told her, holding her against him while the water beat down on them. "Consider it purely therapeutic."

He let the steam from the heat surround them until he felt her stiffen in his arms again.

"I'm naked," she said and looked up at him with something like fear in her eyes.

He grinned. "That's the usual procedure for showering." He reached for the handle and turned off the water. "Come on. I think you're warmed up enough now."

He pulled a towel from a hook, dried her, and wrapped her in it. He quickly wrapped another around his waist and knotted it at his hips before digging a T-shirt out of his drawer and slipping it over Dana's head. Lifting her to the counter, he found another towel to wrap around her head and squeeze out most of the water.

"I think that's the best we can do for now." His voice was still soft. Calming. He tossed the towel over a bar, carried her back to bed, put her beneath the covers, and slid in next to her. She tried to push him away and sit up, but he kept his arms around her.

"Uh-uh. You need my body heat. It's better than medicine after a nightmare."

She stiffened again. "I can go back to sleep now. I'm fine."

"Darlin', you are many things, but at the moment, fine isn't one of them. You have had a hellacious day, and your mind is fighting back. Just relax. Come on. Let it go."

They lay there for long minutes, his hand stroking the graceful line of her back, the smoothness of her skin. The swell of her hip. Her breasts pushed against him through the T-shirt, and he prayed his body would behave. But his cock seemed to have a mind of its own, swelling and poking at her soft skin. He rolled her resisting body over, so she faced away from him and spooned her against him, but his hot erection pressed against the crevice of her ass, and she jumped as if scalded.

"Cole, I—"

"Shh, shh, shh. It's okay. I won't hurt you."

She lay there stiff as a board again.

Cole sighed. "I promise I'm not going to hurt you, Dana. Or force you to do anything you don't want to. I just want to ease you back to sleep."

"I don't sleep with men in my bed." Her voice sounded very small.

"Ever?" She was thirty-two years old, and he was pretty sure she wasn't a virgin.

"Well...hardly ever." She cleared her throat. "I have...issues."

He waited a heartbeat for her to say more, but when she didn't he asked, "Want to talk about it?"

****

Did she want to talk about it? Tell Cole about the dreams that never left her? That plagued her sleep? Hell, no.

Dana had been back in the barn in her dream, listening to Kylie scream. Feeling the man's hands on her. Hurting her.

When Cole woke her, she was a shivering mess, once again terrified by the horror that had haunted her for years. Her collapse was the only excuse she could find for letting him strip her naked and take her in the shower with his equally naked body. And for finding herself under the covers with him.

The T-shirt and towel weren't a lot of protection. The heat of his body burned against hers through the fabric, her senses rioting at the contact. It startled her that she wasn't afraid. Why didn't her body clench and shrink from his as it usually did at this point? She desperately wanted to figure out why, for the first time in her life, she was responding to a man.

True, he was just holding her. He hadn't made any overt sexual moves, but she was hyperaware of the large cock pressed against her. Of his rock-hard body honed to perfection. Of his muscular legs pressed against hers. And she hadn't panicked yet. Possibly, just possibly…Cole Landry could be the one to unlock that frozen part of her. Maybe.

With all the death and destruction raining down around her, how was it that her body chose *now* to wake up and demand attention?

Or was it because of that very death and destruction? Maybe she needed this—him—to wipe all of that away. Whatever it was, Cole Landry was the first man ever who didn't frighten her. Whose presence gave her comfort and at the same time woke up every long-dormant hormone in her body.

Did she have the courage for this?

She wet her lips. "Cole?"

"What, darlin'?"

God, she loved the way he said that with his deep Texas drawl. It stirred something deep inside her. "I, um… It might be all right for you to…touch me."

Please, please, please. I want to try this.

He chuckled softly, the sound vibrating against her. "In case you hadn't noticed, I am touching you."

"I know. I mean…you know…"

She felt him suck in a breath and let it out. "You mean like this?"

One hand slid beneath the T-shirt to cup her breast,

lightly at first. Then a thumb skimmed her nipple. Heat shot straight to her pussy with an intensity she'd waited all her life to feel. She heard a low moan and realized it came from her.

"Feel good?" he whispered. "Anytime you want me to stop, you just tell me."

She nodded, hardly able to speak for the riot of sensations racing through her. And prayed he'd keep doing what he was doing.

"I could make you feel really good." He nipped the lobe of her ear. "You can trust me, Dana."

"Yes." The word was barely audible.

"I don't know what ghosts you're fighting, but maybe, we can chase them away together. Close your eyes, darlin'. Block everything out but my hand."

"O-okay." She squeezed her eyes shut.

"Don't tense. It's all good, I promise. Feel my hand on your breast? You have wonderful breasts, Dana. And nipples I can't wait to get my mouth around." He pinched one lightly, and again a dull throb pounded clear to that spot between her legs.

"Relax," he murmured. "Just feel."

He spent a long time on her breasts, telling her what he was doing. Playing with her nipples. Palming and rubbing the mounds of flesh. When he slid his hand to her stomach, she tensed again, but Cole continued to speak softly in her ear, soothing her, telling her in explicit erotic detail what he was doing to her.

His hand was warm against her flesh, rubbing light circles, moving farther down in small increments until she felt him between her thighs. Again, she tensed, and again, he whispered and soothed. One finger slipped between the folds of her pussy, finding the hot button of her clit and brushing a fingertip over it. Back and forth. Back and forth. Each caress was like the whisk of a lightning bolt. His mouth worked its magic against her ear, her neck, her jawline, while his finger continued to torment her.

He seemed to have endless patience, as though prepared to do this all night if necessary. The more he worked her clit, the more her anxiety faded, replaced by a tension of a different kind. She moved restlessly, unconsciously opening her legs to give him better access.

The lean finger moved between her labia to stroke up and down her wet slit, again slow. Slow and steady. She knew she was wet, as effortlessly as his finger moved, and to her, it was a real miracle. He lifted one of her legs, rested it on top of his, and resumed that deliberate stroke. And all the while, between nips and kisses, he kept up his erotic murmur in her ear.

"So soft." His voice was husky. "And so wet. See how easily my finger moves against your hot flesh? Pretty soon, I'm going to slide it inside you. Feel those tight muscles clench around it. And when you're ready, I'll slide my cock inside there. God, I can't wait. I could come just thinking about that."

When at last he pushed that finger inside her, a small orgasm racked her body. Her muscles clenched, her pussy tightening on that finger.

Cole's soft chuckle of satisfaction vibrated against her. "That's it, darlin'. See how good this is?"

A second finger joined the first, and she rode his hand, so enthralled by the exquisite feeling she didn't want it to end. When it did, he moved back to her clit again, the bundle of nerves so swollen and sensitive that, in seconds, a new hunger built within her.

Again, he worked his magic, first teasing her clit until she was sure she couldn't stand it and then sliding his fingers deep inside her. Another climax rocketed through her, knocking everything from her mind except the exquisite pleasure he was giving her.

As she lay panting against him, astounded at this unfolding of sexual desire and response, he licked the line of her jaw with the tip of his tongue.

"So. Think you want to take this a little further?"

Oh, yes. She wanted to find out if he could give her all of it. The ultimate satisfaction. "Yes. I do."

Cole reached into his nightstand drawer and pulled out a condom, nearly dropping it in his haste. He rolled it on with hands not quite steady, then shifted them until she was flat on her back. He spread her legs wide and knelt between them. She thought he'd try to enter her and her body tensed, but instead, she felt his open mouth on her clit, his tongue licking, swirling, then probing inside her until she couldn't even think anymore. Until all she wanted was to reach that peak he drove her toward.

Just before she was ready to beg for it, he bent her knees back, positioned himself at her opening and entered her with a long, slow steady stroke. He eased his cock past her tight inner muscles, little by little until at last she'd taken him completely. The tiny pinch of fear that stabbed at her at the first sense of penetration was washed away by the heated pleasure that swamped her as her inner walls clamped around the swollen length of his cock.

OhGodohGodohGod!!!!

It had never felt like this, not with anyone. She was

stretched, full, his cock caressing every single tiny nerve ending in her quivering channel. Holy hell!

"Okay?" Strain edged his voice.

Dana nodded, unable to form words.

"Here we go then. Just feel, darlin'. Just feel."

Long slow strokes, in and out, pulling at her nerves, strumming them, heating her from the inside out. In, out, in, out.

"Jesus, you feel so damn good." His voice was tight. "You're soaking wet. You're like a hot, wet fist around me. Oh, shit, I'm trying to make this last, darlin', but I don't know how long I can."

As the pace of his strokes increased, so did the intensity of her pleasure, the sensation like a wild rollercoaster ride. She rode it with him, hanging on for dear life, not wanting it to end. For the first time during sex, feelings of lust uncoiled inside her and pushed her higher and higher. She moved her hips, matching his rhythm as he took her up, up, up.

They crashed together, her entire body shaking with the force of her climax. He groaned as he found his release, his cock pulsing inside her. Her heart thundered, every muscle in her body clenching with a powerful contraction. This was the most delicious, consuming sensation she'd ever had, one she'd never ever thought to feel.

When the fireworks stopped, she lay limp and spent beneath him. He pressed his mouth to hers, a kiss fierce and gentle at the same time. His tongue searching for hers, dancing with it. A strange emotion threaded through her, one she finally identified as happiness.

Omigod!

He eased carefully from her body, padded to her

bathroom, and returned with a warm washcloth that he used to clean her with, his touch tender and gentle. When he finished, he bent and placed a soft kiss on each nipple and then on the top of her mound. Tears leaked from the corners of her eyes at his consideration.

She reached out a hand, touching the stubble on his square jaw, a day's growth of beard that made him even more masculine, if that was possible. She brushed her hand against his still damp hair, almost black from the moisture, and stared into his eyes, the color of day-old coffee. They held a mixture of concern and…something else. Something she wanted so desperately to believe in.

"Time to go back to sleep." He brushed another kiss over her lips.

Finally, he crawled back into bed with her and spooned her against him, his arms holding her gently but firmly.

"Thank you," she said when they were settled together.

"I should be the one thanking you." He kissed her shoulder. "But there's a lot more where that came from."

Thank God!

Dana felt as if she'd experienced a minor miracle. No, a major one. She let out a soft sigh, closed her eyes, and fell into dreamless sleep.

Chapter Twenty-Three

What the hell was the sheriff thinking, involving Dana in the search for Shannon? When he'd heard about her participation, he nearly lost it. All he needed was for her to stick her pretty little nose into everything. With her curious nature, how long would it be before she connected the dots? He wanted her to have her answers, but not until he reached the end of the game. Not until he made her his final victim.

On top of that, the by-the-book former Marine had called in his Guardian Security team, and they were sending help. That would change the dynamics, which meant he'd have to move up his timetable. Not a terrible glitch, but not good either. He wanted to take his time, plan accordingly, make sure there were no mistakes. But with this new twist, he couldn't afford to stretch things out any longer.

One more girl, and then he'd go after Dana. Carrie, his little flower, the one he'd plucked so many years ago. Would she still be as sweet as she'd been back then? How many others had tasted the sweet nectar of her honey pot? Had any other man squeezed his stiff cock into her little well? His eyes narrowed, and his fists clenched at the thought of someone soiling his little innocent bloom.

Once she was gone, he could return to his delicious hobby and fade into anonymity. His last little bud would be just one more in long list of unsolved cases.

Pondering possibilities for his third victim, fate stepped in and dropped one in his lap. Late yesterday, after Shannon's body was found, he had stopped at Harry's for coffee. And nearly smiled when he overheard a conversation from the booth behind him. Gabriella Marquez, twenty-six and shy, confessed to her friend that she was worried about what was happening.

"I wish they'd catch this maniac," she'd said, and he silently chuckled. "They won't release any details about the killings. Can you imagine how horrifying they must be to keep them under wraps?" She shuddered.

He swallowed a smile. He knew how old Gabriella was, but she still had the fresh-faced look of a teenager. Even Carrie/Dana, in her thirties, looked much younger than she was. At least to him.

"I'm scared living all by myself," Gaby went on to her friend. "This whole thing creeps me out. I'm thinking of leaving town until he's caught."

She looked around as if she could sense someone watching her, and his smile grew brighter as he sipped his coffee.

"But, Gaby," her friend said. "What if he's never caught? Are you going to leave your home forever?"

"If it means saving my life," she retorted.

"Why don't you come stay with Jered and me? We have an extra room."

"For how long? You don't want a permanent house guest."

"I don't want to frighten you any more than you already are," her friend went on, "but living alone is only part of the problem. What scares me most is he could take his next victim right off the street. Just like he did with Leanne and Shannon. It's obviously someone we all know, otherwise he'd never have been able to get close to them."

Gaby looked around, her face pinched with fear. "My God. Doesn't it make you just want to lock yourself inside your house and never leave?"

"No." Her friend shook her head. "Anyway, I think you're overreacting. Those girls were a lot younger than you."

"So that makes me an unappealing target?" Gaby's voice rose on a note of irritation. "Is that what you're saying?"

Her friend frowned. "Make up your mind. Either you want to be appealing to him or you don't."

"How can you even ask that?" Gaby hissed. "Aren't you afraid?"

"Of course. We all are. But all I can do is be as careful as possible." The woman's voice softened. "Drink your tea, Gaby, and come home with me for a while. At least spend the night. You'll feel better tomorrow."

His cell phone vibrated at that moment, and he left the restaurant to take the call, irritated that he'd miss the rest of the conversation. But when he saw Tony's number, he had to answer it alone. This was not a conversation he wanted anyone to overhear.

"Can you meet me tonight, old man?" Tony asked, foregoing any greeting. "I happened to pick up a shipment unexpectedly. Choice meat. We could score some big dollars on this. My boss wants to move it."

"Nothing like last minute," he complained.

"Do you want it or not? Otherwise, I'll call my next customer."

"Hold on, hold on. Let me call my buyer and see if we can hook up. Oh, and Tony?"

"Yeah, old man?"

"Any that are really, really choice? I need some entertainment tonight. Something to take the edge off."

Tony's laugh was anything but humorous. "I got just the one for you. But you gotta be careful."

"Aren't I always?"

"I hear the sheriff's got outside help coming."

Shit. How the hell had Tony found that out?

"That won't interfere with our business at all. You can tell your boss he has my word on that. I'm smarter than these idiots. Anyway, they aren't aware of our business at all, so we're clear."

"If you say so. Okay, call me back in five, man, or I'm on to the next name."

He climbed into his truck and called his buyer who was delighted at the unexpected bounty. He had his own demands to meet. Yes, he'd be happy to meet at their usual place and bring cash with him, as always.

A call back to Tony and the meeting was set. God, he hoped nothing happened to fuck things up.

At home, acting as if everything were normal was extremely difficult. He ate his dinner without tasting any of it, finally making the excuse that he had to run an errand and bolted from the house.

At the usual delivery spot, he paced impatiently, waiting for Tony and the buyer to show. The buyer drove up first, smiling and jovial, excited at the cargo he was about to receive. He opened his briefcase to reveal the money neatly stacked inside. The two men leaned against the truck until a van approached.

Tony climbed out and beamed at them. "I've got ten of the choicest pieces of merchandise you could ever hope to set your eyes on."

"That's what you always say." The buyer laughed good-naturedly.

"Yeah, well, don't take my word for it," Tony said. "Take a look for yourself. These are the freshest yet." He clapped his hands together and rubbed them as he wiggled his eyebrows. "They will give much pleasure."

The exchange was made, money changed hands, and the buyer drove off excited and happy.

"Here's what I got for you, old man," Tony said, sliding open the door of the van again. "Ten years old. You'll love her."

The girl was tiny, almost like his little flowers had been. She had delicate features and long black hair. Her hands were tied behind her back, her ankles were bound, and tape sealed her mouth. Above the tape, her huge dark eyes were wild with fear.

He couldn't help salivating. This would more than satisfy his need tonight. And it would prepare him nicely for tomorrow's adventure. He paid Tony his bonus, lifted the girl into his arms, and carried her to his truck, crooning to her all the while.

"We're going to have fun, little girl. You and me. A lot of fun. I promise."

Pulling away from where he was parked, he began singing his little song.

"There was a little girl, who had a little curl, right in the middle of her forehead. When she was good, she was very, very good, And when she was bad she was a tasty treat."

Chapter Twenty-Four

Cole had retrieved his watch from his bedroom and set the alarm on it before falling asleep last night. He was sure Dana would still be sleeping when it went off, but he was alone in the bed. Big surprise. If she thought she was going to pretend nothing had happened, she was fooling herself. Then he heard the shower running and relaxed fractionally.

In a moment, the shower turned off, and the bathroom door opened. She stood in a cloud of steam, wrapped in one of his big towels, and his cock immediately stood up and demanded attention.

"Oh!" The combination of surprise and embarrassment was appealing.

"Good mornin'," he drawled. "You're up early. And here I worried the alarm would wake you."

"I'm…an early riser."

He studied her face and the line of her body. "Sleep good?"

"Yes. I did." She stood in the doorway, as if waiting for some signal from him. He pushed the covers back and crooked his finger at her. "Come here and let me give you a morning hug."

Could her steps have been any more tentative? But she came to him, just the same, and he felt as if he'd won the jackpot. She lay down next to him, still wrapped in the towel, and he pulled her into him. His hand wandered over her, idly loosening the towel until he touched smooth flesh.

"Dana." He cupped her breasts before letting his hand wander to her tummy. "Whatever's in your past, I think we opened a door between us last night. It was wonderful. Beyond wonderful. And it was more than just medicinal sex so get that thought out of your head."

"But—"

"But nothing." He kissed her shoulder. "It was incredible. If I had time now, we'd do it again."

He was painfully aware of the fact that his raging hard-on was poking her in the ass.

And that she'd tensed.

He soothed her with a trail of kisses down her arm and felt her relax. Nice. He'd better get this killer caught soon so they could get on with this because he wanted to spend a lot of years with her. If he could just gentle her. She reminded him of a skittish colt.

"Whatever you're about to say, save it for another time. We have something here, Dana. Right now, life's getting in the way, but nobody's ever hit me the way you have. And it isn't just the physical stuff. Far from it."

"But—"

"Shh, shh. Sometimes in extreme situations, feelings start out as one thing, then turn real fast into something else. Because all your senses are in high gear. So put this in your Day Planner. I'm catching this killer, then moving into your life. Whatever problems are giving you nightmares, we'll deal with them together."

As if she'd been holding herself together through sheer willpower, she crumbled. Her body curled into his, and he held her tightly, vowing to protect her from harm. And to help her banish her demons.

At last, she turned around, so he could see her face. Her smile was weak, but it was there. "Can I fix you some breakfast?"

"Thanks, but no. Coffee's good, but then I'll just go through the cafe drive-through. I really need to get going. I want to make sure your car's in the driveway in case you need it, but Dana?"

"Mmm?"

"Don't go anywhere for a while today, okay? Let me get this meeting out of the way and patrols out on the road, so there are people around if you need them."

She tensed. "You think someone will attack me?"

"After what happened to your house, I just don't want to take any chances." He sat up, taking her with him. "I know I've got frozen waffles and some other stuff."

"Cole, I can't hide out here. I have things to do."

"Just until I call you." He stood up, taking her with him. "I'll get someone from Guardian out to your house today to take care of the damage, but you may need to call the realtor's office first."

She groaned. "That means calling Jane Milburn."

He kissed her forehead. "You can handle it. Come with me. I want to show you something."

"What?"

"Just come on."

He walked her to his bedroom, ignoring the fact he was completely naked and her towel was in disarray. With a flick of his fingers, he opened the blinds on the full-length window and was rewarded with a small gasp.

"Cole! It's beautiful."

Yes, it was. It still took his breath away. Behind the house, the barn, and corral sat in the rising sun, the pastures rolling away and glistening with morning dew. In the distance, the tall hills ringing the property were silhouetted against the sky. A battered pickup stood beside the barn, and the horses were getting their morning play in the corral.

"Is-is someone here?"

"Just the kid I pay to take care of the horses in the morning when I need him. Usually, I ride before heading into the office, but right now, that's on the back burner. I called him last night. He'll be gone in a little bit. He's got school." He kissed the top of her head. "Much as I'd rather stand here with you, I need to shower and get to the office. You take your time and don't leave here until you talk to me first. Where's your cell?"

"In my—the bedroom." She hurried to get it.

Cole punched some numbers in and handed it back to her. "Now you've got my cell number in there. You can bypass the switchboard."

"Thank you. And Cole? Take care of yourself today. Use everything Guardian gives you. They have extensive resources. I've worked with them before, and sometimes, it was actually a pleasant experience. This town is on the verge of imploding, and I don't want you to be at the epicenter."

"I'll be fine." He cupped her chin. "I hope you brought enough for a few nights because I'm not letting you go back to your house."

"I can't stay here forever."

Oh, yeah. You really can.

"Let's catch this killer, and we'll go from there. Meanwhile, I can work better if I'm not worrying about you at night."

"Yes. Okay. Sure." She gave him a shaky grin. "I'll hit the store today and have something for you to eat."

"I don't know what time it will be."

"That doesn't matter."

"Remember, don't leave until you hear from me." He brushed a kiss over her mouth. "And you're not sleeping in the guest room."

By the time he was ready to leave, she was dressed and stood in the doorway, waving to him as he jogged to his truck, whistling. He wouldn't have been in such a good mood if he'd known exactly how tied up he'd be for the rest of the day and why.

Chapter Twenty-Five

Dana took her coffee out to the patio and sat in one of the lounge chairs, watching daylight fill the sky and the lingering traces of night fade away. Last night had been unusual to say the least. It was the first time she'd actually *slept* under the same roof with a man. In the same bed. Had outstanding sex. And not been afraid.

Usually, when she shared a bed with someone, they left before morning light, after an unsuccessful attempt to coax a response from her unwilling body. Sometimes, they came back, other times not. But Cole Landry made her feel desired, unafraid, special. He'd been patient and coaxing, stopping and starting even though she knew what it must have cost him in self-control.

A chill raced through her as she wondered for what seemed like the hundredth time how he'd react if she told him the real reason she was here. Why she obviously had a problem with sex.

Although apparently not with him. Her face heated as she remembered the things they'd done. And she'd enjoyed them. But if she shared the details of the attack and the warped years of her life since then, would he pity her? Be disgusted? Think her less of a woman because of her history with men?

Shoving her cell phone in her pocket, she walked down to the corral where the horses were still enjoying the air, doing an elegant cakewalk for her, tails up, manes ruffled in the morning breeze. When she inhaled, the scent was a heady mixture of horseflesh and hay.

For the first time since she was seven, the aroma of hay didn't wrap tentacles of fear around her and take her back to that terrible night. Instead, an unfamiliar feeling of peace stole over her. She wondered what it would be like to live here, in this place. This house.

With Cole.

The ringing of the cell phone in her pocket jerked her out of her reverie.

"Oh, Dana, I'm so glad I caught you." The voice was breathless. "It's Ivy. Ivy Winslow."

"Yes, Ivy. Good morning." Dana hoped the woman had some news for her. She took a deep breath and let it out slowly, wiping her damp palms on her shorts.

"I made some calls, and I've managed to persuade a couple of the others to talk to you. They're a little skittish, but I promised them they could trust you."

A rush of thankfulness spread through Dana. "Ivy, thank you so much. When? Where?"

"This morning. My House. Ten o'clock. Is that convenient? Did I give you enough notice?" Ivy's voice was anxious.

"Absolutely." Her car was parked in front of the house, keys in the ignition. Cole would just have to deal with her leaving. Anyway, he already had cars out on patrol, and she knew they'd spot her and keep an eye on her. "This is a top priority. I'll see you then."

A tiny finger of excitement danced over her skin as she disconnected the call. Her first major breakthrough. Maybe, if she was lucky, she'd have more information for Cole after the meeting.

Cole. She found herself actually anticipating seeing him again tonight, and her body quivered with a new hunger.

****

Gabriella Marquez finally gave in to Stacy's urging and spent the night with her and her husband in their small home. Not that she felt that much safer. She still had to go out on the streets. Shop in stores. Put gas in her car. Move around the town. The county. Whoever was doing this, if he happened to target her, could jump her at any number of places. Any time of day.

She'd slept fitfully during the night, waking often, gripped by some nameless terror. This morning she was more exhausted than when she'd put her head on the pillow. She slipped out of the house while Stacy and Jered were still sleeping, leaving them a note thanking them for their hospitality. She needed to go home, shower and change, so she could get to the office on time.

She loved her work. Her accounting degree was like an invisible medal she wore proudly, having worked two jobs to pay for her schooling and graduating with honors. When Manny Sandoval hired her to work for him she thought she'd won the brass ring. Two years now, and things just kept getting better.

Not so with her personal life. Maybe she was just too picky. Maybe, like Stacy said, she should find some nice guy and settle down.

And who knew? Maybe she would, but not until the monster on the loose was caught. Until then, she could hardly think of anything else.

When she pulled into her parking space behind Manny's little building, she saw that she was the first to arrive. No other cars in the lot yet. Good. She liked having the first few moments of the workday to herself. She could organize things before the routine took over.

As she was locking her car, a truck pulled up behind her. She looked up and smiled at the man sitting behind the wheel.

"Hi, Gaby. You the first one here?"

"Looks that way. Do you need something?"

He got out of his truck and came around to where she was standing. "Manny said he left an envelope for me on the receptionist's desk. As long as I was around, I thought I'd pick it up. Okay if I come in and get it?"

"Oh, sure. Come on in."

But as she turned toward the back door, an arm banded around her waist and a heavy hand slapped a foul-smelling cloth over her face. As she lost consciousness, all she could think was how stupid she'd been to think she was safe anywhere.

****

Cole met Tate very early at the drive-through for a quick breakfast. He was grateful his uncle didn't mind hauling his ass into town practically at sunup so Cole could unload on him. He ran Dana's theories past him, and Tate just listened, stirring his coffee. When Cole finished, he leaned back in the booth, waiting for Tate's response.

"I'm not saying she's right," his uncle said. "But in case she is, she could be a target, too. The wisest and safest thing she can do is get the hell out of here as fast as possible."

Cole snorted. "Don't you think I know that? But I'd have more luck moving a tank."

"You want to move a tank?" John Garrett slid into

the booth next to Tate, holding his mug of coffee.

"He just wants to find a way to get Dana Moretti out of town."

"Oh, well, good luck with that. She's one stubborn woman."

That was the most productive statement to come out of the meeting.

When Cole reached his office, he made a call to get the mess at Dana's house taken care of. He was working his way through his first cup of Grace's poison, sorting reports into a folder for Guardian when Grace buzzed him.

"Your visitor's here," she told him.

"He's not a visitor, Grace." He bit back his impatience. "He's here to help us. Send him on back."

Cole slid a folder across the desk as Scott Clayton lowered himself into one of the chairs.

"Autopsy and crime scene reports, although in both cases the victims were actually killed elsewhere. I've also included all the interviews we've conducted. And thanks for stepping up here."

The thread of apprehension wrapped around his guts began to unwind. Maybe with the Guardian team coming in this morning, they could fast forward on this a little bit before another body turned up. "The quicker we get a handle on this guy, the faster we can identify him."

Scott rested the ankle of one booted foot on the knee of the other, getting comfortable in the chair. "I don't suppose you've got any coffee around this place. I was at the office at six this morning to talk to Zak and Nick before heading out here."

"You drink Grace's coffee at your own risk," Cole

warned. "But if you're willing to chance it, I'll get you some while you take a look at what's in that folder."

"I gather you drink it, and you're still alive," he joked. "So yes, that'll be fine. Thanks."

Gaylen leaned against the counter in the break room, sipping his coffee. "I've got everyone on regular duty until we know what Guardian wants. That okay with you?"

Cole nodded. "That's good. Let me get my bearings with Scott. Then I'd like you to sit in with us."

Gaylen gave him a penetrating look. "Thanks, Cole."

That was all he said, but for Cole, that and the look spoke volumes. Whatever had stood between him and Gaylen Kleist for the past three years—if anything—was gone, and a new bond was forged.

Scott Clayton was still reading reports when Cole set the mug of coffee in front of him.

"Your people do a good job," he said without looking up. "I'm impressed."

Cole relaxed a fraction. "Thanks. They'll be pleased to hear that."

"What would be the best time for me to meet with everyone?"

"Shift change. I already gave them a heads up." Cole sat back down in his chair. "I'd like to include my senior deputy as much as possible when Nick and Zak get here."

Scott looked up at him and grinned. "Competition or cooperation?"

Cole lifted one corner of his mouth. "Cooperation. Hard won."

"Good enough."

The phone on Cole's desk buzzed again. "Yes, Grace."

"Nita Sanchez is here. Do you want her to wait?"

"No. Send her in. Her timing's great." He hung up the phone and looked at Scott. "The coroner's here with the final autopsy report on the latest victim. I thought you'd like to hear it firsthand."

"Thanks." He closed the folder and stood up as the door opened.

Cole made introductions.

Settling into her chair, Nita opened the large envelope in her hand.

"Why don't I just take it from the top?" She looked from one man to the other. "Stop me any time you have any questions."

Cole nodded. "Go ahead."

He noted that, while Scott kept his face deliberately impassive, the shock at the brutality Nita related was evident in his eyes. He was the first to say something when she was finished.

"This is more than an abduction, rape, and murder syndrome." His voice was cold and hard, and all business. It was impossible to miss the controlled fury behind it as he outlined his perception of the killer. "People who do this are not hitting on all cylinders to begin with, but this guy has some very serious mental problems."

"Do you think it's someone who's been treated by a doctor?" Nita asked. "Maybe has a history of mental illness?"

"Possible, but not likely. It's more logical that he's someone you see every day, someone you'd sit down to dinner with or attend a community event with."

"Jesus." The word hissed through Cole's teeth. This was exactly what Dana had said. "You know how scary that is?"

Scott nodded. "I do. Because this is the most dangerous kind of predator to pinpoint. I see a lot of controlled rage in these acts, probably of long standing and an almost pathological desire to cause pain. This isn't about sexual assault. This is about control. It's about inflicting as much torture as possible. His gratification is coming from the suffering of the victim, not the sexual act itself."

"Are you sure?" Cole had to hear it confirmed for his own mind to accept it.

"I think he's right," Nita said before Scott could answer. "The things the killer does are not about pleasure, his or theirs. It's about pain for pain's sake."

"Right." Scott looked to Cole. "And that's what gets him off. He probably keeps them awake, so he can see the terror in their eyes as he abuses them."

Cole ran a hand down his face in an attempt to wipe away the filth that suddenly seemed to cling to his skin. "It's hard to believe someone I maybe see every day is capable of doing these kinds of things."

"We've all said that," Nita murmured.

Scott nodded. "These two crimes occurred close together, too. Something's driving him. Almost as if he has a deadline. Does that mean anything to you? Is there anything different going on around here that might be a catalyst?"

Nita and Cole exchanged a look, and Cole cleared his throat.

"Dana Moretti, the true crime novelist, is in town doing research on an old case. She's been here about a week. Maybe a little more."

Scott lifted an eyebrow. "Moretti? I've read a couple of her books. One of my buddies in the Tampa office worked with her on one of the cases she wrote about."

"What did he say about her?" Nita was perched on the edge of her chair, every line in her body screaming her skepticism about the woman.

"Actually, he had a lot of very good comments. Said she's bright, has good ideas and the mind of a researcher. She knew when to step forward and when to stay out of the way."

Cole relaxed fractionally. "She has a theory," he began, watching Nita carefully for her reaction.

"And?" Scott prompted.

"She's researching a crime spree from twenty-five years ago."

Scott's eyes narrowed. "How bad?"

Cole shifted uncomfortably in his chair. "Pretty bad." He looked at Nita's impassive face again then back at Scott. "For about eighteen months someone was abducting little girls between the ages of five and seven years. He brutally raped each one of them, then killed them."

"How many?" Scott asked.

"How many?"

"Yes. How many children in all?"

Cole fiddled with the folder on his desk. He knew he was about to get jumped on. "Eleven. No, twelve. There was one who survived."

Nita's eyebrows lifted almost to her hairline. "I didn't know there was a survivor."

"No one's really discussed it since then. He

kidnapped a pair of sisters. One was killed, the other survived, but barely. After the funeral, the parents picked up and moved away." Cole looked across the desk at him. "The killings ended when the last little girl survived. I don't know if he stopped because he feared exposure and identification, but as far as I know, no one was ever named. I don't think the child even knows who it was. I have a hunch the man wore a disguise."

"What kind of disguise would induce a child to run off when I'm sure they all had the big lecture about strangers?"

Cole looked at Nita again.

"My lips are sealed," she told him, "but I'll leave if you'd feel more comfortable."

Cole blew out a breath. "No, because I want to ask Scott something that would involve you."

"Let's hear it," Scott said.

A knock sounded at his door before he could begin. Grace opened the door to let Zak and Nick inside then closed it behind her. Cole had been keeping them in the loop, but he gave them a shortened version of where they were.

"Dana found a common thread in the reports as well as the interviews she's been doing with parents," he said. "It's clowns."

"Clowns?" Nita raised an eyebrow.

Zak nodded. "Makes sense. What kid doesn't love a clown? Great method of enticement."

"It seems, in almost every instance, the family was at a community event. Rodeo, picnic, county fair, one of several public events that go on around here all the time. At least two mothers said their daughters were last seen running toward a clown."

"But no clowns with these latest killings."

"No, but she still thinks the killings could be connected. The difference is those were small children. These victims are teenagers. I wanted to get your take on having Nita look at all the old autopsy reports for similarities."

Nick leaned forward in his chair. "Maybe the girls are older because he's older. Maybe his preference has changed over the years. And we don't know what he's been doing all this time, if it is the same perp."

"Dana brought that up, too. Suggested he might have moved his activities to another county to keep from being identified here."

"Entirely possible," Zak agreed, nodding.

Nita looked from one to the other. "But that would mean the perp in the old case wasn't a transient like everyone said. That it's someone who lives around here. Has for a long time."

"That's right. And we have to accept that possibility." Cole turned to Scott. "Okay, then. Can you profile this perp for us?"

"As soon as I have more information. I don't suppose the old files are on computer."

"Unfortunately, no. But I can have someone scan and email them to you."

"Nita and I can start with the new cases until they can bring us the old ones." Scott snatched a pad of paper and pen from Cole's desk and began making notes.

Cole leaned forward. "Next. Zak, can you reach out to your contacts in the FBI to check for similar crimes during the twenty-five-year interim? We could find out if this guy's been killing all this time somewhere else or just in hibernation, brought out by some perceived danger. I don't want any more bodies turning up."

Zak gave him a piercing look. "You really think Dana Moretti's the trigger for this, don't you?"

Cole exhaled slowly. "Yes. I do. I know she's worried about it, too. He may be creating a situation that will overshadow what she's trying to do. Keep us all so busy no one has time to talk to her, and she'll give up and leave."

"Or he could be working up to her," Scott pointed out. "She showed up, and now he's nervous."

A sudden chill skittered through Cole's blood. He'd tried to avoid thinking that very thing, but now, it was staring him in the face. He heard Nita's indrawn breath.

"I've thought of that," he said, his throat suddenly too tight. "I keep hoping I'm wrong, just connecting too many dots."

No one said a thing for a very long minute. Then Scott stood up. "All right. Is there someplace Nita and I can work?"

"The conference room. I'll put a note on the door and keep everyone out. You'll have to break to meet with the deputies because it's the only space we have for that."

"No problem." Scott turned to Cole. "When we're finished, I'd like you and your senior deputy to join us, and we'll see where we're at."

"Okay." A they all exited his office, his cell rang. He pressed Talk. "Hey, darlin'. What's up?"

"Don't be mad at me, but Ivy Winslow called. She's gotten some of the mothers to meet with me at her place. I'm heading there now."

"Dana, listen." His hand tightened on the phone.

"I know what you're going to say, but what can happen to me at the Winslows? And I'll keep checking in with you. Please, Cole? This is a real breakthrough."

"I guess I can't stop you, right?"

"I promise to be careful. Really."

"You call me when you get ready to leave there. You hear?"

"Word of honor." Her voice lowered. "I'll see you tonight."

"No doubt about it."

When he disconnected the call, he couldn't help the smile tugging at his mouth. Something good came out of everything.

Chapter Twenty-Six

Dana knew Cole was unhappy and worried for her safety, but she couldn't let him lock her away until this was over. Especially now when things were beginning to turn her way.

The women seated around the table in Ivy's sunny kitchen wore expressions that were a mixture of fear and defiance. There were five of them, as Ivy had said, and she introduced each one to Dana. Natalie Grimes. Sharon Colton. Letha Milton. Sonja Escobedo. Mila Garza, who was on her list. Two of them, Ivy had told her, never recovered from the crimes, so Dana was surprised they'd agreed to come.

She slipped into the vacant seat at the head of the table, accepted a cup of coffee from Ivy and smiled softly at everyone. But when she brought out her little tape recorder—her phone wouldn't be enough for this meeting—the women froze.

"If you'd rather I didn't use this, I'll shut it off. But I find if I'm taking notes, I'm not paying full attention to what everyone's saying."

"We had it on when I talked with Dana yesterday," Ivy put in. "If there's something on there you want her to erase or not use, all you have to do is ask."

"First of all," Dana told them, "let me assure you, I'm not looking to sensationalize what happened. If any of you have read my books, you'll know I turn them

259

into full length books based on truth, and I'm very matter of fact about things. I don't want you to say anything you don't want to, and I'm not looking to hurt anyone."

"I'd like to ask a question." Natalie's voice was tentative. "If you don't mind."

Dana nodded. "Anything at all."

"Why do you do this? Dig up all this…this"—she opened her hands—"sludge and slime? Make celebrities out of the people who do these awful things?"

It was a question Dana had often been asked. She looked at each woman as she answered. "I'm not trying to glorify them or give them celebrity status. I'm trying to solve a puzzle, to finally give people answers they've never had. And to let them see the rotten underbelly that could easily belong to the person sitting next to them in a restaurant. Maybe help people be more aware of the evil that's out there and how to avoid it."

"It's a wonder you don't have nightmares," Sharon put in.

You don't know the half of it.

"What exactly are you looking for with this book?" Mila asked, slightly defensive. "Haven't we been through enough?"

"Answers for everyone. When a crime is never solved, when there's no resolution, it's very hard to move past the heartache." She let her eyes travel from face to face as she spoke. "I'm hoping to either turn up new evidence, as I've managed to do many times before, or find a different angle. I'm looking for anything that might make people take a new look at things. Maybe even solve the case."

"Do you think this is someone who lived here?"

Sonja wanted to know. "Who maybe still lives here?"

So. Not everyone had bought the party line about an itinerant stranger.

Dana nodded. "I hate to say this, but it's entirely possible."

"What's he been doing all this time, then?" Sonja persisted. "Did he just stop? I heard people who do the kind of things he did can't control themselves."

Dana pursed her lips. "That's not exactly true. They control themselves until the urge builds and builds, then they seek relief again. I have a theory that he's been active someplace else all this time, and we don't know about it."

They peppered her with questions, which she answered the best she could. She didn't want to cut anyone off because it would be hard to get them talking again. This was almost a gift. Usually, she had to light a stick of dynamite to get her interviews completed.

Ivy kept everyone's coffee cups filled and warm cinnamon rolls on the table. The women talked, the recorder hummed, and Dana listened to every word carefully. Some of these women were still holding themselves and their marriages together with frangible glue. Others had managed to center themselves, as Ivy had, for the sake of their other children.

But as Dana had expected, all the stories had one thread in common.

Clowns.

They had all been at events with clowns. The little knot of expectation inside her began to expand.

"Do you think the Chamber would still have records of who they hired?" she asked when the conversation began to wind down.

"I don't know," Letha answered. "But I could find out. I volunteered there back then."

"I'd really appreciate it." Dana handed over her business card with her cell number written on the back. "I hate to push, but the sooner you can do this the better. The sheriff said he might call in the FBI to help on the recent cases, and I'm hoping to interest them into looking at this."

Ivy stopped in the midst of lifting her coffee cup to her lips. "The FBI's here? Really? And you think they'd take a look at these murders after all this time?"

"Not yet, but I think it'll happen, and I hope so. The more information I can give them, the better chance I have."

Letha pushed her chair back and stood up. "I'll go see what I can find out right now. Mila? We rode together. Are you okay with leaving now?"

Mila Garza swallowed the last of her coffee. "Yes. I volunteered back then, too. Maybe I can help you."

The two women made quick goodbyes and hurried out to Letha's car.

"Well." Ivy looked around the table. "Maybe we're finally getting somewhere."

"It would be nice to have some answers after all this time," Natalie said, her face pinched with bitterness. "Maybe Frank and I could figure out a way to talk to each other again. Twenty-five years is a long time to live with a ghost."

"I want to thank you for this," Dana said. "You've helped me immeasurably."

"If you can do anything to find answers for us after all this time, I'll tell you anything you want to know." This from Sharon, who had such sadness in her eyes that Dana wanted to weep for her.

Somehow, in some strange way, it was helping her with her own problems to see other people who'd been affected by what happened. She wasn't alone in her grief or in the damage to families. But she was the only survivor. She was the only one with nightmares so personal that her life was frozen by them.

At least until Cole.

Oh, yes. Cole.

She swallowed a tiny smile.

Chapter Twenty-Seven

"So. Finally, awake." He looked at the woman tied naked to the bed.

Her eyes widened with fear as she looked at him, then around the one room cabin.

"I've been watching you." He laughed when she tugged at the restraints and disbelief mingled with the fear in her eyes. He knew what she was thinking. He was everyone's friend, a pillar of the community. Well respected. His best disguise.

"I think anticipation is part of the enjoyment, don't you, Gaby?" He laughed as she struggled more, but he'd tied her good and tight. "Yes, I've found that to be true. So, I'm going to leave you here for a while, to contemplate the exciting things we're going to do together. But I won't be long."

He started toward the door but turned back. "Oh, and don't count on anyone accidentally finding you. If anyone ever knew about this place, they've long since forgotten. No, you'll be nice and safe until I get back. See you in a little while."

Chapter Twenty-Eight

Cole looked at his watch. Again. Scott, Zak, Nick and Nita had been closeted in the conference room for nearly two hours, and he wondered if they were making any progress reviewing all those cases. If they had something to tell him, they would, but all of this was making him very jittery. Probably because of Dana.

He'd busied himself with paperwork. Making phone calls. Fending off questions from his deputies. Finally, at eleven o'clock he gave it up and told Grace he was going to Harry's. "Call me there as soon as the door to the conference room opens. I can be back here in five."

"Got it."

He clapped his Stetson on as he headed toward the door. "Where's Gaylen?"

"In his office."

Cole stopped in the doorway to the small cubicle. "Care to go to Harry's with me? I'm about to jump out of my skin."

Gaylen shook his head. "I've put off these traffic reports too long. My boss might fire me."

Cole chuckled. "That'll be the day. Okay, I'll be back soon."

The pre-lunch crowd was beginning to fill up the restaurant when he swung open the door to Harry's. He spotted Adele and Tate Bishop in a booth toward the back and headed toward them.

"Twice in one day," he joked with his uncle.

Adele slid over to make room for him, leaning toward him to plant a kiss on his cheek.

"We hardly see you these days, Cole," she complained. "The other night you took off before I could hardly say hello. Do I have to come into town at the crack of dawn like Tate does to have a meal with you?"

He took off his hat and reached around her to put it on the little ledge next to the booth, giving her a quick hug as he did so. "Just as soon as I get this case put to bed, you won't be able to get rid of me."

"You work too hard," she told him.

"The boy's in the middle of a mess, Del," Tate pointed out. "Leave him be. When he gets it put away, he'll need a dinner to patch him back up."

"I'm not used to seeing both of you in town in the middle of the day," Cole commented. He accepted coffee from the waitress then waved her away.

"Adele had an eye doctor's appointment," Tate explained. "She had to have her eyes dilated so she can't drive. I'm playing chauffeur."

"Besides," she grinned, "this way I get a free lunch."

Cole was about to lift his mug when someone stuck a folded newspaper under his nose. He looked up to see John Garrett standing beside him.

"Hot off the presses," the older man told him. "Let me know what you think."

"I will. Thanks." He unfolded the paper and began the front-page story.

"Would you like to join us, John?" Adele asked.

"Maybe just for a minute."

But before he could slide into the booth, another man called to them. Cole looked up to see Jed Nickels standing next to John. The man was nearly as tall as both Tate Bishop and John Garrett, but he'd let himself go somewhat to seed physically when he'd left office. His belly pushed a little too hard against his belt and a double chin softened his jawline. The former sheriff nodded to everyone.

"I stopped by your office, Cole, and Grace told me you were here. I thought I'd see if that security company is doing you any good."

Cole laid the newspaper down on the table. "I'll let you know in a little while. They're going over the crime reports and the autopsies with Nita right now. I got antsy waiting around, so I came over here to get some relief from that poison Grace brews."

He stopped himself just short of mentioning what was happening with the old cases. He didn't want Jed to think they were second-guessing him after all this time until he had something concrete to go on.

"Well, give me a call if you need me." Jed winked at him. "I still might have an idea or two, no matter how old I am."

Cole reached out to shake the old man's hand. "I don't think you'll ever be too old, Jed. And I might just take you up on your offer."

"Say, you know this Moretti woman, Cole?"

Cole forced himself to remain calm. "Yes. I do. Why?"

"She called my house the other day. I hear she's poking into those cases from long ago." He shook his head. "Bad business, Cole. Bad. Making a lot of people angry. You need to tell her to quit before she gets hurt."

Cole clenched his teeth so tightly he was afraid his jaw would crack. "You sending some kind of message, Jed?"

The man looked at him for an endless moment. Then he shook his head. "Just letting you know the climate. Well, I need to get going, then. Have to run a couple of errands before heading home."

"I'm on my way, too," Garrett said. "What do you think, Cole? About the article?"

"Good job from what I read so far. I really appreciate it." He looked at the others. "I asked John to write something that would help keep the town from exploding."

"If I'd known everyone was here, I'd have brought extra copies," John apologized. "I have a stop to make, but if you go by the paper, they'll give you one. Anyone who wants it."

"I might do that," Jed said and dipped his head in a farewell gesture. "Later, folks."

"We have to get going, too," Tate said. "I have some business to take care of this afternoon, and I need to get Adele home first."

"Honey, I'd be happy to go with you," she told him. "No sense doing all that back and forth driving."

"You'd just be bored, sweetheart." He patted her hand. "I'll finish up as soon as I can."

"Boy, do I know how to clear a room or what?" Cole joked. At that moment, his cell phone vibrated, and he looked at the readout. Grace. He clapped the phone to his ear. "Yes?"

"You're being paged," she told him.

"I'm right there."

****

Dana debated stopping at Cole's office to let him know the results of her meeting. No, bad idea. He'd be caught up in a million things. Better to call first. Anyway, she knew he'd expect to hear from her.

She hadn't known whether to laugh or cry when she left the Winslows' and saw a sheriff's patrol car gliding down the road and back again. On the way to town, it passed her, but then she spotted another one.

I'm all right, Cole.

She punched in his cell number, listening as the phone rang four times and then kicked over to voice mail.

"I know you're busy," she said, "but I learned some things this morning you really need to know. Please call me when you get a chance. I'll be…at your place. Working." She made a couple of quick stops before letting herself into his house with the key he'd given her. After changing into shorts and a T-shirt, she fixed a plate with the food she'd just bought at Don's Deli. Settling herself at the kitchen table, she booted up her laptop and went to work.

She tried to keep from checking her watch every ten minutes, hoping Cole would be able to return her call soon. She really wanted to tell him more about the clowns.

****

Scott, Zak, Nick, and Nita wore identical looks when Cole walked into the conference room. Sick. Angry. Even murderous.

"Zak's contact at the Bureau, Clark Lorimer, already has us up and running with the files we faxed." Scott sorted his notes into piles on the conference room table. "I asked—begged—them to get the BAU on a complete profile right away. Like yesterday. This monster's got to be stopped. Now."

"Don't I know it," Cole muttered.

"I also called the office," Nick added. "Sent them the same files and asked them to do a search for cases similar to the old ones here."

"What do you think?" Cole asked Scott, dropping into a chair next to him.

"I think Dana Moretti has a valid point." He looked across the table. "Nita?"

"I've gone through every one of the old autopsy reports, line by line. Too bad there are no photos, but I'm betting old Jed wanted to spare the parents and the community from what's in these things," She motioned to the stack of folders.

"I don't like pointing fingers, but there was a bad bit of police work at the time." Scott looked grim. "Give Cole the short version, Nita."

She cleared her throat and squared the stack of papers in front of her. "There are too many similarities between those cases and the two new ones for it not to be the same guy. Either that or it's an amazing copycat and the Guardians and I aren't buying it."

Cole hid his smile as his friends winced at her new nickname for them.

"Very little of the information about these cases was ever released to the public," Scott reminded him. "The only one who should know the details, the only one capable of duplicating them would be the guy responsible for the first crimes."

Cole rubbed his jaw, a sick feeling lodging in his stomach. "But where has he been all this time?"

"That's the jackpot question. I called Clark and filled him in. He's going to have someone run it through the databases and see what comes up. He promised to call me back this afternoon."

"Good. And thanks."

Scott glanced down at the files in front of him then back up at Cole. "I hate to say this, but if this *is* the same guy from twenty-five years ago, the whole complexion of this case just changed. You know the FBI will probably step in and take over."

"You won't get any argument from me," Cole said. "I still believe Dana is his ultimate target." He told them about the damage to Dana's house the day before. "If he's working up to her, all the more reason I want this bastard caught yesterday."

Zak narrowed his eyes. "Is there something more here we should know?"

Cole shrugged. "Not a topic for discussion. Whatever, it won't interfere with my focus on the case. Go ahead with what you were saying, Scott."

Scott began ticking off a list on his fingers. "With each of his victims, he's escalating the age. Leanne was sixteen, Shannon was older. Not much, but older. The next one's going to be older still. Again, he's establishing a pattern."

"Jesus." Cole scrubbed his hands over his face. "How do I possibly protect every teenager in the county?"

"You can't. And even if the FBI sent every man on the roster here, they couldn't do it, either. The best you can do is get the message out to every young girl not to get in a vehicle or go near anyone except her parents. No matter how well she knows the man. And with the escalation in age, you might need to expand the parameters."

"I'll have to figure out how best to do that without scaring the shit out of everyone and causing a riot." Cole pulled out his ever-present small notebook and began jotting things down. "I can certainly call the schools. They're back in session today, and the principals can send notices to all the teachers."

"John Garrett could make up flyers to post around town," Nita suggested.

Cole nodded. "And the post office can deliver them with the mail, too."

"Will they do that?" Scott asked. "The post office, I mean."

Cole was about to answer him when there was a knock on the door. Grace rushed in. Her face was so white he thought she might be sick, and she collapsed into the nearest chair.

"Grace? What is it? Are you okay?"

She had to swallow twice before she could get any words out. "Stacy Corona just called in. Gaby Marquez is missing."

"Oh, sweet Jesus," Nita breathed.

Cole went to the door and yelled loud enough to be heard on the other side of the county. "Gaylen. Haul ass in here. And bring some water for Grace."

He sat back down and took Grace's hand. Nita had moved up to the chair next to her.

"Grace, listen to me." He kept his voice low and even. "This could be a false alarm. She's a lot older than the others. This could be something different altogether."

She shook her head. Gaylen had appeared with a

glass of water and handed it to her. Her hands were shaking so badly she almost spilled it.

"Gaby called me last night. She was scared to death. I tried to tell her she didn't have anything to worry about." Grace took a deep breath and let it out slowly, making an obvious effort to keep herself together. "She's so much older than Leanne and Shannon that I didn't even think of her as a target. But she looks a lot younger." She raised her eyes to Cole's. "Do you think he's killing them based on age? Shannon was older than Leanne, and Gaby a lot older than Shannon."

An unpleasant thought tried to work its way through Cole's brain, but he couldn't quite make it come to life. "What else, Grace?"

"She was scared. She wanted to leave town until this maniac is caught, but Stacy talked her into spending the night with them. I said she could move in with me for a while, but I thought she was seeing bogeymen in the closet." She set the glass on the table and dropped her head into her hands. "Oh, God. What have I done?"

"Grace?" Cole prodded. "How did Stacy know she's missing?"

"Gaby's boss, Manny Sandoval called her. He didn't get to the office until almost noon. Gaby's car was in the parking lot, but she wasn't in her office. The dizzy receptionist said she hadn't seen her and didn't know anything about her car. Manny called Stacy, and she called here. Oh, Cole. I just know he's got her."

Cole looked at Nita. "Can you take care of her?"

"Of course. Do what you have to."

Cole introduced his chief deputy to Scott, Nick,

and Zak. "Gaylen, how many deputies can we get here right now?"

The answer was immediate. "Fifteen. Not counting you and me."

"Count us in," Zak said. "I'll call Reno. I'm sure he'll send in more troops."

"Okay." Cole looked back at Gaylen. "Get everyone on the horn right now. Start searching the area around Gaby's house. This guy has left the bodies in convenient places, so we need to cover the area sector by sector."

"I'll get it done." Gaylen had already picked up the dispatch microphone to send out a message to everyone on the road.

Scott looked up at Cole. "You'd better call Dana Moretti and let her know what's happened. There's a possibility this guy is escalating. If there's any chance she's next on his list, she needs to be warned."

"Right, right. Okay. Give me a few minutes, and we'll get started."

Back in his office, Cole closed the door to his office and sat down behind his desk, taking a moment to pull himself together before pulling out his cell phone. He'd set it on vibrate when he returned to the office so he wouldn't be interrupted, but now, he saw Dana had tried calling him. He listened to the message, then pressed the button to return the call.

"Oh, good. You got my message." Her voice was breathless, touched with suppressed excitement.

"Yeah. Just now. Sorry, darlin'. I turned it off while I was in with Nita and the guys and just now turned it back on. Listen, Dana—"

"I wanted to tell you about the meeting Ivy set up

for me. Cole, I have some information that I think is very important."

"Can you hold on with that for a minute?" He forced a calm into his voice he didn't feel. "Right now, you need to know there's been another abduction. Gaby Marquez. Twenty-six years old."

"What? But that's way beyond his age preference."

"Yeah, except for one thing. Scott agrees that your appearance here opening the old cases might have been the trigger. If so, you could very well be his ultimate target, and he's working his way up to you in steps."

"Oh, God." Silence hummed across the connection for seconds.

"I'm worried about you. You're at my place, right?"

"Yes. I said I'd come back here."

"I want you to stay there until this madman is caught. If you need anything from your house, I'll get it for you."

"Okay."

There was a long pause and he wondered if she'd just hung up. When she spoke again, her voice sounded small and shaky. "I have something to tell you, Cole. And not just what came out of this morning's meeting. I…know how busy you are, but I don't want to tell you this over the phone."

His heart thudded. Was she finally going to tell him her secret? "Can it wait, darlin'? We've got every available resource including me on this search for Gaby."

"Please, Cole? I know how urgent Gaby's situation is, but this, um, may help you."

If he knew anything, it was that with her

background, she wouldn't ask this of him, in this situation, unless it was really urgent.

He raked his fingers through his hair. Gaylen would just have to take over for a bit. "Okay. I'll leave right now. And Dana?"

"Yes?"

"Do not let anyone in but me."

"But Cole, this is *your* place. No one's going to come after me here."

"Humor me, okay? I'll call you as soon as I turn into the driveway."

"Okay. Hurry."

Chapter Twenty-Nine

He could tell his victim had been fighting to get free while he was gone. Her wrists were raw and bloody where she'd been pulling against the ropes. Tears streaked her face. He leaned down and licked them off. He loved their tears. They were better than the sweetest candy.

She tried to pull her face away, but he clamped his hand around her jaw.

"Don't do that, or I'll have to punish you. Yes, I know you're a good girl. That's your appeal. That's why I chose you. And why I'm going to enjoy it so much."

And then he began the song in a high-pitched voice. "There was a little girl, who had a little curl, right in the middle of her forehead…"

Behind the tape, she screamed into the silence.

Chapter Thirty

"Nita called Grace's husband to tell him she'd be bringing his wife home," Gaylen said as Cole made his way to the front door. "She explained the situation to him."

"Tell her thanks."

"I also made more copies of the maps we used the other day when we searched for Shannon," he went on. "Same sectors and all and handed them out to the deputies. But we're starting close to her home."

"Can you guys hold the fort for a few? I have a quick errand to run, but I won't be gone long."

"It must be urgent to pull you away now," Scott commented.

"It is," he growled. "Trust me."

He floored it on the way to his place, and in the driveway, he called Dana from his cell. "It's me. Look out the window. Then you can open the door."

She was standing just inside, holding her hands together, but she couldn't hide the trembling. He pulled her into his arms, and she folded into them, letting him wrap himself around her. Tremors racked her entire body. She was coming unglued, falling apart before his eyes, and he ached so badly for her. If only he could take all the pain for her himself.

After a while, he lifted her in his arms and carried her into the living room, sitting her down on the couch.

"I think a shot of whiskey is called for again."

When he brought it back to the living room, he set it on the side table, picked Dana up, and sat down with her in his lap. Then he held the glass to her lips.

"Drink. Not too fast, but get it all down."

"A-are you trying to get me drunk?" She tried to force a grin.

"Darlin', when I'm trying to get you drunk, you'll know about it. Now, start sipping."

It took a while, but she finally got most of it down. By the time she finished, she'd stopped shaking.

At last, she straightened up and looked at him. "I should have told you this before now." She moistened her lips with the tip of her tongue. "If I hadn't waited this long, maybe you wouldn't be out looking for Gaby Marquez. And maybe Leanne and Shannon wouldn't be in the morgue."

"I'm sure you had a good reason for holding back."

"Only my own screwed up mind." She let out a breath. "I've buried this deep inside me for so long, but it's past time for me to do this. The monster's loose again. And you need everything you can get to catch him."

"Dana?" He tilted her face up to his and kissed her softly, gently. "Whatever it is, it's okay. Understand that."

She dropped her gaze to her lap. "I can't look at you when I tell you this. Can you just…hold me?"

"For as long as you want. Forever." He tightened his arms around her.

"You might not feel that way when you hear what I have to say. Please, please, please try not to hate me for not telling you before."

"I couldn't possibly hate you for anything." He kissed the top of her head, his hand still stroking her arm.

He had no idea how to calm her except to cradle her against him and stroke her body, hoping his touch reassured her. His fingers sifted idly through the corn silk of her hair before his hand lowered again, following the line of her rich curves, so unexpected on such a slender body.

She took a deep breath. "The first thing I have to tell you is my real name isn't Dana Moretti. It's Carrie Nolan. I'm sure you recognize it."

Cole did his best to hide the shock he felt, but he saw the realization in Dana's eyes that he knew all too well who Carrie was. Their hazel was now greener, the thick lashes unable to hide the pain that still lived inside her.

The story she launched into chilled him to the bone. It took a long time because once she started, every detail she'd kept tucked away in her secret places came spilling out. As she described what had happened in the barn, Cole was afraid he might be sick. He was shocked to his very soul, agonizing for Dana at the nightmare she'd endured. For the first time in his life, he knew what it was like to actually want to murder someone.

But he forced himself to push his emotions aside. This wasn't about him. This was about Dana. So, he let her talk, and he held her and rocked her and soothed her until, at last, she got it all out. Every detail. Every impression of the man. Things she'd probably buried all this time.

"Jesus," he breathed. "No wonder you've been

afraid of men. And sex."

"I've never been able to really talk about it in detail with anyone." She had a slight catch in her voice, and silent tears ran down her cheeks. "Not even the multitude of therapists I've seen since it happened. It's like there were certain things I was too ashamed for anyone to know about me."

"Ashamed?" His square jaw tensed. A muscle ticked in his cheek. "Why the hell would you be ashamed? You did nothing wrong."

In a small voice, she said, "I didn't save my sister."

Silently, Cole cursed the pedophile, calling him every vile name he could think of. Swearing at the damage he'd done to an innocent child. Many innocent children.

"It wasn't your fault, Dana. You have to believe that. For myself, I'm damn glad you survived so you could come into my life." He kissed the top of her head. "Very glad."

She chewed her bottom lip. "I've had the strangest feeling since the first day I got here. Cole, I think he's here, and he's seen me. Recognized me. It's been like he's watching me, waiting for something. As if he was finally going to finish me off after all these years. That's why that thing at my house freaked me out so much."

"I'm pretty damn sure this bastard never thought Carrie Nolan would ever come back here. Seeing you must have scared him shitless." He brushed her hair back from her face. "He's wondering when you'll look at him and make the connection."

"If he really wants to kill me, why would he trash my house and tell me to leave? If I did go, I'd be out of his reach."

"To scare you. Put you off your guard, so he could get closer to you. The thing he didn't expect was that I'd bring you here to stay with me."

She frowned. "Do you think he knows?"

"I didn't exactly broadcast it, but you know yourself this is a small community. Just in case, I'll have the deputies come by regularly while they're out covering the county.

"I should have insisted my parents let me talk to the police." She was trembling again. "I could have done something."

"Are you kidding? You were a child. Dana, listen to me." He tightened his hold, his cheek pressed to her hair. "None of this was your fault. None of it."

She leaned her head against his chest again, her tears soaking his shirt. "But I didn't save Kylie. I was the big sister, and I didn't help her."

Oh, god. How much guilt had eaten her up all these years? How had she even survived? No wonder she lived with a wall around herself, working every day not to fall apart, seeking salvation as she helped others in similar situations.

"You were seven years old, darlin'. You could barely save yourself."

She shook her head against his chest. "No, I was the one who told her we could go. It's my fault, Cole. My parents always knew it."

"Wait." He tipped her face up so he could see it. With his thumb, he wiped away the tears glistening on her cheeks. "Are you telling me your parents blamed you for what happened?"

"Not in so many words. But I was the older sister. I

knew better than to go off with strangers."

"Oh, Dana. What a mess people made of your life." He kissed the top of her head. "I'm thinking your parents didn't know how to handle their own grief, so they dumped it on you. But never, ever blame yourself for what happened."

"It's been so hard," she whispered.

"I know, but now, it will get easier."

"Maybe. I think telling you was the worst of it. Now…"

"Yes, darlin'. Now." He sat up with her and pulled his cell phone from its clip on his belt. "Give me just a minute here. I need to check in with Gaylen."

"Will you tell him? About me?"

"Not until I get back to the station. I don't want to take a chance someone might overhear the conversation."

"You know I never actually saw him. When I came to, I was blindfolded." She swiped at her damp cheeks again. "But I remember the man had an odor about him. Something I can't identify. Something really strong that made my eyes water."

"Maybe from the clown greasepaint he was wearing?" Cole ventured.

"No." She shook her head. "I've smelled greasepaint since then. This was more like cologne, but not one I've ever come in contact with since then. And he was singing."

Cole stared at her. "Singing? Singing what?"

"That's the problem," she cried. "I can't remember it. I pushed it so far out of my mind it won't come back."

"Do you remember anything about it?"

"No." She shook her head vehemently. "I never wanted to hear it again. I guess I've done too good a job blanking it out."

"Who could blame you? Okay, let me just check in and see if there's any update. Let Gaylen know I'm on the way back."

When he finished the call, he stood up, taking her with him and setting her on her feet. His mouth brushed against hers. "I don't want to leave you, but I have to."

"I know, I know. Gaby's out there somewhere, and you have to find her." She leaned into him. "I wish I'd had the courage to tell you about this sooner."

"Dana. Honey. It's all right," he assured her. "It took a lot of courage to tell me at all."

"But if I'd told you earlier, maybe none of this would have happened," she protested, misery tightening her voice.

"Your arrival may have stuck a pin in him, but we don't think he's been idle all this time, either. Don't beat yourself up over it."

"I just want to have this over with once and for all," she sniffed, clutching at his shirt. She rubbed her cheek against the curls of dark chest hair peeking out over the vee of his shirt, somehow taking comfort from them. "To stop the killing and put him away, so I can try to be a normal woman. That's all. Is that asking so much?"

"Of course not." He tightened his arms around her.

Although he still heard a tremor in her voice, she sounded stronger than before, as if getting this all out was cathartic for her. And maybe it was.

She shivered in his arms. "Cole, what am I going to do?"

"Stay right in this house until we catch him. And that's an order. I don't intend to let anything happen to you."

Suddenly, she smacked her forehead with her palm. "The news about Gaby drove everything else out of my mind. I called you to begin with because of the meeting this morning. Cole, every one of those women mentioned clowns being at the event where their children disappeared. Just like with Kylie and me. The same situation. When I checked back over the reports, all but two of them mentioned clowns. But I couldn't find where anyone had ever checked on that."

"You're right." Again, he felt irritation at the sloppy police work. "I looked, but I couldn't find anything, either. Pissed me off."

"Shouldn't that have been the first thing they jumped on?"

Cole snorted. "And let word get out that Salado County was letting a murdering pedophile run loose? Besides, the county commission and the chamber were the ones who hired the clowns. No one wanted to point fingers at them on this."

"Two of the women this morning who used to volunteer at the chamber said they'd try to find the old records," she told him. "See if there was any information, maybe get us some contacts."

Cole's pulse jumped. A lead? After all this time? "When are they supposed to get back to you? We're running out of time here."

"Let me see if I can reach either of them right now." She found her cell phone and tried both numbers. "Busy," she told him. "But I'll keep trying."

"Good." He smoothed his hand over her silky dark

blonde hair.

"Are you checking for similar cases?" she asked.

"As we speak."

She sucked in a deep breath and let it out. "Tell people whatever you have to in order to get this monster. Just get him. Now." She swallowed hard. "Cole, thank you for being so understanding about…everything."

"Understanding? God! I'm amazed at the courage it took for you to live your life. For you to tell me what happened. And I thank you for trusting me enough to do this."

She wrapped her arms around herself, as if that was all that was holding her together. "Will you let me know what's going on?"

"Whenever I get a minute, I'll call you. That's a promise. I'll be checking on you anyway, just to make sure you're okay." He cupped her chin. "And do not let anyone in this house except me unless I call you first. I don't care who it is. I think we both agree you could be high on his list, and I don't want to take any chances with you. I wouldn't leave you now if I didn't have to. As soon as I get to the office and see what's what, I'll get someone over here. In the meantime, stay locked up tight."

"Got it, Sheriff." She gave him a weak smile.

At the door, he turned to her, needing to touch her once more before he left. Her face was pale, the skin taut over her cheekbones, and her hazel eyes showed the fear she was trying so hard to hide. He stood with his hands on her shoulders, urgency pulling at him, but he allowed himself one last kiss. A deep one. A hungry one. She welcomed his tongue gladly and molded her body to his, her soft breasts pushing into his chest.

His cock swelled, and his balls tightened with need. He wished he could forget the ugliness he had to hurry back to, take her to his bedroom, strip her naked, and make luxurious love to her all night long.

With a tremendous effort of will, he broke the kiss. "I'll be back sometime before the night is over."

She touched her fingertips to her lips and pressed them against his. "I'll be waiting."

He leaped down the porch steps with one bound and jogged to his truck. In the midst of depravity and horror, his heart had tumbled right out of his chest and lost itself to that woman. Amazing, what life hits you with when you least expect it.

He was five minutes out from the station when Gaylen radioed him to change course.

"We found her." His voice was heavy with sadness and anger. "Not too far from her house." He gave Cole the address.

"Didn't we search there first thing?"

"Right after we got the word. But it was still light out. Apparently, he waited until it got dark and then dumped her."

Cole wondered if he'd ever get rid of the sick feeling consuming him. "On my way. Listen, do we have anyone you can send to my house?" He paused. "Dana's there, and I'm not sure it's a good idea to leave her alone."

"I'll do my best to cut someone loose," the chief deputy said. "But you know how thin we're staffed, and this new killing isn't helping."

"I know, I know. Okay. See you in a few."

The area at the end of Gaby Marquez's street was

filled with cars and people. Scott, who was standing off to one side, motioned him over.

"I called the SAC and told him the shit has really hit the fan. He's sending four more agents out here, two of them with a forensics van."

"Good. Thanks. We can use all the scientific help you can give us. Mickey and Andi are good, but they're only trained in the basics. Anything we can't handle, we usually ship to Austin." Cole took off his Stetson, raked his hands through his hair, and clapped the hat back on. "I hope to hell they get here soon."

"Trust me. They're probably driving like bats out of hell. I've ridden with them before." The agent pulled a folded sheet of paper from his pocket. "We got a fax back from Quantico with their preliminary profile. Want the short version?"

"Please." Cole was listening but he kept his eyes on the activity around him.

"White male, probably between sixty and seventy years old. The age is based on the twenty-five-year span between crimes," Scott explained. "He's friendly. Maybe even very outgoing. He likes attention—the clown disguise fits his personality. Nice guy, kids love him, he's well liked and well known in the community. He moves easily among the population without sending out any warning signals."

"Jesus. That could be any one of hundreds of men in Salado County."

"This one's sexual needs give him a lot of repressed rage because he can't satisfy them easily. He almost resents the victims for making him feel the way he does. That's why he abuses their bodies so badly."

"I wonder what started him off in the first place?'

"Good question. Usually people with these kinds of problems had a trigger in their early life. Something that still torments them and drives them. Could be a victim of abuse himself." Scott shuffled some papers in front of him. "Listen, I hope you don't mind, but I put one of your deputies going through the voter rolls pulling out the names of anyone we could remotely consider. He'd be more familiar with the people around here."

"No, that's fine. Whatever you want. I should just tell everyone you're in charge anyway."

Scott flapped his hand in the air. "No need. This is working just fine. Besides, your people seem to have a healthy respect for you. I don't want them sticking pins in voodoo dolls because they think I'm discounting you. Anyway, Quantico says he's ramping up his timeline and it won't be long before he chooses his next victim."

"Next victim." Cole swallowed a sour taste in his mouth. "Fucking shit."

"Double that. So. What did you learn from Miss Moretti?"

Cole motioned Scott to move away from the activity where they couldn't be heard. In short, clipped sentences he gave him every detail of Dana's story, leaving nothing out.

Clayton was stunned. "My God, she's lived with that all these years. It had to take a lot of courage for her to come back here and try to face it head on."

"Yeah, and I have to say, no one was too friendly about it at first. Me included. The word asshole comes to mind."

Scott rubbed the back of his neck. "When people

hide a secret that long, they're ten times more resistant to someone pulling out their dirty laundry. Good for her for sticking with it."

"She also told me a couple of things that weren't in the reports since none of the other victims survived." He filled Scott in about the singing and the odor. "She's lived with this so long. Catching him is the only way she'll have peace of mind."

"Christ, a singing predator. Well, it wouldn't be the first time. And I've certainly heard stranger things." He frowned. "I wonder what kind of unusual smell she's talking about. If it was something common, I'd think she'd have been able to identify it."

"I don't know. Not greasepaint. I asked. She thought maybe some kind of cologne."

Scott pulled out his cell. "Let me call Clark again and ask them to run a program on predators who sing. Sing, for Christ's sake!"

When he finished the call, he said, "They think they've found the answer to what our perp has been doing all this time. It's a stretch, but it's a good possibility."

Cole lifted an eyebrow. "More cases like the old one?"

"Maybe." Scott rubbed his hand over his face, now bristly with end of day growth. "They've been trying to track down a human trafficking ring they got a tip on. These perps pick up girls in Mexico, ages ten to fifteen, and bring them over the border to the buyers. Then they're resold all over the world. Nobody's going to notice if a bunch of illegal immigrants disappear."

Cole's stomach pitched and rolled. Too much about this case was making him sick. In the military, he sometimes had to do extreme things to survive and to protect his country. Things that turned his stomach. But this? This was just pure evil.

"You think our unsub is involved in this?"

"Seems like a logical market for him," Scott pointed out. "He'd have the pick out of each group for his own warped amusement. Not quite as tasty as the little ones but close enough."

"Jesus, Mary, and Joseph. This animal needs to be taken out and shot."

"If the law would let us, I'd pull the trigger."

"The law." Cole snorted. "At times, it's hard to uphold something that protects animals like this."

"They're still trying to pinpoint a specific location for the exchange of 'merchandise.' They get a lead on one place, and the ring moves to another. Or they change the days or the time."

Cole turned as he heard his name called and saw Gaylen coming toward him, his face grimmer than ever. Whatever he had to say, Cole knew it wouldn't be good news.

"This will kill Grace." Gaylen shook his head. "I can hardly get over this one myself. Gaby lives in the house she grew up in, right there at the end of River Street." He pointed. "You can see it's the last one on the block. There's nothing past it except these fields and trees."

"Perfect for our killer."

"Whoever this bastard is," Gaylen went on, "he somehow managed to drop her way out in those fields—in that copse of trees just like the other two—and sneak away without being seen. But here's the worst part. He called Stacy pretending to be Gaby and whispered, 'I'm home. Help me.' Then he hung up."

"Bastard." Cole spat the word out.

"Unfortunately, Stacy didn't take time to call us, just hauled ass with her husband over there. When no one answered the door, she opened it with a key she has. But the house was empty, so they started looking around outside. Her husband's the one who found the body."

"Shit." Cole was running out of appropriate words.

"Andi and Mickey have got the scene roped off, as you can see, and Nita's working with the body. Just waiting for the feds to get here."

Scott pulled out his cell. "Let me check with Clark to see how close my people are."

"He held her somewhere else before killing her," Gaylen went on. "Probably some isolated building. We just need to find out where. I've got one of the deputies back at the office pulling up property lists and any other list they can find that would give us some kind of hint."

"Maybe I should ask for the chopper," Scott put in. "It's dark now, but if you can give me any locations to start with, I can get the bird up at first light. If this guy's got a hidey hole somewhere, who knows what else we'll find there. Especially if it ties in with the other thing I told you about."

"Do it," Cole said.

As he moved slowly toward where the body lay, he heard Scott giving information to someone and putting in his request.

Chapter Thirty-One

He managed to get home and into the house without any questions. He was careful about the excuses he used and always meticulous about cleaning himself up before he left his cabin.

Tonight had been the trickiest, but luckily, it was dark out and no one was looking out their windows. He laughed thinking of the irony of tonight's delivery. For years, folks had complained about how dark it was on that street. Hell, he'd been one of the people to lobby the city council to put in a light at the end of the block. Now, he was glad they'd dragged their heels.

His own house was quiet, the only light coming from the bedroom. He'd make himself known, report on his nonexistent meeting, then help himself to a beer. Lord knew he needed one.

But as he made his way back to the kitchen and took a bottle from the fridge, a new rush of excitement coursed through him. Tomorrow would be his finest hour. Tomorrow his prize would be Dana Moretti. Little Carrie Nolan herself.

And once he had her, there would be no rushing. He intended to take a great deal of time with his little flower. No quick session in the truck with her. Like Leanne and Shannon. Oh, no. He'd bring her to the cabin where he could take his time with her. He was going to enjoy himself, and he'd make certain she did, too.

Twenty-five years ago, she hadn't cried out like the others. She'd been quiet, defiant, beautiful. Tomorrow, he would make her cry out in all kinds of ways. He was damn hard thinking about how she'd scream and yell. Maybe, if she was really good, he'd take the tape off her mouth and let her beg.

The idea of his little Carrie begging him to stop hurting her almost made him come, and he had to grab hold of the counter to hold himself together.

Oh, he wanted her. Wanted her like he'd never wanted her when she was just a little bloom. Now, she was a full blossom, a flower that had matured just for his pleasure. He could hardly wait to see her again face to face. To watch her eyes grow wide with knowledge and fear when his hands wrapped around her throat and his thumbs squeezed the life from her.

At last, he would finish the job he'd left undone twenty-five years ago.

Chapter Thirty-Two

The scene near Gaby's house was organized chaos. The FBI agents had finally arrived and two men in dark blue FBI issued coveralls immediately went about their job with neat efficiency. Additional lights illuminated every area of the scene. In the center of it all was Gaby's broken body. Blood-stained and bruised, it bore the signs of unbelievable sexual torture. Like the others, she'd been arranged with her head at an angle to show her broken neck.

Cole walked off into the shadows, pulled out his phone, and made the call he'd been putting off.

"We found Gaby," he told Dana when she answered, not knowing any way to soften the news. He heard the hiss of an indrawn breath.

"Please tell me she was still alive."

"I wish I could, darlin'. I wish I could."

"Oh, Cole." He could hear the tears in her voice. "I am so very, very sorry. How is her family taking it?"

"She doesn't have much family," he told her. "Her parents are both dead. They were killed in an auto accident a few years ago. No sisters or brothers. All she has is Grace and her uncle. And her friend Stacy, who found her."

"Oh, my God." Dana's voice trembled. "How did that happen?"

Cole explained about the phone call, telling her

how the perp had lured Stacy over to the house. "Nita called an ambulance for her, and she's in the hospital, heavily sedated, under the watchful eye of her distraught husband and Barry Engler, Nita's clinic partner."

"That poor woman. Both of them." She paused. "Are you still there? At the scene?"

"Yes. I wanted to let you know what happened and tell you again to be sure every door and window in the house is locked. Do not go out unless it's with me or one of my deputies. Or someone I call you about."

"I can promise you that. Believe me."

"I'll cut someone loose as soon as I can. I promise."

"I'm fine. Really. They all have more important things to do right now, and I don't plan to go anywhere."

He wished he could be there with her, comforting her. Taking comfort *from* her. But he knew he'd be tied up here and then back at the station for hours. The FBI was present now in full force, and everyone would have to be brought up to speed.

"I have no idea what time I'll be through here. I was planning to head home when we're done but that could be really late."

"Cole, I can assure you I don't think I'll be doing much sleeping tonight." A pause. "I'll be waiting for you."

A warm feeling coursed through him. "Then I'll see you whenever."

"Cole?"

"Yes, darlin'?"

"Be careful."

"Always." He clicked off.

Eventually, he left Scott and Gaylen supervising the scene and went back to the station. He was weary in every bone in his body and the night was far from over. One of the rookies was manning dispatch and coordinating everyone out on the road. He sought out another young deputy, the one who was searching records for isolated buildings in the county.

"Find anything?" he asked.

"It's kind of hard to tell, Sheriff," she explained. "I have to pull up the property listings, then the topographical maps and try to match properties with aerial locations."

"Get as much as you can," he told her. "The FBI will have a chopper here first thing in the morning to start a search by air. I'd like to have a list going by then."

"I'm working on it. The problem is, the county's just full of ranches, big ones that have all these line shacks and cabins that haven't been used in years. Mostly people have forgotten about them."

"That's just the kind of place our guy would look to use." He sighed. "I know it's a tedious job. Let me know when you need a break."

"Yes, sir, but I'm fine." She turned back to the computer.

He sat down behind his desk, put his feet up, tilted back his head and tried to sort out everything they knew. He ran down a quick mental list of the ranchers whose property held the most out-buildings and line-shacks. It was actually fairly small.

The first three people were, to his mind, the unlikeliest of the lot—Tate, Jed Nickels, and John

Garrett. John was more into the newspaper than the ranch these days, leaving it to his two sons. Besides, he'd been in town near or with Cole or Dana when at least one of the murders was taking place. That had his mind circling back to Jed and, much as he hated it, his Uncle Tate. Both men used ranch managers now to do most of the work, especially now that both of them were pushing seventy.

He cringed as the words of the profiler came back to mind, 'sixty to seventy years of age.' But Jed and Tate were the last men in the community who would ever get involved in something like this. They were pillars of the community. Visible and popular with everyone. He couldn't see either of them committing these heinous crimes. Or, for that matter, being involved in a sex slave business.

Reaching in his drawer, he pulled out the current list of members of the chamber of commerce in High Ridge. Even people who didn't live in town belonged to it. It was the ruling social organization of the entire county.

Flipping it open, he began slowly going through the list, using a pen to tick off names he'd go back to later. He was still engrossed in the list when there was a tap at his door and Scott came in, closing the door behind him. He dropped into a chair across from Cole, looking weary enough himself.

"I'd give a year's pay for five minutes alone with this bastard when we catch him," he spat. "This goes beyond sickness. This guy is insane."

"Is Nita finished with the body?"

"Only the first pass. I followed her to Drowdy's so I could hear what she had to say. The forensics men are still at the scene and the other two are waiting with Nita until she's finished." He raked his fingers through his hair. "Cole, this time it's the worst. I've never seen anything like it, and I've seen a lot."

"He's escalating, and I think he's getting desperate."

"I think he's losing control," Scott added, "and won't be satisfied until he gets hold of Dana. Then he'll stop. She's his final target."

"Here's another guess for you." Cole showed him the book in his hands and explained what they were doing about properties. "Think about this. If he's the one skimming from the human deliveries to feed his lust, he has to have a place to take them. A place to hide the bodies when he's done with them."

Scott stared at him. "I must be more tired than I thought. That should have occurred to me."

"We need not only an isolated outbuilding, but a place to dump bodies without drawing attention. Or wild animals." He dropped his feet to the floor and strode to the door. "Kelly!"

The young deputy doing the property search turned at the sound of his voice.

"Yes, sir?"

"We need you to check locations for one more thing. Wells. Not the kind with the pump above ground but the old ones. Those not used anymore. Is there such a place to look?"

"Yes, sir. The water district should have a list going back fifty years. They've been tracking those old wells to seal them."

"Good enough, Deputy. Don't let me keep you."

She grinned at him. "Yes, sir."

299

He was still standing in his doorway when the front door to the station opened and Harry and Wanda came in carrying a huge coffee urn and a stack of boxes.

"Thought y'all could use some decent coffee," Harry announced. "It's all made and hot. We just need to plug this thing in. And that's all the donuts and rolls I had. Lean pickings for breakfast tomorrow, but they'll survive."

"Harry, if you weren't so ugly, I'd kiss you," Cole said.

They carried everything into the conference room and set it up on the long table. He and Scott each drew a cup of coffee and went back to his office. The two men drank in silence, just staring at each other across the desktop.

The hot brew settled through Cole's system, washing away some of the fatigue and giving his brain a kick-start. But he felt as if he'd been up for days and discouragement sat heavy on his shoulders.

"Why don't you take a break?" Scott suggested. "My guess is you've been short on sleep since the Pritchard girl's body was found. Gaylen's going to need a break pretty soon and if you're dead on your feet, you won't be able to give it to him."

"I don't know if I feel right about that," Cole protested.

"Why not? Things are wrapping up at the Marquez house, and everyone will be back here before long. I'm going to the High Ridge Motel to crash myself." He gave a short laugh. "Maybe if I close my eyes as soon as I walk in, I won't have to look at that godawful spread. So go on. I'll need you back here when the chopper arrives."

"You're right." Cole drained his cup, crushed it, and tossed it in the trash. "I think I'll do that. I'll get someone to spell Kelly on the computer, check in with Gaylen, then get an hour or two of sack time."

He stopped to call the hospital and learned Stacy Corona was still under heavy sedation. She'd woken up once and was so hysterical Barry had to put her under again. Her husband hadn't left her side, sitting in the chair next to the bed clutching her hand in a death grip.

"I'll check back in the morning," Cole said before hanging up.

The circle of lives being damaged by this whole thing just kept widening.

After telling the deputy handling dispatch to call him in four hours, he finally headed out to the parking lot. He had to force himself not to speed as he headed for his house. In front of the house, he speed dialed Dana's number on his cell.

She picked up at once. "Cole?"

"There better not be any other man calling you at this hour of the night." He tried to inject a little humor in his voice.

She laughed softly. "Where are you?"

"In front of the house." He beeped his horn twice.

"I'll be right there."

He wanted to see her. Needed to see her. He felt steeped in filth and needed her presence to cleanse him.

The front door opened, and she stood there in her sleep shirt, holding the phone to her ear, a smile playing on her lips. "You gave the right signal, so get yourself inside."

He was out of the truck and on the porch in seconds, stuffing his phone into his pocket. As if they'd been doing it forever, he reached for her and she wound her arms around his neck. The kiss was so full of fire he thought they would burn up just from touching each other. Lips and tongues and teeth collided. Hands explored bodies that pressed hard against each other. When they broke the kiss, they were both breathless.

"I think the first order of business is a shower," she told him. "Let's get the traces of the crime scene off of you."

How had she known that was exactly what he needed? He let her lead him to the bathroom—*his* bathroom. Her small hands tugged at his clothes, unbuttoning buttons, unzipping zippers, unbuckling buckles. When his clothes lay in a heap on the floor, she let her eyes roam over him, taking in every detail. When she got to his erection, her eyes widened, and she wet her bottom lip with her tongue.

"I had a little more than staring in mind," he said with a touch of humor.

The pulse at her throat was beating harder. She reached around him and turned on the shower, then waited for him to step inside.

"Go on," she urged. "It will feel good."

"I know something that will feel better," he teased.

"I'll bet it will. Go on now."

He stepped into the shower and was just lathering himself up when the door slid open again and she stepped inside, completely naked. The sight of her took his breath away. He remembered how those full breasts with their wide, dusky nipples felt in his hands. The soft curls covering her pussy sparkled with droplets of water, and he itched to slide himself into her hot channel again. When she turned to adjust the spray, he decided she had the finest ass he'd ever seen in his life.

Her hand trembled slightly as she took the soap from him, but when she looked at him, her eyes told him any fear she'd had was gone now. Slowly, she began to spread the lather over his skin.

Oh, lord. Oh, Jesus.

Whoever's watching over me, I'll be thanking you for the rest of my life.

****

Memories of the previous night washed through Dana as she looked her fill of Cole's naked body. The sight of it made her mouth water—wide shoulders, narrow hips, flat abs, sculpted muscles. The heavy dusting of dark brown curls on his solid chest. And that magnificent cock rising from its nest of thick curls at his groin.

All these years, all the nightmarish episodes, and this man had walked into her life with the key to unlock her hidden sexuality. Not once had her body frozen into its protective mode, defying any attempt to coax a response. In the midst of this horrific situation, she had finally been able to get past her fears of intimacy. Because she'd found a man she knew she could trust implicitly not to hurt her.

His eyes burned on her skin as she stepped into the shower, but she didn't try to hide from his gaze. Starting with his shoulders, the highest point she could reach, she worked the lather down the rich hair covering his hard chest and his dark brown male nipples. Down past his navel where she twirled her finger in the soapsuds, into the wiry hair surrounding the biggest erection she'd ever seen. When she reached his cock, she slid her soapy hands up and down,

303

cupping his balls and teasing them with her fingers.

A strangled groan slipped from him. "Maybe one of these days when I've had enough of you to take the edge off, I won't be so much like a horny teenager the minute I touch you."

He grabbed the bar from her and began to return the favor, soaping every inch of her. He lathered her breasts, pinching her nipples lightly. Moved his hands down her rib cage and forward over her stomach, then down to her already quivering pussy. When he slid two fingers inside her and she clamped down on him, he grinned. "You're sure ready for me, darlin'."

Ready? She wanted him to throw her down on the shower floor and take her there. She rocked back and forth on his fingers, lost in the waves of pleasure. She didn't even tense when he slipped one hand past her hip to the curve of her ass and trailed his fingers through the hot crevice there. The dream burst into her head the moment he touched the ring of her anus and a dark thrill coursed through her. Not tonight, but maybe soon.

They dried each other with frenzied haste. And then they were in his bed, exploring each other, touching every intimate place. He teased her with his fingers and his mouth, drawing moaning pleas from her. With two fingers inside her pussy, he rubbed his thumb back and forth over her clit. The heat building inside her was like a trapped animal screaming for release.

And then, when she was already half out of her mind with need, he stretched out between her thighs, gently opened the pussy lips with his thumbs and lapped the length of her slit.

Every pulse point in her body pounded, her nipples ached, her blood raced with electrified intensity. But then he closed his mouth over her clit and sucked. Hard. And without warning, her orgasm broke over her and she poured into his mouth.

He held her while she shook and trembled. His lips and tongue working her, drawing every last response from her. She was still panting when she pushed at him and moved so she could slide a hand down to find his cock, so thick she could barely wrap her fingers around it. Her thumb brushed lazily over the broad head, swiping at the tiny pearl of liquid. She lifted her finger to her mouth to lick his essence, drawing a groan from him.

"Better quit that, darlin', or it'll be over before it starts."

Moving her hand away, he went back to teasing her, touching her everywhere. He kissed the line of her jaw, the column of her neck, the curve of her shoulder. He licked the hollow of her throat where her pulse had ratcheted up again.

He palmed each breast in turn, gently squeezing as he sucked her nipples, nibbling on them with his teeth and licking them with just the tip of his tongue. He cruised his tongue to her navel and licked the furled flesh before moving his mouth lower again.

"Do you like this?" He traced the crease of hip and thigh with his tongue then kissed the inside of each thigh.

"Yes," she breathed, her hands fisting in the sheet.

"And this?" He lifted one leg to nibble the back of her knee.

"Oh, yes." Her breathing kicked up a notch.

"How about this?" He moved his mouth back to her pussy, lapping her juices.

"Yessss," she cried, arching off the bed to him. She felt like a flower that had been waiting for years to open. But once unfolded, it opened without reservation to the sun.

He described to her in explicit erotic detail what he was doing to her breasts, her nipples, her pussy. How her wet heat felt to him. His words drove her crazy. Made her heartbeat pound furiously and her pussy quiver with need.

He pulled one stiff nipple into his mouth again and sucked on it while his thumb teased her swollen, sensitive clit and his fingers rested lazily in her wet slit. Every pulse point in her body thrummed with anticipation.

He kissed her forehead, her eyelids, her cheeks. Trailed the tip of his tongue around the shell of her ear and down the column of her neck, taking one tiny nip where neck and shoulder joined. Lapping at her nipples, pausing again to ask if she was all right. If everything was okay.

Until she couldn't stand it anymore.

"Please," she begged. "I want you. Now. Please, Cole."

She heard the nightstand drawer open and watched him pull out a condom.

"No, I don't make a habit of bringing women here," he told her when she looked at him curiously. "But I like to be prepared."

His voice was as unsteady as his hands, which were shaking so badly he could barely get the condom out of the nightstand drawer. It thrilled her to know he was that aroused. For *her.*

He stared at her slick center for a long time, the

impact of his gaze ramping up the heat blazing through her. Then he was right there, looking at her as if he could see into her soul. And she into his. Something inside her, the last tight coil, snapped, and she was free. Because he made love to her heart, not just her body. Because her needs were more important to him than his own. Because in his eyes, she saw everything she ever wanted or ever needed to know. The answer to her future.

He turned her over and pulled her to her hands and knees, then stroked her buttocks with a slow glide of his hand. "Does this position frighten you?" His tone was gentle, but there was no mistaking the need in it.

Dana forced herself to think through the erotic haze she found herself in. Frighten her? Maybe with someone else. But not with this man.

"No," she answered softly. "Not with you."

"One of these days when all this is over and there's no question of anything at all, I'm going to take you back here, Dana. But for tonight, this will be the best."

The head of his cock probed at her opening, touching the wet flesh. Then he glided into her so slowly she thought she'd die before he was all the way in. His hands gripped her hips, lean fingers holding her in place as he stroked in and out. It was the most sensual thing she could imagine. She caught the rhythm and moved with him, joining him in a dance they might have been doing forever. He rocked slowly, gauging her reaction, the movement of her inner muscles.

One hand moved around to her pussy again, finding her clit, stroking, stroking, stroking. As he glided in and out, his balls slapped against her, another tactile sensation that ramped up the fire burning inside her. He rode her for a long time, holding back until he knew she was ready.

Tonight, she was ready for him, her body welcoming him. And after all the teasing in the shower, it wasn't long before her climax built within her. His body tightened, and he drove hard into her, taking her over the edge with him, the orgasm shaking her very bones.

She had no idea how long it lasted. A minute? An hour? When the last aftershock died away, when the thundering of their hearts slowed to an acceptable pace, she felt as if she'd been bathed in magic.

Very slowly, he eased from her body, turning her onto her back again. He left her only long enough to dispose of the condom. Then he was back, pulling her against him, wrapping her up in his arms, her head nestled on the pillow next to his.

The last thing she heard him say was, "You're mine now. Don't forget it."

Then he kissed her cheek.

Chapter Thirty-Three

It seemed they had hardly closed their eyes before reality intruded with the ringing of Cole's cell phone. Dana pried her eyes open and watched him stumble out of bed. He cursed as he dragged it out of his pants pocket.

"Landry." He sat back down on the bed and held the phone so Dana could hear, too.

"Sheriff? It's Roy on dispatch. You asked me to call you."

"What?" he rubbed his eyes. "Okay, yeah. Thanks."

"Scott Clayton asked me to let you know the chopper's here. And sir? Kelly wouldn't go home. She says she's got some long lists for you, matched them up with those names in the Chamber booklet. She won't leave until you get here."

Excitement stirred inside Dana. Maybe they were finally getting somewhere. Her gut had told her the clowns would provide the answer.

"I'm on my way." He pressed the End Call button and looked at Dana. "You heard. The FBI chopper's here. We're going to see if we can find this asshole's hidey hole."

She started to push her way off the bed. "I'll get up and make you some coffee."

Cole tugged her back against him, his arm curling

around her. "No need. I'll get some at the office. But I do want you to get up long enough to chain and bolt the door after me, okay?"

"Sure, although I still can't believe even *this* guy would be so bold as to go after me at your place."

"Why not? I don't have any workers around here, and he knows our entire department is focused on the killings. He's probably counting on it. I haven't exactly advertised the fact, but a few people know you're here and information has a way of leaking out around here." He kissed her, just a light touch of lips. "Give me five to take a shower and dress."

Dana grabbed her sleep shirt from the chair where she'd tossed it the night before and pulled it over her head. Looking out the window, she caught the dawn just blossoming on the horizon, fingers of rose and gold reaching into the sky. Prairie grass trembled in a breeze. She imagined Cole mounted on a horse, riding flat out across the pastures. The scene was so peaceful she could almost pretend all the ugliness was happening to someone else. Some *place* else.

The shower stopped at the same time she saw the battered pickup stop at the barn and a tall, skinny boy hop out and go into the barn.

"Your helper's here," she called.

"Good. I'll stop and have a word with him before I leave. Maybe he can stick around."

"Cole, he's just a kid. I don't want him in any danger."

"And I don't want *you* in any danger."

"I told you I'll be careful. That's a promise. And if anyone tries to get in, I'll call right away."

When he was shaved and dressed, his gun and

holster in place, she walked him to the door. He wrapped her in his arms, leaned his head down, and kissed her until her toes curled. His tongue touched every inch of the inside of her mouth, and his hands rubbed up and down her body as if imprinting himself on her. Both of them were breathing hard when he let her go.

"I'll be checking with you during the day, just in case."

She frowned. "Just in case what?"

"Just in case I can't wait another minute to talk to you. Also to let you know what's going on." He brushed his thumb over her cheek. "Listen, Dana," he began. "I want…I feel…that is…"

She smiled. "I know. Me, too."

"When this is over, we're going to make plans."

"Sounds fine to me. Now, get going before the FBI gives you a detention slip."

He smacked her bottom playfully then jogged to his truck.

"Lock the door," he yelled as he climbed behind the wheel.

She waved one more time, then closed the door and fastened all the locks. There was no going back to sleep, so she headed for the kitchen to start a pot of coffee.

****

When Cole walked into the conference room, every deputy not on patrol was there as well as the five Feds. Gaylen had printed out topographical maps of every sector and pinned them up on the wall. He and Scott and a third man were studying them carefully.

Scott turned just as Cole was helping himself to

coffee and one of the leftover donuts.

"Cole, meet our pilot, George Fillipi. Gaylen and I were just going over the different areas with him and trying to decide where to start. Any suggestions?"

Cole looked at each picture carefully. "I'd say these two areas first." He pointed. "They're the most remote and stand the least chance of strangers stumbling on them. Mostly, there's nothing there but herds of cattle that have been moved from one pasture to another. Both places are far away from the ranch houses."

He took the pencil out of Gaylen's hand and marked each photo with a number.

"This is the order I'd hit them. Gaylen? What do you think? Should I make some changes?"

"No." The chief deputy shook his head. "I think you've got it pegged."

"All right." Scott began pulling the photos off the wall then looked at Cole. "Okay if I get one of your deputies to make several copies of each? We thought we'd do land searches with air cover. That way if George spots something we can be on it pretty quick."

"Absolutely. How do you want to split everyone up?"

Gaylen cleared his throat. "I don't want to overstep my bounds here, but Scott and I discussed that. We'll take our five best deputies and pair each one up with an agent. Give them a route to drive."

"Good. And there's no overstepping here. At all. Don't even think about that."

Gaylen looked at him hard. "You're all right, Cole. For a foreigner."

Scott lifted one eyebrow. "Foreigner?"

Cole gave him a rusty laugh. "Not only not born in Texas but not born in the county. It's a heavy burden to carry."

Gaylen nodded, then turned to the deputies waiting in the room. "All right, guys. Let's get to it. Cole, I thought you should be the one to go up with George."

Cole shook his head. "I'd rather it was you. You know the lay of the land better than I do and can spot things I'd miss."

Gaylen gave him a look. "You're sure?"

"Absolutely. Besides, I want to talk to Nita when she brings in her final report, and I'd like to check on Grace and Stacy." He punched Gaylen lightly on the arm. "Go ahead. If I mess up the office, you can fire me when you get back."

Just like that Cole felt the atmosphere between the two of them shift again. Now, he not only had a coworker he could trust, he felt he'd made a friend.

He walked out to the parking lot where the chopper had landed and waited while Gaylen and the pilot climbed in and lifted off. Ten minutes later, everyone else was sorted out and Scott opened the passenger door of the lead car.

"We'll get him before he strikes again. My SAC may be calling while I'm out. I told him to ask for you. Also there could be stuff coming through on the fax machine."

"Got it. Good luck."

Chapter Thirty-Four

He was so furious he wanted to break something. This was not going his way at all. Not one bit. Who knew that Cole would end up being so besotted over Dana Moretti? Or that the boy would decide to call in the FBI. They hadn't done it twenty-five years ago. Didn't Cole understand that wasn't the way things were done around here?

He didn't have much time. The first thing he had to do was call Tony and tell him all deliveries were off until this blew over. He didn't care how he got rid of the merchandise as long as that snot-nosed kid didn't bring it around here. Then he had to figure out exactly how he was going to get his hands on his little flower.

His little escapade at her house had backfired, too. He'd just wanted to throw her off her game. Make her more susceptible. But Cole had to play hero and move her to his house. He was sure Cole had told her to lock herself in the house and not let anyone in. That meant he had to find a way around it, and that couldn't happen until dark. At least Cole didn't run cattle so there were no ranch hands to get in the way.

Raging at the bad luck plaguing him, he prayed that this would be over before anyone located the cabin. Of course, it was very well hidden, so even the stupid chopper probably wouldn't spot it. And the road into it hardly looked like a road at all. Still, he needed to be finished before he pushed his luck too hard.

Chapter Thirty-Five

The day dragged. The chopper radioed in, as did the cars, but they had no success to report. It was slow going all around because thick stands of trees hid so much. By dinnertime, they had barely finished searching two areas and started on a third.

Cole swore under his breath. At this rate, it would take them a week, and he had a sick feeling they didn't have that much time.

The only new piece of information he got was on one of his calls to Dana.

"The ladies came through," she told him. "The clowns were hired through two different agencies in San Antonio. The bill from the agencies was one lump sum. Four clowns. But no one was actually counting them at the events. Things were just too hectic and who figured they had to keep track of clowns?"

"Damn." Cole felt his anger rising again. "Someone saw a good thing and made use of it."

"Well, Letha Milton is trying to find the names of the individual clowns so you can run them down and eliminate them. Trouble is, who knows where they are now."

"Always a cheerful thought."

He called her so many times during the day she told him she might have to move into the sheriff's office to prove to him she was safe.

"Now that's not a bad idea," he told her. "I can pick you up in ten minutes."

She laughed. "I'm fine, Cole. I'm starting to outline the book so I'm busy working. And yes, everything's locked up."

He took time to go by Grace's house. She looked so old and drained he hardly recognized her. Her friends had gathered around her, and Barry had stopped by to check her over. She kept insisting on blaming herself for Gaby.

"I should have listened to her," she said over and over. "I shouldn't have told her she was imagining things."

Cole sat down opposite her and took her cold hands in his warm ones. "Grace, listen to me. It wouldn't have mattered. If he wanted her, he was going to find a way to get her. If she started to leave town, he would have followed her. If anyone's to blame, it's me for not catching him sooner."

Stacy Corona wasn't much better. When he stopped by the hospital, Jered was still sitting in the chair, still holding her hand and murmuring softly to her. She looked like a ghost lying in bed, and Jered blotted the tears on her cheeks with a tissue.

"She won't talk," he told the sheriff. "Won't say a word. Just lays there and cries."

Cole bent down to her. "Stacy, I'm going to tell you the same thing I told Grace. If you want to blame anyone, blame me for not catching him before this. His course was already set. Don't let her death be a waste by dying yourself, please?"

He squeezed her other hand, then clapped Jered on the shoulder.

"You'll let us know the minute you catch him?" the younger man asked, an anxious look on his face.

"Count on it."

Beyond that, he felt he accomplished little. He talked to the SAC in San Antonio and reported on their abysmal progress. There were no further leads on the human trafficking gang either, Lorimer told him.

Still, he had a feeling that somehow he'd forgotten something important.

****

Dana turned on the television to catch the news at five o'clock. Mostly for background noise as she worked at her laptop. But one fragment of a sentence caught her ear.

"…putting on their production of Three Little Girls. The senior class president said…"

And like that, the light went on in her head.

Sweat broke out on her brow, and her hands began to shake. Good god, how had she ever forgotten that horrible song? She'd heard the sing-song phrases over and over in her head for so long she'd finally, consciously blocked it out. But it had hung there, waiting for something to trigger it.

Her hand shook as she picked up the phone and punched in Cole's number, but it went directly to voice mail. Next, she tried the direct line to dispatch.

"I'm sorry, Miss Moretti," the deputy handling the calls told her. "He's gone to see Grace and then he's stopping at the hospital. If he's there now, he'll have to have his cell phone off. Can I help you with something?"

"You can give him a message for me. It's really important, so please don't forget."

"I'll write it down, ma'am. And get him on the radio as soon as I figure he's back in his vehicle."

"Tell him the song I told him about is 'There was a little girl'. He'll know what I mean. Got that?"

"Yes. 'There was a little girl.' I'll see that he gets the message."

"Thank you."

But after pacing the dining room for twenty minutes, she decided to try his cell again. Again, it went to voice mail, so he was probably still with Stacy.

"Call me. I left a message at your office, too."

Then she sat back down at her laptop and tried to focus on the outline. Anything to keep her mind occupied.

Chapter Thirty-Six

He had driven by Cole's place twice, trying to figure out how he was going to get inside. And how would he get her outside without being seen? Driving past the hospital, he saw Cole just leaving the building, no doubt checking on Stacy. An idea popped into his head, and he turned into the parking lot.

"You look like you've been run over twice," he told the younger man when he pulled up next to him.

Cole rubbed his face. "I feel it."

"How's Stacy?"

Cole shook his head. "I don't know how she's ever going to handle this."

"I know you've got the feds in to help, but is there anything I can do? At the moment, I'm feeling sort of useless."

"Me, too, if you want to know the truth." There was anger in every line of his body.

"Damn shame," he said. "Just a damn shame. Well, if you think of something…"

Cole started to shake his head, then snapped his fingers. "Actually, there is something you can do if you wouldn't mind."

"Name it."

"I'm very worried about Dana. We're sure this madman will be after her next, and I can't get away for hours yet. She's at my place. I don't suppose you'd like to invite yourself over there and baby-sit for a while, would you?"

The smile that came to him was genuine, and he gave it without pause. A gift. The boy had given him a damned gift.

"I'm glad you trust me enough to ask this of me."

Cole snorted. "I'd like to think I can take *someone* off the list. Certainly you."

"She doesn't know me," he pointed out. "Will she let me in?"

"I'll call her and tell her you're coming. Pick up a pizza on the way. That'll be your excuse if she gives you a hard time."

"Well, if you think I can help, I'll be happy to do it."

"You'll give me peace of mind, old man. And I'll be more than grateful."

"All right." He could barely contain his glee. "You go on and give her a call, and I'll stop for the pizza. Tell her about half an hour."

As he drove off, Cole was picking up the phone. No doubt calling Dana to tell her what to expect. Only what she got would be something totally different.

Back in his truck, he almost rubbed his hands he was so delighted. He couldn't have planned it better himself. Stopping to see Cole had been a brilliant move on his part. Otherwise, he'd still be racking his brain how to pull this off. And if he did it right, he could call and tell Cole that she was already gone when he got there. He'd tell him that her car was still in the drive, so he was going out to look for her.

And off they'd go. Just him and his little blossom.

Oh, yes. He could see it now, and his body grew excited.

Chapter Thirty-Seven

Just as Cole pulled his cell out of his pocket someone rapped on the window. Gaby's boss, probably visiting Stacy. Cole patiently answered questions, but the man seemed to go on forever. Checking his watch, he realized twenty minutes had ticked off while they were talking.

When he finally powered up his cell, it beeped to let him know he had messages, but he wanted to call Dana before he checked them. He frowned when he got her voice mail. Maybe she couldn't get to the phone fast enough. He left her an explicit message, told her that Tate was on his way over and she should be sure to let him in. He described his uncle and his truck.

"Call me," he said. "I want to make sure you got this."

He was about to check his messages when his radio squawked.

"I'm patching Clayton through," the deputy said.

"Cole?" Scott's voice."

"Anything yet?"

"Nada. We're heading to another sector right now. You on your way back in?"

"Yes. I'll check with you again when I get there."

As he drove something niggled at him, an uneasy feeling that made his neck itch. Then he realized she hadn't called him back yet. And he hadn't checked his messages. He was only a block from his office, so he'd do it when he got there. But the moment he walked in the door Deke Ramirez, the young deputy filling in on dispatch today, came running toward him.

"Someone find something, Deke?" He could only hope.

"No, but Miss Moretti called while you were at the hospital." The young man handed him a pink message slip. "She said to give this to you right away."

Cole looked at the slip. This call came in long before his call to her. "I just tried reaching her, but there was no answer. Did she say she was going out?" He ground his teeth. Surely, she wouldn't ignore his warnings. She knew the risks. More than anyone. "I flat told her to stay put."

"I wrote down the message, so I wouldn't get it wrong. She said she remembered the song. It's 'There was a little girl.' She said you'd know what she meant by that."

Cole's blood chilled at the words. He'd heard that song so many times when he was a kid. He actually used to laugh about it and said they should have a song for boys, too. Closing his eyes against the wave of fear that threatened to overtake him, he scrambled for his cell and punched in Dana's number. It rang and rang. Fear rolled over him as he punched in another even more familiar number.

"Cole." The voice he'd heard a thousand times answered. "I was just about to call you. I got here, and Dana doesn't seem to be in the house. Her car's still here, so I thought I'd take a look around. Did she say anything about visiting anyone in the neighborhood?"

The casual tone made Cole want to reach through the phone and rip the man's face off. He was sick to his stomach at the realization of the demon masquerading as friend.

"Where is she, Tate? Just tell me she's okay, and we can forget this whole thing happened."

"She's fine. Just fine." He paused. "For now. You've put a spoke in my wheel, boy. I thought this game would play out successfully to the end, but now, you've spoiled everything." He cackled. "Oh, not quite everything. I hope you'll take good care of your Aunt Adele after I disappear."

"Damn you, Tate." He ground his teeth, digging for control. "Put Dana on the phone. Right now. Please." Cole's heart was beating so fast he thought it would leap out of his chest. He'd never known such fear or such rage.

"Sorry, she's a little...how shall I say it? Out of it right now." And then he began to sing. "There was a little girl, who had a little curl..."

And the call disconnected.

Cole raced to dispatch and grabbed the microphone from a startled Deke.

"Scott, come in. Are you still out there? Where are you? Where's the chopper?"

At first, all he heard was static. Then Scott Clayton's voice came crackling back to him. "We're here, headed back to the office. So is the chopper. What's up?"

"I know who our killer is, and he's got Dana."

"How do you know he's got her?" Scott asked.

"Because I'm the one who sent the son of a bitch to her." He explained in choppy sentences.

"Jesus." Scott's curse came through even with the static.

"I'm going to give you the description of a truck and my address. Tell the chopper pilot to hover over the area and see if he can spot it. Everyone else hear that?"

Four voices answered affirmatively.

"Here's where I want you." He laid out instructions for everyone. "Gaylen?"

"Right here, Cole," the voice came back.

"I want you there, too. I'm outta here now."

"On my way."

Cole handed the microphone back to Deke. "Did you get all that?"

"Yes, sir."

"Okay, then. You don't budge from here. You're our point of contact." He was already racing for the door.

****

Dana's eyelids felt so heavy it was an effort to open them. And something was making her dizzy and giving her a headache. She tried to rub her eyes, and when she lifted her hands, they were manacled.

She was in a truck, riding down an unfamiliar road, and wondering how she got here. She rolled her head slowly toward the driver, and everything came slamming back to her. The man who introduced himself as Cole's uncle, Tate Bishop.

"My nephew sent me to make sure you're safe." He had smiled when she cracked the front door. "Did you get his message?"

"Yes. I just played his message back a few minutes ago." She drew the chain from the lock and opened the door wider. "This was totally unnecessary but please.

Come on in."

She had greeted him warmly. After all, he was a member of Cole's family. Then the familiar scent from long ago had drifted across her nose, and she stared at him, shocked. Turning away, she had tried to run, but he was on her in seconds and clapping a rag over her face. Just like the man had done twenty-five years ago.

He glanced at her now as she stirred. "I see you're awake. Good, good. Sorry if my medicine offends you. I've had a skin condition all my life, and this is the only thing that keeps it at bay. Just my damn luck that I had to put some on today and you recognized it."

"Cole," she croaked, swallowed, and tried again. "Cole will look for me."

"Oh. I've already spoken to him. Somebody let the cat out of the bag to him. Too bad. Was it you, my dear?"

She moved her hands sideways, feeling for the door handle. Maybe she could throw herself out of the truck.

Tate Bishop backhanded her without taking his eyes off the road. "I know exactly what you're trying to do. Forget it. If I have to disappear, I'm going to have my pleasure first. And finish off what I should have twenty-five years ago."

Dana's head rocked back against the seat, then fell sideways and hit the window glass. She blinked hard to clear her vision. She couldn't die now. Not when she had just found Cole and was finally able to start living.

****

Cole skidded his truck to a stop at the intersection of a state road and a farm-to-market road where he'd asked everyone but the chopper and Scott to meet him.

They were all standing there waiting for him. He could barely get the words out to tell them that the person they were after was his Uncle Tate.

The man who'd married his mother's sister.

The man who had been like a second father to him for so many years.

Had talked him into taking this fucking job!

He was barely finished speaking when he heard his radio crackle and picked up the mic to answer.

"This is Scott. The chopper followed him as far as Fandango Road, but there's no way he didn't notice it. He pulled off the highway into thick trees, and we lost him."

Cole fingers tightened on the mic. "Tell me exactly where you lost him."

He listened to the information. What was it that was tickling the back of his mind? Something from when he was a kid. Someplace...

"I've got it." He turned to Andi. "Let me see your copy of those aerial maps."

Andi reached into her car and pulled it from the dashboard. Cole grabbed it, spread it out on the hood of the SUV, and jammed his finger in one spot.

"Right here in these trees. I remember an old cabin the cowboys used to use when they were riding fence line. It was long before they started using trucks and ATVs." He smacked his head. "And Jesus. Oh Jesus. It's got an old well behind it." He spoke into the mic again. "Scott, remember we talked about..."

But he couldn't finish. The thought of what they'd probably find in the old well nearly made him lose the coffee he'd just finished.

Andi took the mic from him. "Deke, patch me

through to the chopper." When Gaylen answered, she said, "Give these coordinates to George. We need to get started from where we are right away."

"I've got them," Gaylen answered. "Tell Cole we're on our way."

Cole took the mic back. "It's dark. Can the chopper do this at night?"

Scott actually allowed himself a chuckle. "Give George a compass and coordinates and he can fly the Alps blindfolded at midnight. Just tell me the best way to approach the place from where I am now."

Cole gave him the information, then tossed the mic back in his car. He buried his face in his hands, trying to find some semblance of control. "Jesus, Andi, he's got her... He's... Oh, God."

"We'll get to her in time, boss." She squeezed his arm. "Come on. Let's get moving."

****

Dana's head ached unbearably. Tate had tired of her cursing him and yanked a foul-smelling cloth out of the console, pressing it against her nose until she passed out again. She'd lifted her manacled hands to grab at his arm, but the anesthetic had worked too quickly.

She didn't want to open her eyes now, but she had to see where she was. No cedar smell this time, so he wasn't using the old barn. No doubt that place had been written off after the teenage boys had discovered it. Pushing hard to lift her eyelids, she saw Tate standing in front of her, a frightening grin on his face. Carefully, she slid her eyes from left to right. They were in a cabin. An old one from the looks of it.

She tried to sit up and discovered her hands and feet were tied to the bed. Goose bumps stippled her flesh and when she lifted her head to look, she was stark naked.

"That's right, Dana. Or should I say, Carrie. Oh, yes. I know who you are. One good look and I knew." He cackled. "Although you aren't nearly as appealing as when you were a little girl. Still, I can take my pleasure." He rubbed his hands together. "So. Let the games begin."

Anger welled up from deep inside her. This was the man who had turned her entire life into a living emotional hell. The rage surged over the fear.

"You don't scare me anymore," she taunted. "You're nothing but an old man who gets off on torturing people. Hell, you don't even torture people. You torture helpless little girls who can't fight back. What do you think that makes you? You think that makes you a man? What kind of man gets off hurting helpless little girls?"

His face hardened. "You don't want to provoke me, Carrie. That makes me very angry."

"If you're smart, you'll just let me go and get the hell out of here. You know Cole's hot on your trail."

"Even if he remembers this place, it will take him so long to find it again it won't much matter by the time he gets here. Now, shut up. I don't want to have to hit you again."

"Oh, as if you brought me here for a friendly visit."

"Friendly?" He laughed. "My dear, I can be very, very friendly."

Tate sat down next to her on the bed and ran his hand over her, from shoulder to knee. It was difficult, but she made herself not flinch.

"Your breasts are certainly much bigger now. And

such delightful nipples." He took the left one in his fingers and twisted it as hard as he could.

Dana clenched her teeth together and swallowed her scream. She wouldn't give him the satisfaction.

"We'll see just how long you last when the fun really starts." He licked his lips and began to sing. "There was a little girl, who had a little curl, right in the middle of her forehead…"

****

"We need to do this carefully." Cole was in the chopper on the radio with Scott, who'd switched places with Gaylen at the rendezvous.

"Of course." Scott was now riding with Gaylen and one other deputy. "As deranged as this guy is, and knowing the game is up, if we come in with the chopper, he could decide to kill her and take off into the woods."

Thanks to Cole's memory, they were able to spot the cabin from the air, and he was directing the five vehicles from the air since the building was almost completely hidden from sight. But the helo stayed far enough away so if Tate happened to look, they'd just be a speck in the sky.

"Remember," Cole continued, "I'm pretty sure he's still got sensors around the cabin. He's a nut about them. Has them all around the ranch house. The deer are always setting them off and driving my aunt crazy. We need NVGs to be able to spot them."

"Got 'em in the bag I brought along," Scott told him. "Ask and ye shall receive. What's your idea? I'm up for anything."

"I'll tell George where to set me down and give you the spot to meet us. Pass it along to the others. The cabin is two miles in from the road where we'll land."

"Got it," Scott told him.

"We can't all go at the same time. We'd make too much noise and besides, someone would be sure to set off the sensors. But I can lead you in with me. When we get Dana out of there, we can call in the troops. Not until then."

"Are you sure the two of us can do this?"

"Who else do I need?"

But the panic still gripped him.

Oh, baby, hang in there. Please don't let him get to you. Be strong. I know you can do it. Dana. Dana.

Cole repeated her name over and over as he tried to center his mind on what was about to happen.

George set them down in the pasture Cole indicated, and he dropped to the ground. In a moment, the car with Scot and Gaylen bumped along with its headlights off. Scott was out almost before it stopped.

"Here."

He handed Cole a pair of NVGs, putting on a pair himself, and Gaylen passed out radios and flashlights. Cole ran through the plan he'd formulated, letting Gaylen know he was leaving him in charge of everyone else.

"The others should be here any minute," he told the senior deputy. "Tell them what's happening. Remember. Do not head in until I call you. There's no telling what this maniac will do if there's a bunch of people thundering through the woods."

"And if we hear shots?" Gaylen asked.

"If I yell for help, you have my permission to proceed. Not until then. Okay, Scott. Ready?"

Scott checked his gun, made sure a round was chambered, and nodded. "Let's go."

Chapter Thirty-Eight

Dana found her mind drifting back to the barn where Kylie had been killed and she'd barely survived. He'd had all the power back then, but not anymore.

She knew better now. She was no longer a seven-year-old little girl. She was a woman who knew her own mind, and she knew this man was one sick bastard. She wasn't going to let history repeat itself, and she sure as hell wasn't going to let him kill her. She was stronger this time. She was even stronger than him. Cole had given her that strength. She'd find a way to hold herself together until he could get here.

Even letting the monster grope her wasn't so bad as long as she let her mind go somewhere else. Pretend it wasn't happening. She looked at the ceiling made of chinked logs and began counting each of the logs. When she'd counted them twice, she began on the walls.

"If you think your lack of response will make me stop, little girl, you're very much mistaken. It does, in fact, urge me to more bizarre actions to stimulate you." He gave that high cackle again she was familiar with. "But that will be lots of fun, won't it, little girl? I didn't tape your mouth like I did the others, you know. If you are to be my last enjoyment, I want to hear every exciting scream."

He walked over to the dresser, opened a drawer,

and took out a large box. When he came back to the bed and showed her his toys, she finally knew real fear.

****

They crept slowly through the trees, watching for the sensors through the NVGs. They'd be on the surface, made of metal and easy to spot with the goggles. As they got closer to the cabin, the little dots of titanium began to glow in the green light.

Calling on memories from years before, Cole led them in a zigzag pattern avoiding the sensors and taking them around to the front of the cabin, which faced away from them. Tate's truck was parked in the small clearing. Light from one lamp spilled into the woods, and they crouched low, scuttling below the window to avoid being seen.

They had just tiptoed up to the porch when a scream split the night and Cole's blood turned ice cold.

****

Dana watched the man as he moved about the cabin. Every so often, he'd stop by the bed, reach over and pinch her nipples. The pain was so bad she couldn't stifle the scream that ripped from her throat.

"I love that sound," he crooned. "And I've just gotten started. Oh, yes, I expect you'll be screaming until the lovely little throat is raw."

When he picked up a single razor blade, Dana felt the nausea rise at the back of her throat.

"There was a little girl who had a little curl, right in the middle of her forehead…"

Tate Bishop was so busy focusing on her, he never heard the door crash in until it was too late.

Cole leaped on him like a madman, knocking the razor blade loose. His hands were around Tate's throat, squeezing, squeezing, squeezing. Tate tried to grab his wrists and pull him away, but Cole just squeezed harder.

Dana tried to turn her body to hide her nakedness from the stranger who entered with Cole, but he got to her first and covered her with his jacket. Tears rolled down her cheeks, tears of relief as much as pain.

"Cole. Cole, damn it." The stranger pressed his arm around Cole's neck to pull him back, at the same time yanking his radio from his belt. "Come in, everyone. Jesus, get your asses here right now."

"I'm going to kill the bastard." Cole's voice was rough and thick. "I'm going to fucking kill him."

"Think of Dana." The man pulled harder. "Cole, look at her. She needs you. Come on, man."

"Cole?" The word came out as a croak from her raw throat.

Cole blinked hard, looked at her, then slowly released Tate and moved to the bed, leaving the stranger to cuff Tate. "Oh, Dana. Oh, sweetheart. Jesus, God. Let me get you out of here."

He pulled out a pocketknife, opened it, and sliced through the ropes binding her. Then he picked her up gently in his arms.

"Scott." He shouted at the other man in the room. "Get that damn chopper to land in the clearing. I need to get her to the hospital. Now."

"On its way."

Cole's lips landed all over her face, showering her with soft yet desperate kisses.

"I'll be all right," she tried to assure him. "I just need…a little time to heal. I held on for you, Cole. I knew you'd come for me." More tears ran down her face.

She could tell he wanted to hug her so tightly neither of them would be able to breathe, but he was restraining himself, not sure how badly she was hurt. And the rage in his eyes was a terrible thing to see.

"I told you," she assured him, her voice still raw. "I'll be all right."

"Why isn't that chopper here yet?" he yelled.

Even as he spoke, they all heard the whir of the rotor blades and the roaring sound as the bird set down. Then Cole was running from the cabin with Dana in his arms, protecting her from the rotor wash as he lifted her into the chopper, setting her on the seat while he climbed in after her.

"Get this thing up in the air," he told George. "You can radio Salado General. They're set up to accept Life Flite so I know they can handle us. Do you need their frequency?"

George shook his head. "Gaylen got us all set up just in case."

Just before he increased the speed of the blades, they heard Gaylen yell, "Hey, Scott. Your men need to see what's back here. If you aren't sick yet, you will be in a minute."

****

A medical team was waiting at the helipad on the roof of Salado General hospital when the chopper set down. They raced forward and literally pried Dana from Cole's arms, placing her gently on the gurney. Before he could climb down himself, they'd rushed her through the glass doors. He waved at George before hurrying after them. He had to stop someone to find out where the trauma center was, then fumed impatiently as he waited for the elevator.

He nearly wore out the tile in the trauma waiting area pacing in front of the treatment room where doctors were checking Dana over. Luckily, they'd gotten to her before she suffered any real injuries, but they wanted to make sure the chloroform was out of her system and that none of her bruises were serious. He was sorry Scott had pulled him away from his uncle. When he saw Dana on the bed, tied and naked, the killing need in him had been so strong a red haze clouded his vision.

The agent had been right, of course, to point out that Dana needed him. A lot of good he'd do her sitting in jail for murder. But now they'd been at the hospital for more than an hour, and no one would come and tell him a thing.

About the time he was ready to storm the room, and to hell with the consequences, a woman in scrubs and a white lab coat came through the swinging door. "Sheriff Landry?"

"Yes."

"I'm Dr. Hallowell."

He was almost afraid to hear what the doctor had to say. "How is she?"

She gave him a tired smile. "She has a lot of bruising over her body from her breasts to her thighs. But from what she tells me, you got there before he could do any real damage to her. Any worse damage," she corrected herself. "I gave her a shot for pain, just in case."

Cole had to swallow twice to keep from being sick.

The doctor shoved her hands in her pockets. "She told me she was the only survivor of his victims twenty-five years ago. I'd recommend she see a therapist after she's released. This is a shattering experience for anyone. In her case, she'll need all the help she can get just to get through it." She tilted her head and looked up at him. "May I ask what your relationship is with her? It's obviously well past the official stage of sheriff and victim."

"I'm going to marry her." He hadn't known it until that moment, but he felt the rightness of it clear through him.

She gave him a hard look. "I see. Well, then. I hope you'll be able to give her the love and support she'll need. She's been through a horrendous ordeal. She may have some latent issues resurface..."

"I'll do whatever is needed to help her on the road to recovery. Both physically and mentally." His voiced grew louder. "Are we clear on that?"

"Sheriff, I have perfect hearing. It's not necessary to shout." She smiled. "I get the message."

"When can I see her?" he demanded.

"She asked for you several times. I think she'd feel better if you were with her. You can—"

Cole brushed past her and pushed his way into the room. Dana was lying on a treatment bed, eyes closed, her skin whiter than the sheets. He pulled a rolling stool over, sat down, and took her small hand in his.

"We got him, darlin'." He lifted her hand, kissed the knuckles. "He'll never hurt you or anyone else ever again. And it's all because you wouldn't quit. Because you came back here and stirred things up. You get full credit for this."

She moaned softly.

"I'm so sorry I sent him to you. I didn't know. I

swear it. I thought I was keeping you safe. I love you, Dana. Is it fast? Sure. But it doesn't have to take a long time to fall in love. My plan is to take care of you for the rest of your life." He squeezed her hand.

She squeezed his hand back. "I know. I love you, too. And Cole? Your uncle? That's on him, not you."

Cole Landry felt his heart crack. He was emotionally battered and physically drained. The man who'd been like a second father to him had turned out to be the vilest of creatures. He felt as if the heart had been ripped out. He had no idea how he'd face his aunt or his cousins. Or if the town and the county would think he was tainted by his uncle's actions. He hated to even think that Tate had helped him get this job so he could control any investigation that popped up into the old cases. Except for Dana, his entire life as he'd known it had disintegrated like wet tissue.

He leaned his arm on the side rail of the bed, put his head down on his forearm, and finally let himself fall apart. Clutching Dana's hand, he cried harder than he had since he was ten years old.

He was just pulling himself together when the doctor came back in.

"I assume you're going back to your office?"

He nodded. "In a little while. I have a lot to wrap up." He glanced at Dana. "But not just yet."

"My opinion is, she shouldn't be alone right now. If there's no one to stay with her I think we should keep her here until you can pick her up." She smiled. "And you can check in with me whenever you need to."

Two hours later, he was in the office, having been literally forced from Dana's side so she could sleep. Fortifying himself with Harry's coffee, he sat with

Scott and Gaylen, answering questions about Dana's condition and getting a full report from them.

"Bishop's on his way to San Antonio to federal lockup," Scott told him. "His wrists and ankles are flex cuffed, and I sent two men with him, fully armed. I don't trust that bastard for anything."

"Andi, Mickey, and the two federal CSI's collected every bit of evidence." Gaylen looked as if he had a bad taste in his mouth. "Fingerprints, his so-called toys. Can you believe the son of a bitch even took pictures? We found his stash."

Cole swallowed some coffee, wishing it was something stronger. "I'm sure he thought he was safe. He has been all these years."

But it was the gruesome discovery in the back that had everyone losing whatever they'd had for dinner.

"There was a dry well back there," Scott told him. "It was a pile of bones and rotting flesh, some so new the stench was nearly unbearable when the cover was lifted."

"I had two deputies tossing a coin to see which one had to go down into the well," Gaylen added, "and send up the remains."

"We'll need a forensic anthropologist to sort all this out," Scott added. "I called Clark and put in the request. We've got two of my men and two of yours out there until George gets back with enough body bags for all the remains."

Nita Sanchez walked into the room, cursing steadily in two languages. "I hope they give that son of a bitch a three-hundred-pound roommate in jail who wants a piece of his ass at least twice a day. Even that wouldn't be enough."

"A lot of people are going to be shocked when this comes out," Cole said in a heavy voice. "Has anyone talked to my aunt?"

Gaylen nodded. "I roused her pastor, filled him in, and sent him over there."

"I'm sure she's in shock. I'll have to make time to get over there today." He rubbed his face. "I just don't know what to say to her. What about the girls?"

Scott stared at him. "What girls?"

"He has two daughters. My cousins."

"I know they're your relatives, Cole, but how the hell could a man with daughters of his own do this to so many innocent little girls?"

"Makes one wonder, doesn't it?" Nita said.

"Yeah, and then some." Scott grimaced. "It doesn't matter how long I do this job, there are still some things that will never stop surprising me."

"Me either," Nita agreed.

"The pastor can get their numbers from Adele's phone book. He knows them. I'm sure they'll fly in right away. God." Cole shook his head. "What a mess."

"My guys found his cell phone." Scot pulled it from his pocket. "Lucky for us, all the numbers he calls were still in the history and they led us right to the trafficking ring. I'm sending everything back with the FBI. They'll get a task force together to start rounding up all the people involved." He paused. "Go on, Cole. Get back to your lady. We've got things under control here."

By the time Cole returned to the hospital, Dana was in a private room. Cole pulled up the big armchair and reached through the rails to capture her hand. She slept fitfully through the night, panicked each time she woke, then relaxing when Cole squeezed her hand and murmured to her reassuringly.

Early in the morning, Gaylen and Scott stopped in to bring him up to date.

"George brought us back a load of body bags and a forensic anthropologist to supervise moving the remains. There's no telling how many bodies are down there."

"God." Cole wondered if he'd ever get rid of the sick feeling.

"Some are so old there are just bones. After we get all of them out, she and the bodies will go back to San Antonio and begin the work of trying to identify them."

"That may be impossible if they were smuggled over the border," Cole pointed out. "What about my aunt? How's she holding up?"

"I went out to the ranch," Gaylen told him. "The pastor was smart enough to get Barry Engler out there. He gave her a sedative. Your cousins are already flying in. I'm sending deputies to pick them up."

"Thanks. I appreciate it." Cole scrubbed his eyes. "My God, I don't know if they'll ever recover from this."

Scott cocked an eyebrow at him. "How did you figure out who it was? Nothing specifically pointed to him."

"It was the song."

"The song?"

"Dana finally remembered. When he had her and Kylie in the barn, he sang that old nursery rhyme song. You know. There was a little girl?"

"And?"

"I remembered when I was a kid at the ranch

343

hearing Tate sing that to his daughters all the time. Then he'd laugh and pinch their butts. Until they got older and told him it was stupid." He stared at Scott. "Jesus. You don't think he molested his girls, do you?"

The agent shook his head. "Not from the reaction Gaylen had from Adele. But he obviously spent a lot of time directing his energies elsewhere."

"Shows you just how little you know about someone."

"Well, we're digging into his background. Someplace there, we'll find the trigger."

Because he knew he'd be at the office until morning, catching a nap whenever he could, he agreed with Dr. Hallowell that Dana should stay at the hospital overnight. It was late morning by the time he got to her room.

"You look like shit, Sheriff. Go home, shower, and change. And get a cup of something besides this hospital coffee."

"Why can't I take her now? Is she…" Cole swallowed, afraid to ask any questions.

"She's doing fine."

"Hello," Dana broke in. "I'm right here. I can speak for myself. I'm good to go."

"And I want to take her," Cole insisted.

The doctor laughed. "If she's willing to walk out of here with someone looking as mangy as you do, it must be true love."

At his house he insisted on carrying Dana inside, even though she protested that she was more than able to walk. When he had her settled in his bed, he stripped off his clothes and headed for his bathroom.

By noon, Cole was showered and shaved and

dressed in jeans and T-shirt. He scrambled eggs and fixed toast for himself and Dana, insisting she eat in bed.

"I'm not an invalid," she told him.

"Just humor me today, okay?" He kissed her lips, doing his best to restrain himself from leaping into bed next to her.

Finally, he called the office and asked for Gaylen, so the man could bring him up to speed.

"We're set here," the deputy told him. "Tate will be tried in a federal court. SAC Clark Lorimer is rolling the task force to take down the trafficking ring."

"I just can hardly believe it," Cole said for what must have been the hundredth time. "I've known this man for years. Spent summers at his ranch. God, my mother will have a stroke when she finds out."

"Cole, I hope you don't mind, but I already called her. She's flying out today to be with her sister. She said she'll call you when she gets in. Your father might come, too."

"Oh." Cole was startled. "Thank you."

"I probably should have waited for you, but I didn't know when you'd leave the hospital, and your aunt and cousins were falling apart in little pieces. And I figured you could use a shoulder yourself."

"No, no. That's all good. My mother's a tiger. She'll handle things just fine."

"You might be interested to know that Tate Bishop's father died when he was about five. He was left alone with his mother who always wanted a girl. She's the one who taught him the song, tried to put him in dresses. Made him the object of bullies."

"We never knew. Adele met him when he came to

work on a ranch here. One he eventually bought. He told us all his relatives were dead." Cole shook his head. "I don't give a shit what happened to him when he was a kid. There's no excuse for what he is. He's a sick coward who tormented little girls. Nothing that happened could ever justify what he did to those girls or their families."

"Scott and I talked to John Garrett. He nearly had a stroke himself when we gave him the details, but he'll handle the local story."

Cole raked a hand through his hair then down his face. "Listen, can you handle the other media for a little while? They're gathering outside like a hungry pack of wolves. If you can stall them, I'll give them a statement this afternoon. I'd like Scott and I to do it jointly. But not until we have our facts straight as to what we'll tell them."

"No problem. He went back to the motel to shower and change. I'll catch him as soon as he gets back. Go on back to Dana. I know she needs you."

"Thanks. I owe you big time for this."

"Just take care of the lady. She's a keeper."

Cole smiled for the first time in hours. "Don't I know it."

Epilogue

Dana and Cole pulled their horses to a stop on a slight rise and looked back toward the ranch house. She didn't think she'd ever get tired of this view. The ranch house was lit by the dying rays of the sun, and the horses still frolicked in the corral, one last romp before being penned for the night. Summer had arrived like a blast furnace, but this evening had cooled down enough for them to sit outside.

Learning to ride was one of Dana's greatest pleasures. She wondered if it was the freedom of racing the horse across the open pasture or watching Cole in his work shirt and worn jean sitting his fine ass so well in the saddle. Either way, it made her happy.

She was actually excited when Cole fetched all her things from San Antonio and listed the house with an agent. He even set up the third bedroom as an office for her when she was ready to write again. Each night, as they slept in his big bed, he cradled her tenderly in his arms and let her know she was safe, with him. And that he loved her beyond reason.

The media, not unexpectedly, had indulged in a feeding frenzy. Only now was the story fading from the national news. Tate had yet to come to trial, confined as he was in a secure mental facility. Cole hoped they never tried him, sparing Dana the agony of having to testify.

"I heard from Adele today," he said, breaking the peaceful silence.

"How is she?" Dana knew all too well how shattered the whole family was by the revelations.

"Still trying to come to terms that the man she was married to for nearly forty years actually didn't exist." He blew out a breath. "It's been good for her, staying with my cousin all this time."

"I heard the sale of the ranch went through," Dana commented.

"Finally. Hard selling property owned by a pedophile." He lifted his Stetson, raked his fingers through his hair, and placed the hat back on his head. "Saw Jed Nickels at the post office."

"Oh?" Dana lifted her eyebrows. "They should have run *him* out of town on a rail, too."

"No kidding." Cole spat on the ground. "Turns out he suspected his friend at the time and didn't want to, as he said, 'cause anyone embarrassment.' He wasn't too happy when I pointed out to him how many little girls died a horrific death because of that."

"John Garret said the Nickels place is for sale, too."

"Good riddance." Cole swung down from his horse and helped Dana from Diamond, then led her over to their usual spot by the creek. "We should talk.".

She grinned. "I thought that's what we've been doing for the last few months?"

He planted a soft kiss on her lips then held the wine glass for her to sip. "I mean about the future."

She tensed in his arms.

He kissed her again. "Good talk, okay?" He rested his arms on his knees. "The county commission wants to extend my contract, with a substantial raise. Margene said they were satisfied with the way I handled the whole situation." He snorted. "Satisfied. Now there's an inadequate word for you."

"I think they don't know what to say to you," Dana pointed out. "Satisfied isn't so bad."

"Anyway, there's a point to all this. Point number one. I want to marry you. As fast as we can get it done." He kissed her temple. "I love you, Dana. I hope you believe that."

She grinned. "As many times as you've told me the past few months, and for everything you've gone through with me willingly, it would be hard not to know it." She slid her gaze to his. "But I hope you know I love you just as much."

"So that's a yes?" he prodded.

She smiled again. "Yes. That's a yes."

"Great! Now, that brings me back to the commission and their offer. We don't have to stay here. This place has a lot of bad memories for you. Me, too. And there are bound to be other opportunities out there for me. Reno has offered me a place at Guardian Security as a partner if I want it."

"Really? That's great." She leaned her head against his shoulder. "You're right about the bad memories, but you know? This place has grown on me. And people have been unbelievably wonderful. Not to mention the fact I think everyone's learned a good lesson. About protecting their children as well as protecting their friends. So, if you're asking me if I'd be happy living here, that's a yes, too. As long as I'm with you, that's all that matters."

He stood up so he could reach into his pants pocket

and pulled out a small box. "I stopped at the jewelry store today, just in case." He looked at her. "You know I like to be prepared."

She laughed because the phrase brought back one of the first times they'd made love. And the last, she thought soberly, as her body and her mind had taken the time to heal. He lifted her to her feet to slip a magnificent emerald cut diamond mounted on a white gold band on her finger.

"Elegant. Just like you." He kissed her, a long, lingering kiss.

Dana wound her arms around him, holding his head to hers, her mouth opening to invite him in.

"I can think of a better way to seal this deal," she whispered against his lips. "And frankly, I can't wait another moment."

"Then I say let's start the rest of our lives together, right here, right now."

She lifted his Stetson from his head and tossed it on the soft blanket of grass behind them. "Anything you say, Sheriff."

About the Author

USA Today best-selling and award-winning author Desiree Holt writes everything from romantic suspense and contemporary on a variety of heat levels up to erotic, a genre in which she is the oldest living author. She has been referred to by USA Today as the Nora Roberts of erotic romance and is a winner of the EPIC E-Book Award, the Holt Medallion, and a Romantic Times Reviewers Choice nominee. She has been featured on CBS Sunday Morning and in The Village Voice, The Daily Beast, USA Today, The (London) Daily Mail, The New Delhi Times and numerous other national and international publications.

~*~

Visit Desiree at
www.desireeholt.com

Thank you for purchasing
this publication of The Wild Rose Press, Inc.

For questions or more
information contact us at
info@thewildrosepress.com